W9-AHE-582

# FOR TODAY I AM A BOY

*For Today*

# I AM A BOY

# KIM FU

*Houghton Mifflin Harcourt*

Boston   New York   2014

Copyright © 2014 by Kim Fu

All rights reserved

For information about permission to reproduce selections from this book,
write to Permissions, Houghton Mifflin Harcourt Publishing Company,
215 Park Avenue South, New York, New York 10003.

www.hmhco.com

*Library of Congress Cataloging-in-Publication Data*
Fu, Kim.
For today I am a boy / Kim Fu.
pages cm
ISBN 978-0-544-03472-3 (hardback)
1. Brothers and sisters — Fiction. 2. Fathers and sons — Fiction.
3. Chinese — Canada — Fiction. 4. Gender identity — Fiction.
5. Psychological fiction. I. Title.
PR9199.4.F8F67 2014
813'.6 — dc23
2013027720

Printed in the United States of America
DOC 10 9 8 7 6 5 4 3 2 1

Lines from "For Today I Am a Boy" written by Antony Hegarty.
Performed by Antony and the Johnsons. Rebis Music, LLC.

FOR MY FATHER

One day I'll grow up, I'll be a beautiful woman.
One day I'll grow up, I'll be a beautiful girl.
But for today, I am a child. For today, I am a boy.

— ANTONY AND THE JOHNSONS, "For Today I Am a Boy"

# *Prologue*

O N T H E  D A Y  my sister Adele is born, my mother goes
to the butcher. It is January 3, 1969. Her belly, hard as
packed snow, bobs outside of her unzipped parka as she walks
up to the counter. An enormous sow is laid out in the display
case. In her mind, Mother replaces the pig's body with her
own: her legs hanging on hooks at the back; her tiny feet en-
cased in rounded, hoof-like leather boots; the shinbone ready
to be held in a vise and shaved for charcuterie. Her torso is
cut below the breast and lies flat, showing a white cross-sec-
tion of vertebrae. Her head is intact, eyes clouded yellow
and rolled upward. The dried-out edges of her ears let light
through. Human ears probably taste similar to pig's ears, she
thinks. A glutinous outer layer with crisp cartilage underneath. She could stew them, char them in a skillet, watch her
skin blister and pop.

The butcher asks my mother what she wants. "A pound of
sausages," she says. She feels a stab—homesickness, maybe,
or dread at the thought of more burned sausages and boiled

potatoes. The pain arcs from one side to the other, as though her hipbones are electrodes lighting up the space between. Her legs give out and she lands on her hands and knees.

The butcher calls for an ambulance. He hangs up on the dispatcher while he's still giving instructions and kneels on the floor beside my mother with his rubber apron on. He's ready.

Mother makes it to the hospital in time, though the butcher tells differently. The story goes that a woman gave birth on the concrete floor of the butcher's shop, a child born in pig's blood, the cord cut with a cleaver. He never says who the baby was, and is never contradicted.

Fort Michel, Ontario, had a population of thirty thousand people — an awkward, middling size, large enough that you waited in line with strangers at the grocery store and didn't recognize the names in the newspaper obituaries, small enough to count each business: the one butcher, the one Chinese restaurant, the old theater and the new theater, the good bar and the bad bar. Not a small town, by any means, but if every man, woman, and child came out of their homes at the same time, we couldn't have filled a football stadium. The right size for the story of the butcher-shop baby to live on.

My mother's version omits the butcher. It begins with her in the back of an ambulance watching fluid travel down an IV line. The moment it reaches the hollow of her elbow, her entire body goes slack. The world tilts to the left and slides into itself, leaving only black.

Then she's walking. In the middle of the street outside our house. Snow falls, light but insidious, building up fast on the ground. The wind lifts the split in her open-back hospital gown. She unties it, and the string whips her exposed backside.

She starts walking faster. She feels the house is chasing her, accusing her; its shabbiness and empty rooms are an indictment of her character. Three bedrooms crammed onto one floor, growing off the combined kitchen–living room like tumors. Gravel in the front, woods beginning quickly in the back. On the rounded hill that leads into the woods, grass grows in tufts, like hair on a balding man's temples. No one who ever lived there had been able to afford to re-sod the lawn. The houses stop shortly after ours in a freshly razed commercial strip, holding promise. Concrete bases in open pits can become anything. (In 1969, there was no way to know that so many of them would languish for decades, the posted architectural paintings growing increasingly outdated and green as the reds bleached out.)

Mother runs barefoot on the asphalt, past the pits, toward the edge of town. She's almost out. She sees a figure up ahead, through the snow. A man stands in the road, his feet astride the yellow line. She hesitates—she fears him more than the house.

It's my father. A short man who stands tall in people's minds; they're surprised when they see him against a point of reference, surprised that his chin doesn't reach their shoulders when he comes close. He wears a gray vest over a white shirt, the sleeves rolled up to the elbows. His black hair is gelled back into a ducktail. Mother takes a few steps forward. There is a brutal, magnetic beauty to his features.

A chair appears behind him. He sits. He has always been sitting. He holds a baby in his lap as casually as if it were a briefcase. The baby's arms are flung backward. Mother peers into the pursed, demanding shape of the baby's mouth. A flash of violence passes through her mind—tearing, heat, gore, broken bones—and then is lost to her forever.

Mother is in a hospital bed. Mother has always been in a hospital bed. She looks down. She has pulled herself upright by the guardrails, gripping so hard her knuckles are white. Sleep calls her back. My father sits in a chair beside her, holding their first child, my oldest sister, Adele.

Mother wants to ask where the baby came from.

Father misreads the question in her eyes. "We'll try again for a boy," he says.

Soon afterward, as soon as Mother's broken pelvis has healed, Father begins to whisper in her ear, "A boy, a boy, a boy." She pushes him away. He slides down her body and repeats it into her navel, as though calling down a long tunnel. "A boy, a boy, a boy!" Mother laughs.

He lifts her slip over her head. He mouths the word: the aspirated *b* and the rounded, open press of the *oy*. Her eyes roll back. Even in these moments, they don't speak to each other in Cantonese. Father has fixed their first language in the past. He's decided to outgrow it the way a child decides to outgrow a beloved toy after being mocked.

Nine months later, Helen is born.

Father regards Helen with increasing suspicion as the years go by. Eight years, and still no sons. She has inherited his flat features and coarse hair; Adele has our mother's delicate nose, her fine, weightless hair. He begins to think Helen sealed the spirit door behind her. He begins to think of her as the murderer of his son. Then he remembers he's trying to shed his old superstitions, as a child remembers he *doesn't like the stu-*

*pid toy anyway,* and he brings Helen gifts: books, a bone-handled letter opener from Toronto's Chinatown. What could an eight-year-old girl do with that? Helen just likes to hold it.

The last time my mother hears Father speak in Cantonese, it's a name. A boy's name: *Juan Chaun.* "Powerful king." He thought she was sleeping from the way her eyelids twitched like moth wings against the hospital linen. It's a strange name —too many harsh sounds, too severe for a newborn. She grabs his pant leg as he walks by carrying their firstborn son.

"Make it his middle name," she says.

The birth certificate contains no middle name at all: Peter Huang, born at Fort Michel Hospital, April 11, 1979. She signs it anyway. The name exists, if not legally. They crowned their king.

During these early, blissful days, all my father knows about me is the nub of penis that extends from my torso. He grabs my mother from behind in the middle of a Sunday afternoon. "Now that you make boys, let's have a dozen," he says.

My sister Bonnie is their last child.

# 1

## *Boy*

WE CALLED THE wooden bleachers the Big Steps. They overlooked a pit of dust and gravel, generously called the field. I sat on the Big Steps and watched as two boys in my grade rooted around the edge of the field as though searching for a lost ball.

They emerged, each holding a long strip of wild grass. Ollie, the smaller of the two, didn't have all his permanent teeth yet, so he wouldn't give more than an unnerving, close-mouthed smile. Roger Foher, tall, ugly, and hulking, had ruddy-brown hair and a crooked nose.

I skipped down the Big Steps with some of the other boys. Half hidden around the corner, the playground teacher smoked and dropped ashes onto her gray dress, trying to set herself on fire. We formed a circle around Roger and Ollie. Another boy shoved me out of the way to get in close. He cheered with his fists balled.

Roger struck first, backhanding the grass in the circular sweep of a swordsman. I could still hear, over the shouting, the grass slicing through the air. It left a red welt on the milky skin of Ollie's calf.

Ollie raised the grass over his head like a lion tamer with a whip. He cracked it on the shoulder of Roger's T-shirt. The sound—the impact—was muffled by the fabric, and Roger laughed. Ollie stayed grim and silent; the first boy to cry out or bleed lost the game.

Roger struck the same spot again, crossing the welt into an X. Ollie's grass wrapped limply around Roger's side. Roger turned the X into an asterisk. Ollie got one solid hit, on the fleshy part of Roger's upper arm. Roger continued to criss-cross the same spot on Ollie's leg.

I could smell the teacher's cigarette, see its muted red dot against the gray sky. The boy beside me stamped his feet, stirring up the dust around us, throwing gravel against the back of my legs.

It was Roger's turn. He paused, expectant, like an animal when it hears movement in the brush. Squinting his eyes, he pointed at Ollie's leg. The jagged ladder of skin peaked in a spot too bright to be just a mark.

Roger raised his arms and spun around. Champion of the world. The other boys were quiet. The strong had beaten the weak; there was nothing exciting about that. The boy who had shoved me went to walk Ollie off the field. Ollie shoved him away.

The boys dispersed. I stuck around. Roger noticed me. "You played before?" he said, gesturing with his strand of grass, green and impotent now. I shook my head. "You should try it. It'll make a man out of you."

Two years earlier, in the first grade, we did all of our assignments in a slim composition book to be collected at the end of the year. I couldn't imagine consequences that far away. Maybe I'd be dead by then, or living on the moon.

One of our assignments was What I Want to Be When I Grow Up. Our teacher had written several suggestions on the board: *doctor, astronaut, policeman, scientist, businessman,* and *Mommy. Mommy* was the only one with a capital letter.

Working in studious silence, I drew myself as a Mommy. I thought of the mommies in magazine ads and picture books, always bending at the waist over their tied aprons with their breasts on display—serving pancakes, wrapping presents, patting the heads of puppies, vacuuming sparkling-clean floors. I drew myself with a stiff halo of hair, swaddled babies around my feet. A satisfied smile from ear to ear. "I want to be a Mommy."

Two days later, I found my notebook lying open on my bed. That page was ripped out. I asked Bonnie, my younger sister, if she'd done it. The evidence didn't point to Bonnie: she could hardly have ripped so neatly, right from the staples, making it seem as though the page had never been there to begin with. There was no one else in the family I was willing to confront.

The year I became friends with Roger, we were asked again. I said *fireman*. A picture was optional. I worked furiously on mine. The fireman had an ax in one hand and a woman in the other, and his muscles were as bulbous as snow peas. Flames danced all around. I could imagine only being the woman, my arms around the thick neck of my savior, a high-heeled shoe dangling from my raised foot. I left my notebook open on the coffee table when I went to bed.

My father came into the room I shared with Bonnie after we were supposed to be asleep. I watched his shape swoop down like a bird to kiss Bonnie on the forehead. He stopped near my bed and saw the whites of my eyes. He patted me on the foot through the blanket. The door clicked shut. I stayed awake for a long time afterward, wiggling my warmed toes.

Ollie and I waited at the base of the Big Steps for Roger. I asked Ollie about his leg and he gave me a withering look, like I had asked something overly intimate. I tried to think of a topic that would interest him. I was used to talking with my sisters. "How did Roger break his nose?"

Ollie pointed to the end of the field, where Roger was jogging toward us. "One time, he said it was in a fight with his cousin, who lives across town. Another time, he said he tried to skateboard off his roof. Some girl asked him yesterday and he said he got struck by lightning."

The boy who'd shoved me the day before came to join us. "Hey, Lester," said Ollie. They nodded to each other.

"Hi, Peter," Lester said. I gave him the same knowing nod and crossed my arms over my chest the way they did.

We didn't speak until Roger arrived. "New game," he said. No fear crossed Ollie's and Lester's faces.

"I put three big rocks at the other end of the field," Roger went on. "Last guy there gets them all thrown at him."

Ollie and Lester nodded. I looked back. Behind us, I could see the yard teacher chastising a girl for chewing gum. There was no reason to bother with us. This was what boys did.

"Okay. Go!"

Ollie shot off immediately. Lester and Roger were close on his heels, and I followed. We broke right through some kids who were kicking a ball back and forth. Their shouts fell behind us.

My lungs seized up. I ran as fast as I could. The distance

between me and their backs grew, became unbridgeable. As I watched Ollie crash into the fence with his arms out, and Lester and Roger slow to a stop, I considered turning and running the other way.

By the time I reached the end of the field, each of the boys held a stone in his hands. Roger tossed his back and forth between his palms. I doubled over, my hands on my thighs, and stared through my knees. I could hear a jump-rope rhyme coming from somewhere — musical voices, an even meter.

"Straighten up," Roger said.

I tried to stand tall, but the moment they drew their arms back, I instinctively crouched and threw my hands over my face. With my eyes closed, I heard the stones hit: *Thump. Thump. Thump.*

They'd all missed.

Roger barked, "Peter! Stand still!"

They gathered up their stones again. Ollie caught my eye and quickly looked away. He was enjoying this — the victor at last, his fast, mousy frame good for something.

I couldn't help myself. The stones left their hands and I dropped instantly down. The stones flew over my head.

"This isn't working," Lester said.

Roger's even gaze told me I should have stood still. What happened next was my own fault. "Lie down on your stomach."

Gravel dug into my face, my palms, my knees. The boys stood over me. I stared at Ollie's white shoelaces, the hole at the toe of his sneaker. The dust stung my eyes. I closed them. The girls were still jumping rope somewhere, under the watchful gaze of the gray dress and the whistle. Singsong patterns.

I sank down. All my weight toward the center of the earth.

The first stone fell from above, like rain. It struck me high up on my back, just left of my spine. The second landed on the flat of my tailbone. The last one landed on the ground by my ear, loud as thunder. Someone had aimed for my head.

"You're a good man, Peter," Roger said.

One afternoon back when I was in first grade, my sisters and I came home from school and the house reeked of boiling sugar. My mother was making white-fungus soup. She said her mother used to make it.

Father lifted the pot from the stove, went outside without his shoes, and dumped it on the lawn. It wasn't because of the smell. The sweet broth sank into the earth, leaving behind a heap of frilly white. On the first day, it looked like a girl had stripped off her nightgown and abandoned it there. On the second day, like a pile of bleached bones.

The next night, she made split-pea soup with ham. The six members of my family crowded around our table meant for four, and my sisters worked dutifully through the sludge. I put a spoonful in my mouth and retched. The soup ran out the sides of my mouth and back into the bowl.

My father stood up and came over to me. His head blocked the overhead light, like an eclipse. He took my hands in his. He shaped them into an upturned bowl, as though I were begging.

He looked at my sisters and my mother. I followed his gaze. Adele, Helen, and Bonnie: the same black eyes, so dark that the iris blended into the pupil. My father put my soup bowl in my hands. "Drink."

My own saliva pooled clear on top of the dense slime.

"Drink, or eat nothing tomorrow," he said. No anger in his voice.

Trying to make the soup skip my tongue, I inhaled it like air, straight into the back of my mouth. It left a slug's trail down my throat. Fleshy, pink chunks remained at the bottom of my bowl. My father sat down again.

He turned to my mother, lifting his spoonful of ham. "It's good." ·

We followed Roger farther and farther from the playground. We had to sprint back to class when the bell rang, while Roger just sauntered in tardy. I wasn't in his class. He claimed to have flipped off his teacher when she called him out for being late.

Ollie had to explain the gesture to me. Lester, Ollie, Roger, and I sat in the grass ditch for the field's rain runoff, below the sightline of the playground. A long drought had dried out the ground. The grass the boys used to whip each other was starting to yellow and sprout. "It's like swearing."

"But why?"

"Because it looks like a dick, I think."

Lester and I stuck up our middle fingers to examine them.

"Not really," I said.

Lester said, "It's more like, 'Stick this finger up your bum!'"

"That does sound rude," I agreed.

"But why is that an insult?" Ollie said. "Isn't that worse for the person who says it, since he has his finger up someone's ass?"

"Well, it doesn't look like a dick," Lester said, defending his theory.

"Sure it does. Your other two fingers are the balls, see?" Ollie held out his fist with the finger sticking up.

"Don't point that at me."

Roger hadn't spoken in a while. He lay on his back staring

up at the sky, the wheels turning in his head. He batted the empty juice bottle from his lunch against his stomach. His mind was somewhere beyond us. It was like being caged with a sleeping lion.

"New game," he said.

Ollie didn't react. "Come on, man. Lunch is almost over."

Roger stood up. "New. Game," he repeated. He used the juice bottle to grind a hole in the dirt the size of the bottle's base so the bottle stood upright on its own. "Stand three steps back and try to piss in the bottle. Whoever can't do it has to drink from the bottle."

I felt a wave of panic. I never peed standing up. When I had to, I thought of my body as a machine, a robot that did my bidding. A combination of arms and legs and heart and lungs. It had nothing to do with me. My real body was somewhere else, waiting for me. It looked like my sisters' bodies.

Lester and Ollie were still sitting down. "Come on," Roger ordered. "You guys chicken?"

Ollie pushed himself up. Roger had said the magic word. "Not chicken," Ollie said. He went over to the bottle and counted his steps backward. "One, two, three." He unbuttoned his corduroys. Boys were ugly and foreign, like another species. Like baboons. I was not one of them. The evidence was right there, all the time, tucked into my tight underwear, but I still didn't believe it. I didn't have one of those things, that little-boy tab of flesh.

The bottle tipped in the dirt as it got struck. Ollie managed to get some inside, filling up about a finger's worth of yellow. Roger went next. Lester nudged me. "Let me go last," he said.

I shook my head. "No. I want to go last." Maybe the bell

would ring first. Would that be enough? Would Roger let us go? Probably not. His games trumped class. There'd be no leaving until it was over.

Roger couldn't do it. His stream arched downward before it reached the bottle. He kept trying until it petered out entirely. Ollie hooted. "Ha! You have to drink it!"

Roger zipped up his pants. His dead stare was frightening. Ollie kept pressing. "That's what you said! Whoever can't do it has to drink it!" He shoved Lester. "Come on. It's your turn. Then Peter. Then Roger has to drink it!"

The bell rang. The distance made it sound low and benign. "Bell," Roger said.

"Screw the bell," Ollie said. "We'll finish it."

"Bell," Roger repeated.

"You have to drink it! That's what you said. Those are the rules! Don't be such a chicken!"

Roger punched Ollie in the ear. Ollie toppled into the ditch next to me and Lester. "Fuck you!" he shouted.

Roger stood over us, casting a shadow into the grassy pit. I had a sudden vision of him pouring dirt over the ditch and burying us there. He probably had the same idea. "The bell means it's over," he said. "I make the rules, not you."

Bonnie and I, five and six years old, sat on the floor outside of Adele and Helen's bedroom. I pressed my ear to the door. Whitney Houston came out muffled, more beat than melody. Bonnie tried to shove me out of the way. We both tumbled through their door. "Hi!" Bonnie said, flat on her back. "Can we do the hair thing?"

"I have to study," Helen said. The corkboard above her desk threatened to crush her, overloaded with medals and awards.

Adele was reading a magazine, lying on top of her made bed. "Sure. Close the door."

Even inside their room, the radio was barely audible. Bonnie sat cross-legged on the floor. Adele sat behind her and ran a comb through her hair. I sat behind Adele and combed her hair, handling it like bone china.

Helen shut her history textbook and sat down behind me, grabbing a brush from the basket on the table between their beds. She always tugged a little too hard, leaving my scalp raw.

We all looked alike then. The same eyes in our unmolded faces, the same blue-black hair, even though Adele's fell straight and limp and Helen's frizzed in a thick heap like an animal pelt. Bonnie and I had matching haircuts from our mother, two button mushrooms. Sitting in a line, connected by hairbrushes and raking fingers, the perfumed air of the room settling over all of us, nothing that split me apart.

A knock at the door.

We rolled to the side, out of position. I grabbed all the brushes and combs and stuffed them back into the basket. Adele threw some paper and pencils at me and Bonnie. Bonnie started writing out numbers. Helen sat down at her desk and tossed a textbook to Adele as she turned off the radio.

"Come in," Adele said.

The door swung open. Half of my father was visible. An arm, a shoulder, a waning moon of face.

"Ba-ba." Adele had memories I couldn't imagine. "Father," she corrected. "We were just studying."

Father nodded. "This door stays open." None of us were looking directly at our father, our necks curved forward like sickles. "Send Peter when you're finished."

He disappeared into the shadows of the hallway. I stopped

holding my breath. "I don't think Father likes you spending so much time with us," Adele said.

"Why?" I asked. I wanted to hear it said out loud, in real words. I wanted to understand it, not just sense it in my gut.

"He wants to spend time with you," Adele said. Her smile was so kind, it bordered on pity.

"Why?" I asked again. I focused on Adele's gentle, reluctant face and avoided Helen's shrewd eyes, her eyebrows that sloped to a point.

"Because he wants you to be like him," Helen said.

Adele added, "Big and strong like him."

"But I want to be like you," I said, grabbing Adele's knee. "I want to have hair like you. I want to be pretty like you." Her sad, saintly expression frightened me.

"You can't." Helen had turned in her chair. Adele glared at her. "What?" Helen said. "He can't. You can't, Peter. You can be handsome, like Father or Bruce Lee." She pointed at a poster of theirs, one that Father disapproved of: dot-pixelated like a comic book, a shirtless Bruce Lee posed in fighting stance, his body warped wide with muscle. I stared at the poster in horror. I started to cry.

"You're a boy." Helen said it like she thought it would be comforting.

"I am not! I am not!"

Bonnie was always delighted when someone older than her cried. She started poking me in the side. "A boy! A boy! A boy!"

Adele knelt down. "Peter, there's nothing wrong with being a boy. There're a lot of great things about being a boy. Sometimes I wish I were one."

I started to wail, a bland, continuous cry, not pausing to take a breath. I felt out of control. A boy! A boy! A boy!

Helen turned a page in her textbook. "Father's going to hear him and we're all going to catch shit."

Adele nodded. She pulled me into the closet and shut the door behind us. The seam of the hinge let in the only light, and my heaving breaths seemed louder in the tight space. I felt Adele's thin arms close around me.

Bonnie pounded on the door, angry at being excluded. The sound was distant and unimportant. Adele whispered close to my ear, "You can be pretty. You can be pretty."

Roger wasn't at school on his birthday. He'd been talking for weeks about the party he was going to have. There'd be horses, he said, and arcade machines, and BB guns. He mimed popping off a shotgun on his shoulder, then watching an invisible bird tumbling from a tree.

As we left school that day, Roger was standing by the front door. Ollie and Lester walked together. I chased behind. They stopped abruptly and I crashed into their backs.

"Hi, losers," Roger said. The scar on his nose was more noticeable than usual, throbbing over the spot where the bridge curved away from straight.

"Happy birthday," Lester said. Ollie smiled without opening his mouth.

We waited for the front of the school to empty. Kids rushed past us. I saw Bonnie heading for the bus home. She looked just like me from behind: a helmet of black hair, a pair of Helen's old overalls. I watched a version of myself stay with the crowd, get on the bus, go home. Home to my sisters.

"Where were you today?" Ollie asked.

"Pa took me to a baseball game," Roger said. He looked us up and down, searching for something.

"What baseball game?" Ollie challenged.

"Blue Jays. Out in Toronto."

"Then how come you're back already?" Lester asked.

I'd believed in Roger's birthday party.

"Yeah," Ollie said. "When did this game end, so you could be back by three o'clock?"

"Morning game," Roger said, vaguely. "You losers bring me presents?"

I said, "I got you something. It's at home. I was going to bring it to your party."

Roger sucked on his teeth, drawing his cheeks in. He addressed Lester and Ollie. "What about you two?"

Lester shrugged. Ollie brought something out of his bag: a gift wrapped in brown paper and kitchen string. Roger grabbed it out of his hands and tore a hole in the paper.

I saw the glint of metal. I couldn't read the expression on Roger's face as he stared at the half-opened present. "You're a dick," he said.

"What?" Ollie said, the words coming out the side of his shut mouth.

Roger ripped the paper off entirely. "This is your old lunchbox. I *seen* it."

Ollie's face twitched. Maybe a smile.

Roger kicked at the scraps of brown paper. They drifted up and down daintily, as though mocking him. "Fuck you guys." He squinted, his cheeks squishing upward. Astonished, I wondered if he was going to cry. His eyes opened. His hands closed slowly around the collar of Ollie's shirt. As Ollie's breath caught, I could see him remembering how big Roger was.

Lester pushed them apart. "Cut it out. Someone's coming."

A small figure skipped toward us. As she came closer, I recognized her—a girl from my class, Shauna. Her desk was in front of mine, and I found it soothing to look at her. Her blond hair was always parted neatly in the center, clipped in barrettes that stayed in place all day. The glassy blue eyes of a doll. She looked like the child of the Mommy I'd wanted to be, the one receiving the plate of pancakes, the one in white socks and patent-leather Mary Janes that never left muddy footprints behind.

She seemed oblivious to us as she tried to go past and into the building. She wore a yellow skirt that bounced as she walked, short over her shapeless legs. Roger let go of Ollie, who started to cough. He reached out and grabbed Shauna by the arm. "Where are you going?"

"I forgot my pencil case." Roger's fingers sank into her chubby arm. "Let go. You're hurting me." The last part came out as a whine.

"Roger," Lester said. "Come on, man. Let's go to the corner store. We'll buy you a Coke or something."

"Shut up," Roger said, deadpan. He stayed focused on Shauna. "It's my birthday today. Did you know that?"

"What?" Shauna tried to struggle free. "Let me go!"

"Wish me a happy birthday first."

"Fine. Happy birthday. Let go!"

The possibility of letting go, of ending it there, rose and died in Roger's eyes. "Come with us," he said.

After I had calmed down enough to leave the closet, Helen reminded me that our father wanted to see me. I headed out of my sisters' bedroom and went down the short hallway like I was on a death march. My mother, who was nothing like the mommies in the magazines, was washing down the kitchen table. My mother, more like a wind than a person: visible only in her aftermath, the cleanliness and destruction she left behind, forgettable until a tornado blew off the roof. She motioned me silently toward their bedroom door.

I went into their room. My father stood by the window in the dark. The house was shaped so that the light from the kitchen window came through their bedroom window. My father's white shirt glowed, revealing the muscles of his back. For the first time, I thought about what his body might look like. Did he have square pectorals like Bruce Lee, divided abs, all those sharp, frightening angles?

"Come with me," he said. He walked toward their connected bathroom, and I crept after him. My eyes were starting to adjust. He pushed a stool against the sink. I hopped on the stool without being told. We stood side by side in the dark, facing the mirror.

I heard the light switch snap. In the flood of light, my father's face was momentarily washed out, drained of its tawny color, his burnished tan. My own face was softened, blurred at the edges where I couldn't focus my eyes. In the mirror, a white man and a girl.

Then — pupils contracted — just us again.

"Today's special, for father and son. You learn to shave," my father said. He winced at the sound of his own voice, mouthed the words a second time. Nobody heard his accent more acutely than he did. "I'm going to teach you how to shave."

I ran my hand over my smooth chin, a wordless reminder that I was six years old. "Do what I do," he said. He mixed the shaving cream in a cracked wooden bowl. I looked around their bathroom. There was a curious lack of feminine things, the oils and creams and powders of the bathroom I shared with my sisters. No evidence of my mother.

Father lathered up his face and neck and I did the same. He handed me a disposable plastic razor. It was easier to look at his reflection in the mirror than at him, like seeing the sun through a pinhole projector. I followed his example, clearing away the foam from my hairless face in strips. "Did your mother ever tell you your Chinese name?" he asked.

I didn't want to get my mother in trouble, but I was more afraid of lying. I nodded. I couldn't remember the actual syllables she had whispered. I remembered they rhymed. "Powerful king," I said. We rinsed off our razors in a second bowl of water.

"Adele's Chinese name is her middle name. It will make her life hard when she's a doctor." He paused. I didn't know Adele wanted to be a doctor. "Maybe she will change it."

He ran the blade over his Adam's apple. "We waited a long time for you. In a family, the man is the king. Without you, I die—no king."

I slid the razor over my flat throat. It caught on the skin. "*Hah.*" A line of blood appeared.

My father glanced over, unalarmed. He ripped off a piece of toilet paper. He held the back of my neck and pressed hard with his other hand to stop the bleeding; it felt like being strangled. "It's okay. Just part of being a man." I stared up at his face, my head hanging back like a dancer's in a dip, this strange embrace. "Women bleed much more."

The space under the Big Steps was closed off on one side. There was only one way in or out. Cracks of light came through the bleachers, throwing the shadows of a prison window.

Roger dragged Shauna there by the arm. Our feet crunched on the gravel. We herded her toward the back of the hollow, blocking the entrance with our bodies. The momentum felt unstoppable. Lester's elbow dug into my side as he tried to get closer, just as it had at Ollie and Roger's grass fight. His expression was the same: manic, nauseated.

Shauna had lost a barrette somewhere along the way. Her mother would ask about that, I thought. Her socks were stained by the pale dust under the gravel. She cried. Not like I cried, not the way I heaved and sobbed into Adele's chest in a closet. Soundless tears, as though crying were impolite.

"Lift up your skirt," Roger said.

She blinked. I could smell Ollie's sour breath. It came out in short, excited bursts. She raised the hem of her skirt by the corners, not quickly, not slowly. With a knowing I hadn't expected. Like she'd done this before.

Roger's eyes fixed to the spot. "Peter, pull down her underwear."

I looked into Shauna's eyes. My hands on her small hipbones. I tried to tell her that I was sorry. That we were both victims. I wanted her to see who I really was. The one who took a stone in the back. The one who combed his sisters' hair. In her eyes, I could see only the reflections of four attackers, four boys in that dead, marble blue, like you could see the sky right through her.

There. Shauna's ankles bound together. A bald, pink wound.

Shauna's legs trembled and then buckled. She hit the ground on her knees. Her skirt pooled protectively over her thighs. Better to be one of us, better to be standing on this side than kneeling and weeping in the gravel while they leer, that was all my father wanted from me, to be one of them, to be a king.

But I belonged in her place, holding something so stunning they'd steal for it, they'd stare into its hot center even as it blinded them.

We took a long time walking home, not talking. The streetlights were already on. We passed through the undeveloped area between the school and our houses. The corner store, a garage, a laundromat, a stretch of empty lots. We lingered for a while over a dead rat, steamrolled flat by tire treads. The tail was the most recognizable part.

We came to my house first. I stayed on our gravel driveway and watched them walk away. The road rose uphill and then went down, creating the illusion that the boys disappeared into the horizon faster than they should.

I pushed open the front door. My father was sitting at the kitchen table. Mother sat on the floor by our shoes. My sisters were nowhere to be seen. They knew. Shauna's parents must have called.

Mother picked me up by my armpits. She could barely lift me; my head hovered above hers, my feet dragged on the ground. She held me at arm's length like a bag of garbage. She carried me into their bedroom and dropped me hard into a chair.

Father came in behind us. He leaned on the wall by the door. Mother opened her mouth and a long stream of invective came out in a language I barely recognized, a language of hard, short sounds, a language of pain. My father put his hand on her shoulder to stop her. She wasn't supposed to speak to us in Cantonese. Our English would come out wrong, he'd insisted. Like theirs.

Deprived of that weapon, she used the only other one she had: she slapped me in the face. For a moment, no one moved, as if the sound of her palm cracking against my cheek needed time to echo. Mother walked out. The door hung open.

I met my father's gaze. He stayed leaning on the wall across from me, his expression inscrutable. Slowly, deliberately, he straightened up. He was smiling. He didn't speak for a long time, just smiled. I felt his approval like a warm glow.

He said, "Bonnie is moving into Helen's room. You get your own room, son."

My father loved me.

# 2

## *Eighteen*

LOVE AN EIGHTEEN NIGHT," Adele sang over Eddie
Rabbitt's "I Love a Rainy Night," dancing with her hands al-
ternating over her head like pistons. For the summer after she
turned eighteen, we replaced any two-syllable word in songs
on the radio with *eighteen*. Bon Jovi was livin' on an eighteen.
Janet Jackson told eighteen boys that they don't mean a thing.
Adele skipped through the house singing, *"Bam-ba, eighteen!
Bam-ba, eighteen!"*

I was eight years old, the summer before Shauna and
Roger and being marooned in my own bedroom. Adele
would be leaving soon. Helen had been waiting seventeen
years for her own room, and she would lose it within a few
months. It wouldn't surprise her; nothing did.

Bonnie and I imitated Adele's steps in our white socks
and plastic slippers. Adele drew circles in the air with her
hips while Bonnie snapped just off the beat, marked by jolts
of electric guitar. Adele and I leaned in toward each other,
mouths moving in unison. "Yeah, I love an *eighteen* night."

Helen sat at her desk, hunched so far over that her shoulders rose above her neck. She'd signed herself up for an SAT prep course that was run out of the high school, otherwise dormant for the summer. I danced over to her chair and asked if I could help her study. Rather than answer, she handed me one of her vocabulary lists. I couldn't pronounce the first word. "That's what I thought," she said. She went back to her practice set of math problems. We sang straight into her addled brain: B can clean the house in half the time it takes A. If they cleaned it together in three hours, how many hours would it take for A to clean the house all by himself? Eighteen hours.

Bonnie slipped and fell onto the gray carpeting. Adele grabbed her chubby hands and pulled her upright. "Well, I love an *eighteen* night." She spun Bonnie around. I took weaving jazz steps backward.

Helen leaned on her elbows, resting an index finger in each ear. In a class of seventy-two students, forty-one students are taking French, twenty-two are taking German, and nine are taking both French and German. How many students are not enrolled in either course? Eighteen students.

As the guitar began to wail on its own, Bonnie and I stopped trying to mimic Adele's long-limbed grace. We jumped up and down, shook our arms free like monkeys. Adele, her small butt still swaying back and forth, picked up one of Helen's markers and blacked out two of the digits in the year on the calendar: 1987 became 18.

"I need that," Helen said. Adele tossed the marker in Helen's general direction. The three of us joined hands and danced in a circle through the end of the song. Helen groped for the marker on the floor.

She went back to filling in the bubbles. Sarah is twice as

old as John. Six years ago, Sarah was four times as old as John. How old is Sarah? Sarah is eighteen. Helen's own numbers: the lesser seventeen, the imperfect 150 on her PSATs.

When the envelopes came, I knew what they meant. Businesslike, Adele's typed name visible in the clear plastic windows. Crests with Latin words in tight circles, silhouetted birds.

The letters arrived within a few days of one another and were stacked on the hall table with the junk mail no one had thrown away yet. I caught Helen flipping through them. She was irritated that they went unopened, that Adele didn't care which ones were small and white and cursory and which ones were thick and yellow and welcoming.

After Helen left, I wrapped them all up in a grocery-store flyer—*Save eighteen cents per pound on roasted ham*—and shoved them through the swinging lid of the kitchen trash. I thought of it as a portal. Things went in and were never seen again.

They were back on the hall table within a few hours, still wrapped in the flyer. The ghost of eighteen dug them out from the bin. A streak of coffee grinds over a university logo, the hall reeking of eggs and orange peels. The smell caught Adele's attention.

All summer long, Helen volunteered for one thing after another, so she could put the activities on her college applications. Adele took me with her when she visited Helen at the local nursing home. The first floor looked like a hospital —white reflecting on white, a long corridor of doors with numbered boxes and clipboards, a strip of wooden paneling running along each wall. The linoleum smelled freshly bleached. Unlike in a hospital, there was no one around. No one greeted us or asked us what we were doing there. A cart of medical supplies was abandoned at an angle in the hallway.

We got into the elevator and went up to the fourth floor, where Helen worked. The silence persisted. On this floor, many of the doors were closed. I stuck my head into an open door as we walked by and saw a man lying face-down in bed with a bathrobe bunched up around his hips. His bare buttocks looked like empty sacks sliding off his spine. Adele shut his door for him.

We found Helen in the lounge. She was spoon-feeding a woman fortified pudding, a beige substance that looked like it had come from a caulking gun. The woman tried to say something. "Just eat," Helen interrupted, shoving the spoon into her mouth.

I flopped down into an armchair. The remote control for the shelf television was attached to the armrest by a cord. I turned on the TV. It was muted. Hitting the mute button didn't do anything. I turned to channel 18.

The woman reminded me of a snowman, a human shape drawn broad and round, sinking deep into her wheelchair. The hard egg of her belly was pinned under a seat belt. She shoved the spoon away. "Where are my real shoes?" Her feet were elevated on the footrest of her chair, in soft-looking leather moccasins.

The spoon knocked against the woman's teeth. "Eat," Helen repeated.

The woman turned to Adele. "Do you know where my shoes are?"

Adele perked up. "Nope." Her voice bright, singsong. She

got to her knees and pretended to look under the sofa. "Not here." She opened the fridge. "Not here either."

The woman nodded solemnly. "Try the cabinets."

Adele walked around, loudly opening and closing all the cupboard doors. "Is it in this one? Nope. This one?"

The woman tapped her chin. "Maybe someone hid them."

"Maybe," Adele agreed.

"She can't wear shoes because her feet are too swollen," Helen said. "Don't turn her against the nurses and the volunteers by telling her we steal her shoes."

"But you do," I said.

The woman looked at me. She smiled. "Hello, Alfie."

I didn't know what to do. "Hi," I said.

She gestured for me to come closer. Adele nudged my back, so I got out of the chair and stepped forward. The woman's lips had sores in different states of healing, dry and wet. "How's school, Alfie?"

Helen held the woman's chin firmly between her two fingers and turned her head. "You need to eat, Mrs. Harrison. It's important."

"School is fine," I said.

Mrs. Harrison grabbed the spoon from Helen and wagged it at me. "Would you like some pudding, Alfie?"

"No, thank you."

"Alfie's dead, Mrs. Harrison," Helen said.

"No, he isn't," she said. "He's right here. What are you, blind?"

Helen knelt down between me and Mrs. Harrison. "What did Alfie look like?"

She seemed confused. Her eyes dimmed as she glanced between us. Adele couldn't stand it. "Of course this is Alfie," she exclaimed, putting her hands on my shoulders. "He came just to see you."

Mrs. Harrison looked more foggy-eyed than ever, but she relaxed again. "That's nice," she said. She tucked her blanket around herself.

Helen stood up. She pulled Adele over by the arm. "What are you doing?"

Mrs. Harrison and I continued to smile dumbly at each other. "What harm does it do?" Adele asked. "It makes her happy."

"It's a lie."

Mrs. Harrison patted the back of my hand. Adele said, "So? Why tell her if she's just going to forget? Why make her relive Alfie's death over and over again?"

"Because those are her real memories." Helen wiped her hands on her uniform smock. "You disrespect her dead son by encouraging her to forget him. What he looked like. How he died."

Adele continued to smile gently. "Why not just let her be happy?"

Mrs. Harrison picked the pudding container up off the table. She held it out to me. "You need to eat, Alfie," she mimicked. "It's important." Mrs. Harrison and I both glanced sideways at Helen, and we laughed together.

Helen plucked the pudding out of her hand. To me and Adele, she said, "I think you should go now."

Helen once told me that her favorite volunteer job had been picking up trash by the highway, because it gave her time to think. Even though she once had to scoop up human feces in between the discarded cans and waist-high dandelions. I asked her how she knew it wasn't left by a dog, or a coyote, or a bear. "The size and the shape," she said.

Our mother told the four of us to go see a movie, which meant she was sick of us. Helen mouthed SAT words as we walked: *abasement, harangue, obdurate*. We passed the laundromat, the forever-unsold lot. There were two theaters in town. We went to the one that was closing down, that showed only old movies. The Luther's marquee announced that for its final week, it was showing *Sabrina*, from 1954. Neon light blazed in the middle of a sunny afternoon, red and blue flourishes down the Luther's vertical sign.

Adele paid for our tickets. The man in the ticket booth looked at Adele with the eyes of a child who is hungry but no longer expects to be fed. As she took the tickets and change, she rested her fingers in his palm for a long moment. He shuddered from his sneakers to the tips of his long white hair.

I looked back at him as we passed under the red curtain. He was old, but he probably smelled like popcorn all the time, buttery and warm. "The ticket guy likes you," I said. "Maybe you should stay and date him."

"Maybe," Adele said. Helen snorted.

We let the afternoon pass in an air-conditioned haze. The movie was a modern Cinderella story: The unnoticed chauffeur's daughter falls in love with one of the sons of the main house, played by William Holden. She goes to Paris a girl and comes back a woman, finally attracting his attention. Humphrey Bogart plays Holden's older brother; he tries to discourage their romance by pretending to be in love with her too. Every frame was like a photograph, champagne and ball gowns in black and white. I watched Adele as much as

I watched the screen, the scene changes playing out as light and dark on her face. She had her hands pressed to her mouth in delight. I thought she looked just like Audrey Hepburn — the gamine smile, the swan-necked beauty.

As we left the theater, I noticed that the bakery next door had a bank-foreclosure notice in the window. The whole town was shutting down because Adele was leaving. At least the Luther exited with class, running up an electric bill of daytime neon.

Time felt loose. We meandered in the opposite direction of home and came to the new bridge. It led to a housing development whose funders had run out of money while it was still concrete foundations in a pit. Helen had begun to speak out loud. *"Ensconce, lachrymose, crepuscular."* She looked at me meaningfully. Now that she wanted me to ask her what the words meant, I'd lost interest. Her gaze drifted southward, past the river. Toward her future in the States.

Bonnie dropped her arms down over the railing of the bridge. Cars rumbled behind us, a few at a time. They weren't in a hurry either. "How do they build bridges?" Bonnie asked. She pushed her toe against a large bolt jutting up through the metal.

I remembered the hollow frame being lowered on a hook. "Cranes," I said.

"Like the bird?" Bonnie traced a split in the concrete with her foot.

"Sort of," Adele said. "They're a lot like birds. They dip their beaks, pick up parts of the bridge, and raise them up high."

Bonnie nodded. Giant white cranes with ink-stained wing-tips and red crowns built the world, steel crossbeams balanced on their stick legs. She traced the groove in the concrete again. "And what are these lines for?"

"I don't know," Adele said.

Helen had walked ahead a few steps, her back to us. "Those are expansion joints," she said. The wind carried the words back to Bonnie.

"What does that mean?"

"So that the bridge doesn't break when it expands and contracts with the temperature."

Bonnie stared down at her feet in horror. "What?" I asked.

"Heat makes it expand, cold makes it contract," Helen finished. Her hands were in her pockets and she leaned back on her heels.

"Why?" I asked.

Bonnie climbed up the railing, trying to get her feet off the bridge that might collapse at any moment. Adele went to hold her safe. "Concrete's like people," she explained. "When it's hot, each little bit of concrete tries to get away from every other little bit. Like how it sucks to share a bed with someone in the summer. When it's cold . . ." — Adele squeezed Bonnie hard until she had to giggle — "they snuggle together close. Like you two, always climbing into my bed in the winter and sticking your cold feet on my back."

"That's not it at all," Helen said, still facing away from us. "The kinetic energy increases as you heat something, so the particles vibrate at higher amplitudes, increasing their average distance from one another."

Adele tickled Bonnie, who hooted and arched backward over the railing, almost falling. "That's what I just said."

Helen turned around. Her chin-length hair tangled in her face from the hot wind. Her shoulders broadened. Expanding. "That is *not* what you just said." She gestured at Bonnie and me. "They believe whatever bullshit you say, you know. They're going to think concrete has feelings."

"Of course not," Bonnie protested. She slid to the ground, toed the bridge sympathetically. "It just doesn't like to be cold."

In August, the flies and bees came in from the lakes, swarmed like a fog through town. The four of us sat on the two-meter strip of grass behind the house, the bit of lawn that was ours in front of the sparse trees that belonged to no one. It was the last summer that we would all be together.

Bonnie poured orange soda on her hand and held it out, watched in fascination as the flies swarmed the back of her knuckles, tasting it with their feet. The heat forced Helen to study by osmosis. She pressed the cool cover of her SAT prep manual to her forehead. The glossy cardboard soaked up her sweat, and the knowledge flowed into her bloodstream. She pictured the problem in her head: a sheet of paper folded in half and then in half again, the constellation of holes and half-holes. Four holes in seemingly random places, one half-hole like a bite mark along the edge. How many holes will there be when the paper is unfolded? Eighteen holes.

Adele, in a white bikini, rested on her stomach on a towel. She dealt in small joys: bringing Alfie to life, letting the ticket-taker at the Luther touch her hand. Wearing a bikini on our lawn where boys could slow down their cars and gawk, too stunned to honk.

I drew on her back in black Sharpie. I was drawing angel wings, feather by feather. She let me wear one of her old bikini tops, as long as I wore a boy T-shirt over the top. I felt the warm sunshine through my T-shirt, and I hoped I was getting a tan around the halter straps of the bikini. I held my elbows in tight as I stroked her back with the felt pen. It squished the flat skin over my sternum into ridges that were not completely unlike Adele's shelf of cleavage.

"That tickles." Adele yawned.

The SAT manual blocked Helen's face completely. It looked like it had replaced her head. "All the toxins in the ink are seeping into your skin," she said, muffled.

My angel wings were elaborate, eighteen pointed ovals, one wing sloping out of each of Adele's shoulder blades. She shrugged and the wings shifted. When she showered that night, the soap foam would run black.

Soon there were boxes at the foot of Adele's bed marked Home and Away, like opposing teams. While Adele was in the bathroom getting ready to go out—writing 18 in lipstick on the mirror and wiping it off with her arm—I went into Adele and Helen's bedroom. I started pulling things out of the Away boxes. Helen stayed at her desk and didn't stop me, which I took as tacit blessing.

Helen lived at her desk. She ate handfuls of dry bran cereal and drank coffee that was dark as river silt. Already the seed of the woman she would become was visible, the woman who would crush multivitamins to a powder with the back of a chef's knife, who would believe eating disorders were things that happened to young girls; grown women could not be too thin. I moved Adele's winter sweaters into a Home box. I threw some books onto the ground. I flung her sneakers across the room, then followed them with a long volley of balled-up socks and underwear, the panties blooming open midair like juggling scarves. I counted them as I threw: eighteen pairs of socks and eighteen pairs of panties. I pulled out a tangled string of fake pearls and put it on over my head.

I paused briefly at a thin photo album. Open to a random page, it showed Adele as a child, her stick legs in a yellow sundress. Almond eyes wide with invitation. It had been worse then: She made grown men sweat, made their thoughts dribble from their temples. Made them question what kind of men they were.

When the box was light enough, I dumped the rest out onto Adele's bed. I rolled on top, right in the center of the mess, a makeup compact digging briefly into my back. I pulled it out from underneath me and snapped it open. In its tiny mirror, there was just a small circle of the center of my face. I fluffed blush onto my cheekbones, trying to sharpen them into Adele's high angles.

Bouncing near me on the mattress was a pot of violet eye shadow that made me think of an eye forced open. I brushed it onto my eyelids. I wet my thumb on my tongue and smeared the shadow into an opaque layer, all the way from the tear ducts to the outside corners.

"Don't mess with her makeup, Peter," Helen said, as though that were the worst of the things I'd done. She tapped a pen against her lips. She made no effort to stand. "You look insane."

I peered into the compact mirror again. I thought I looked lovely.

I popped open Adele's clear plastic umbrella with a border of roses at the bottom and held it over my head, like I was in a bubble. I heard the bathroom door open. I sat up, crossing one leg over the other above the knee, keeping my back primly straight. Adele stopped in the doorway. She took in the sight of her things strewn across the room and the miniature version of herself. I announced, "Now you can't leave."

Adele pried my fingers gently from the umbrella. For a

moment, she held it so easily it seemed to hover. Then she pulled it shut. The umbrella went back in the box.

She scooped clothes off the floor in piles. She shoved the Away box up against the edge of the bed, and, in a few sweeps of her arms, everything tumbled back in again—rumpled, disorganized, but back in the box. I couldn't believe how quickly my plan had unraveled. She gave me an uninterested, affectionate pinch on the shoulder and left the room.

Adele and Helen were once offered a ride home by a stranger. Helen was twelve and Adele was thirteen, the more interesting age.

The man was not entirely a stranger, Adele would later argue—a friend of a friend's father. She still remembered him as handsome, wearing a white jacket with large lapels like a preacher on TV. Unsustainably clean.

He gestured to them from the window. She remembered noticing his neatly trimmed fingernails. There was a fine rain. Adele got into the car. Helen refused, so Adele gave her the umbrella. Helen watched the car disappear through a watery blur of pink roses. She thought Adele would never come home, and she couldn't make herself feel bad about that. When you behave that stupidly, there are consequences: maybe the river would be dredged for bodies two weeks later.

Helen and Adele arrived home at the same time. The coughing gray Lincoln Continental stopped at the house next door and Adele stepped out. One leg and then the other, like a movie star. Smiled and waved at the driver as he pulled off. Helen told herself that she was glad Adele wasn't murdered, that she hadn't wanted to tell the news cameras that she was the smart one, the one who didn't get in the car, the one who knew it was better to squish down the sidewalk in waterlogged shoes than risk getting strangled by a pervert. She watched Adele wiping her mouth on the back of her hand.

I ran from the bathroom back to Helen's post. The one thing Helen and I had in common was our lack of friends. Bonnie sometimes disappeared to other little girls' houses, and Adele had a wide territory through town. She could be anywhere.

"Helen, help." Helen looked up and saw me frantically rubbing my eyes, purple- and pink-stained, as wide as raccoon markings. "It won't come off. It won't come off! Dad will be home soon!"

Helen watched my agonized dance as I hopped from foot to foot like I had to pee. Her face said *I hope you've learned something*. She ushered me back to the bathroom. She knelt to get into one of the cupboards, and her seventeen-year-old knees cracked.

"Here." She handed me a tub of cold cream. "Put it on top of the makeup, then wipe it away, then wash your face again." I spread a thick layer over my entire face, leaving holes for my eyes. A Halloween mask. Helen crossed her arms. "Why did you put it on?"

I was too busy dunking my head under the tap to answer. Water flooded in and out of my nose. "You want to look like her," she said. I didn't deny it. "You're too young to understand how pathetic she is. How badly she needs people to like her." I pressed a towel to my face and inspected it in the mirror for blush and shadow. My skin was dried out from the scrubbing. "You look at her and you think that beauty is all that matters."

My face was clean. Colorless and uninteresting as Helen's.

Everyone could see that Adele was the superior creature: the ticket-seller at the Luther, the man who drove her home and left Helen standing smart and unwanted on the curb.

The night before Adele was supposed to leave, I was determined not to sleep. I sat up in bed, convinced there was some way I could stop it from happening. I'd hidden her bus ticket in the pantry, but that was only a stopgap.

I heard Bonnie shifting in her bed. "Hey, Peter?"

"Yeah?"

"The cranes aren't birds, are they."

"No."

We sat in the dark, both of us picturing giant white birds sleeping in construction yards. Their heads were tucked under their wings, beaks harder than steel. Who would give us these visions? Who would take us to black-and-white films, let us draw on her back and wear her clothes? When Adele left, all beauty would pass from the world.

The sun seemed explosively bright when I woke up, though our bedside clock said it was only six o'clock. I got dressed without waking Bonnie. Her leg hung off the edge of the bed and twitched as she slept.

I stepped silently through the hallway and the living room. Adele's boxes and suitcases were lined up by the door, the stacks varying in height like siblings in a family portrait. They were the symbols of her leaving. They were the agents of her leaving. I was going to bury them in the ground.

I decided to start with the heaviest box I could carry, leaving the easier boxes and the wheeled suitcases for later, when I was tired. I carried it as far as the backyard before I had to flop down. I took a moment to breathe then dragged it into the trees, digging my heels in the dirt.

Adele would be able to dig them up later, once she'd been convinced of her mistake. The boxes were sealed with tape. The contents would stay clean. I was doing her a favor.

In the copse of spindly birches, some of them dead but still standing, the trees were too far apart to provide much cover. I left the box between them anyway. I went back to get the metal snow shovel from where it hung behind the house. It was heavy. Another body to drag.

It took all of my strength to lift the shovel up and drop it, point down, to the ground. It bounced off the hard earth. There was no way I could dig a hole here, let alone one deep enough to contain the Away box. I slid down and rested against the shovel, picturing the boxes and suitcases waiting by the door, their passive victory.

As my breathing slowed, I became aware of the sound of moving water—a slow, babbling flow. I left the box and shovel and climbed the slight slope. I caught sight of a narrow tributary below me, a stream that flowed into the larger river that went through town, the one with the bridge that didn't like to be cold.

Maybe the dirt would be softer closer to the stream. More like mud.

I couldn't lift the box this time, so I shoved it up the ridge. Once it was over the hill, I gave it one solid push so that it rolled down to the river's edge. I threw the shovel after it and stumbled down to them. The box was dusty and streaked with mud, the corners crushed inward, making it more like a ball.

I started to scrape at the bank with my shovel. It didn't

really make a hole—the dirt just broke away and crumbled into the river.

"Peter!"

I looked back. A figure stood on top of the ridge, the eastern sun behind. Even in silhouette, I knew it was Helen from the threat of her stance. She edged down the hill sideways, arms out like a surfer's.

I sat down, defeated, putting my butt squarely in the mud.

Helen stopped in front of me. She looked at the shovel. She looked at my tired face, my stained clothes. At the dirty, still-sealed box now with only the *Aw* of *Away* legible. She watched the box tensely, as though it were a wound-up jack-in-the-box.

She knelt down. Mud and water got into her sandals. With both arms, she thrust the box into the stream.

The box sank down with a sucking *blomp*, then bobbed up again. Only the top was visible, like an iceberg. The box moved leisurely with the current. When it struck the rocks along the bank slightly farther down, not very hard, the tape came loose from the sodden cardboard. The flaps popped open.

Helen and I watched as Adele's possessions flowed away and the box buoyed more and more easily to the surface. Glossy paperback covers jumped like iridescent fish. A coveted leather jacket floated on its inner lining, looking like an eel, sleek and menacing. Everything migrated slowly downstream.

I felt numb, more conscious of the wet seat of my pants than anything else. Helen extended her hand to me. I took it and she pulled me up. We walked back to the house. At the back door, Helen took off her sandals and wiped her bare feet on the mat. She lined up her shoes neatly. I kicked my sneakers off and left them where they landed.

Adele was standing with her boxes and suitcases by the front door. She paced a small circle. The house still had the anticipatory air that it had when my parents were sleeping, their authority latent. Adele's face—eyebrows knit in confusion, not accusation—made me realize what we'd done. I started to cry.

Adele opened her arms and I rushed for her knees. "I just wanted you to stay," I mumbled, muffled by the bottom of her nightshirt. Even then, I knew my eight-year-old tears were crocodilian. I knew what I was saying: *I don't care if you're happy, as long as you're here.*

I could feel Adele and Helen meeting eyes over my head. Helen stayed a safe distance away from our embrace, her head held high and her stare blank.

Adele's stuff washed up on the riverbank a day later. Someone phoned the police, thinking there had been a drowning, that all those clothes implied a body. It was in the local paper.

Another family would have reported what had actually happened, saved the town from speculation. Ours ignored it. The explanation was too complicated, too private. I had guilty nightmares. In my dreams, policemen stood at the edge of the river, carefully skimming the water with butterfly nets. They moved as gingerly as archaeologists, gathering pieces of a teenage girl's life. They ignored their radio and the screams of real crimes.

Adele went to study at the University of Western Ontario, in another Ontario town that sprawled through strip malls and industrial lands, hardly different from the one she'd started in. Helen left a year later. She went to UCLA on a cocktail of scholarships and bursaries that just covered her first year.

On a weekend, she drove by herself to Santa Monica. She bought a sandwich and sat on the Venice Beach boardwalk, laughing reedily at artists hawking sketches, musicians in the costumes of their subcultures thrusting tapes at passersby, the deluded parade of people who thought they'd *make it* one day. Helen went to California like a gold-rush miner, expecting to find a place where dreamers were ground underfoot by the hard-working, the wise. She would return wearing a suit of gold or she wouldn't return at all.

We drove as a family to drop Adele off at the bus station. The buses picked up from a long strip like an airfield. She wore impractical traveling clothes: high heels and a cinched blazer, both in electric blue. Her hourglass figure shimmied away with the distinct ticktock of her shoes on the asphalt. Bonnie and I held hands as we watched her go. We were the same height, had the same baby plumpness, the same sweaty palms. At a certain point, we couldn't tell if Adele was walking toward us or away.

I have no memory of Helen's leaving. If it was by plane, train, or bus. If we said goodbye. I have only memories of events that took place before she left and memories of events that took place after. It was as though when she left, she vanished in the night, unnoticed.

# 3

## *Thursdays*

EVERY DAY BUT THURSDAY, Bonnie and I came straight home from school. We did our homework at the kitchen table. Bonnie turned my threes into birds and sideways pairs of breasts. I watched the back of our mother as she shelled shrimp in the sink, her spine rigid and visible through a cotton shift. She inhaled sharply as she cut her finger on a spiky leg. She lifted her finger high enough for me to see the drop of red falling into the bowl of naked shrimp, and then she went on. Their briny gray juices got into her wound, and she went on. We would eat her blood for dinner.

The doorbell rang. My mother jumped as though slapped awake. She went to open the door. "Yes?"

Bonnie climbed over me to see who it was, and I followed. We strained to see past our mother.

The woman at the door was pale and thin and seemed to quiver at the edges, like she was made of water. She had limp red hair. Her freckles were a handful of sand tossed in her face. "Hi," she said. "I'm Lisa Becker. I live down the block."

My mother stayed mostly behind the door. "Did you just move in?"

"No, we've lived here for a few years."

"What do you want?"

"Well, I, uh . . ." Mrs. Becker seemed to have forgotten why she had come. She glanced around for an explanation. Her gaze landed on the plastic box in her hands. "Oh, right. I heard you had a little boy and girl. I had some toys we don't need, so I thought I'd give them to you." She opened the container: a rag doll and some toy cars.

"My son is fourteen and my daughter is thirteen. But thank you." My mother started to close the door. Something in Mrs. Becker's face stopped her. "How old are your children?"

"I don't have any children." She moved her head and hands constantly, like a bird, and it made it hard to concentrate on what she was saying. "I had a miscarriage a few years ago and my mother had already bought me the toys. You know —whether it was a boy or girl, we'd be ready." She closed the container. "I guess they would have been more useful to you back then."

I couldn't see my mother's face, but I could feel the distaste radiating off her back. What kind of woman talks about miscarriages at a stranger's front door? "Thank you for the offer, Mrs. Becker."

If my mother breathed out too hard, Mrs. Becker would blow away like a plastic bag. "No problem, Mrs. Huang." She started down the front steps. She was wearing white sneakers, the same discount-store brand as my mother.

"How did she know our name?" Bonnie asked.

"Who cares," Mother said, going back to the sink.

· · ·

Bonnie was born fourteen months after me, more like a twin than a younger sister. When she was twelve and I was thirteen, she stole a pair of earrings from a friend's house. She walked into the jewelry store of the nearest mall and tried to sell them. The clerk called the cops. Bonnie told them she had taken it from her own mother's jewelry box. The cop called our house.

I was home. I hated answering the phone, so I stood by the machine and listened to the long, grave message. The moment he hung up my hand shot out and hit the Delete button.

Bonnie was delivered home. She didn't learn any of the things the cops had intended to teach her. She learned to go to pawnshops downtown, wear heels, not look twelve.

When Bonnie was five and I was six, we popped out of our shared gray bathwater and went into the kitchen. It was exam season, when Adele claimed to be studying at the library in the afternoons and Helen actually was. Our mother, hiding from us in the bedroom, had left dinner to simmer. Bonnie wet her hands in the beet juices on the cutting board and convinced me to do the same. She reached back and squeezed her own buttocks, leaving a pink imprint of cupping hands. I grabbed the sides of her face. Magenta tribal paint. She pushed back on my shoulders, giggling.

Key in the lock. Our father walked in the front door and our mother walked out of her bedroom to greet him. The beet soup started to boil. We were covered in each other's red fingerprints, smudged meaningless. Our hands were puckered from the bath, and the sunken stains highlighted the creases. "What are you doing?" Mother asked.

Bonnie and I looked at each other, puzzled. It had made sense a moment before.

My father took off his shoes, leaning his hand against the wall. He announced to no one in particular that a boy and a girl were too old to bathe together at our age. He disappeared into their room.

My mother snapped back to life. She dragged us by the arms to the bathroom. Bonnie sat on the closed toilet seat, swinging her legs and examining her rosy blotches, while I sat in the tub and my mother scrubbed me with the back of a sponge. My mother concentrated on each stain, scraping the rough side against my skin until I cried, rubbing and rubbing as though she could erase us both.

My mother worked part-time as a telemarketer. She came home later on Thursdays. My father thought it would be good for her to get out of the house and talk to people. People in far-off cities, mostly in America, screamed abuse in varying accents, their voices slightly hollow from the distance. As though cursing her from the bottom of a tin can.

On Thursdays, Bonnie and her friends went to a pool hall on the other side of town that didn't card. They drank coolers in glass bottles, mostly sugar and dye.

One night, Bonnie came home running. I watched her through the window over the kitchen sink, running in zigzags down the long driveway as though someone were chasing her. *She's drunk,* I thought, *or she thinks she is.*

I went to meet her at the door. She burst in and kissed me just to the side of my mouth. My face felt tight where she left a glazed mark. I licked it and it tasted like candy. "Mom is behind me," she said.

Our mother had gotten onto the same bus. She had sat

down near the front immediately and didn't see Bonnie at the back. Bonnie looked out the bus's window when Mother got on: they were stopped at the Chinese Association, a brick building covered in tangled graffiti, mostly black, like a ball of steel wool. "The Chinese Assoc," Bonnie said to me, pronouncing it "a-sock" because that's what was on the building; the rest of the gold-painted letters had fallen off and never been replaced.

Bonnie had slunk off the bus one stop early and bolted home through unfenced yards. She told me this once we had moved to the bathroom, where she could brush her teeth, both of us listening for the door. "The call center is nowhere near there," I said.

Bonnie bared her foamy teeth. "I guess she doesn't work on Thursdays." She bent over the sink and spat. "What did you make for dinner? It smells great."

"Pasta," I said.

"What's in it? In case they ask again."

"Ground beef, cream, chicken stock, peas."

We went out into the kitchen. Mother was already hanging up her coat, having slipped into the house without a sound. "Hi, Mom," Bonnie said.

"Hi. Thank you for making dinner, Bonnie."

"No problem."

"Your father will be late today," Mother said. "So we can go ahead and eat without him."

I was disappointed. I got a secondhand thrill when my father praised Bonnie for her cooking, slapped her hard on the shoulder. No one had explicitly forbidden me to cook, but my father, just once, had reached out an arm to stop me when I went to help my mother with the dishes. "Women's work," he said.

We sat at the kitchen table and Mother served Bonnie and me. Bonnie ate like a hearty drunk. I watched my mother wander back behind the counter, slowly constructing her own bowl. Forgetting we were there, a distant look on her face, she took a mahjong tile out of her pocket and brought it to her mouth. I could just hear the sound of her teeth on the plastic, as though testing whether or not it was real.

Years later, after my mother died, I went to see the Chinese Association building again. The *c* in *Assoc* had fallen off, and the remaining *o* had been spray-painted over as a joke. I wondered why the letters fell from right to left. Some workman on a ladder, putting in the studs, losing faith as he went. The longer he worked, the looser the letters became: tight *A*, then *s*, then another *s*, then *o*, then what was the point, what was the point of this language, while people yelled at him from below: *You interrupted my dinner, you woke my baby, how did you get my number, this number is supposed to be off your fucking lists, you people are the scum of the earth, how do you sleep at night?* The workman had mounted *Chinese* first and it stuck.

In the rare solitude of Thursdays, I cleaned the house. I wore a full-length apron that my father had bought for my mother and that she had never used. It was made of cheap-looking acrylic with machine lace for the trim, the color of a pearl. Naked except for the apron, I pushed the vacuum across the floor, scrubbed the bathroom on my knees.

As I made dinner, I watched a cooking show on the portable black-and-white television, another gift in which my mother had no interest. I had lost most of the feeling in my fingertips from constant burning. I dipped my little finger in sauces while they were still in the pan to taste them, making a seductive face at the TV screen, imitating the show's host: an older Italian woman, fifty and sumptuous as an overstuffed sofa. She hacked lamb shanks with a cleaver while wearing a brief slip dress. She pouted and I pouted. "Half the flavor is in the presentation," we said in unison.

Before anyone came home, I folded and put away the apron, first pausing to hold it to my face. It was starting to get the rubbery smell of my own body.

When my parents first came to Fort Michel, Father did the books at an import-export store near the Chinese Association. He entered receipts for rugs and furniture in English and Chinese into a ledger. His desk was inside a metal cage with the safe and the register. Adele told me about the Chinese couple who owned the store. They affected a goofy, stumbling servility for their white customers, grabbing their hands and bowing deeply with every sale. "Thank you, thank you, thank you!" Then they'd head into the back to write it up, muttering to my father, "*Sei-gwai-lo.* Idiots."

He managed a McDonald's off the highway for a while after that. Helen remembered the smell when he came home, the distinct beef-tallow perfume they sprayed onto the french fries. He wore a jacket and tie every day, and our mother spent her nights scrubbing stains out of the wool. He managed a gas station. He managed a sporting-goods store. He liked to be in charge of people. He liked the respect demanded by *manager;* he would accept any pay but no other title. Father never stayed at one job for long. He always felt he wasn't climbing fast enough.

Eventually he was hired by the Passport Canada office near us, part of a federal visible-minorities program. Nothing could be more antithetical to the way my father saw himself. Under the Languages Spoken sign, they added a slate: Cantonese. The rare Chinese customers always ended up at his window. Father forced them to speak English. He was patient but unrelenting.

There were only three offices with doors behind the service windows, and within two years, one of them was my father's. Being a civil servant fit his white-collar idea of prosperity. Everyone dressed the way he always had—jackets, ties, shined shoes. No burgers. But their pale faces in the fluorescence reminded him how he'd gotten there, by being *visible*. He comforted himself with pictures of his two eldest daughters, away at university. Adele would be an invisible doctor and Helen would be an invisible lawyer. He'd laid it out for them, and they had expressed no resistance. Bonnie and I had much simpler orders. Be a little girl forever, be a boy.

My father called to say he was working late again. My mother said, "Mmm-hmm," and hung up. We ate my canned-tuna casserole. I thought about roasted lamb with rosemary.

Mother read the paper while she ate. Bonnie and I played hangman on the comics page. She wrote out a long string of spaces, her lips dark and ragged at the edges.

"*A,*" I said. "*D.*"

Her six-word phrase turned out to be *Made out with old bar guy.*

When it was my turn, I drew thirteen lines, four words. A question mark at the end. *What was it like?*

The phone rang again and Bonnie ran to answer it. *I gave him my number,* she mouthed at me over her shoulder.

*Are you insane?* I mouthed back, and she grinned.

When she came back, her face was unreadable. She sat down in a slow, brittle way, holding her knees tightly together, like someone under the table was trying to look up her skirt. "Was it him?" I whispered.

"Who was it?" my mother asked.

Bonnie took so long to answer that my mother put down the paper. She looked tiny holding it, the newspaper almost longer than her body. Bonnie started piercing food with her fork. The largest chunk of tuna on her plate, a piece of pasta, a pea on each tine. "It was Dad's office," she said. "He left his wallet."

"Oh," Mother replied, opening the paper again. "Tell him when he gets home."

Our father came home three hours later. I listened to him and my mother in the bathroom at the same time. The toilet flushed. The sink ran. He didn't shower. They moved into the bedroom, and the lights went out. Neither of them spoke loudly enough to be heard.

I tried to imagine my father's mistress. The culmination of his immigrant fantasy, blond as Marilyn Monroe, breasts like party balloons, a loudmouthed vixen fattened on abundant grain and milk in the great fields of America. Or maybe, the way sex squeezes irony out of us, she was a Chinese seamstress, almond eyes squinting more and more, her vision vanishing at the point of her needle. Maybe my father wanted to push his tongue against the sounds of the old language; maybe she was silent and docile, scrawny from the voyage, still wearing a stash of incongruous peasant clothes that looked like linen pajamas. My mother before my father had begun his project of westernization, my father the conqueror.

Years later, visiting home, I went to see the bar where Bonnie had given her number to old men. It was open at ten in the morning, dank and empty. I saw Mrs. Becker's husband sleeping on his arms in a booth. The bartender didn't seem to care. I sat at Mr. Becker's table and we talked about his wife. I knew she'd died in an accident soon after we met her and that Mr. Becker was the one who had found her. Neither my mother nor the kids at school could elaborate any further—an accident, a tragic accident on our street.

"My bus was never late," he said. "I was home every day at seven forty. On the dot."

He told me that Mrs. Becker liked to eat sour candies crusted with sugar by pressing them to the top of her mouth. She didn't like pain in general, he said drunkenly, least of all in bed—just that, crystals cutting in and wearing away her soft palate, often doing it until she bled. He could taste it when he kissed her. "Like sucking on pennies," he said.

Another Thursday. I walked home from school, anticipating an empty house. As I rounded the corner, I saw Mrs. Becker standing in her yard and watching the sprinkler spit its twitching lines like it needed supervision. Sprinklers were an odd sight in our neighborhood of scraggly trees and poisoned soil. She spotted me as I tried to run past. "Hello there!"

"Hi."

She held out her hand. I shook it. Her white glove was dry and cool. "I'm Mrs. Becker. You live in the house at the end of the road, right?"

"Yes." In full sunlight, she looked even paler. The light shone through her skin to the blue veins along her forehead.

"What's your name?"

"Peter."

"It's nice to meet you, Peter. Can I ask you a question?"

"Sure, I guess."

"What does your mother like?" Mrs. Becker clasped her hands together in a position of prayer. "I feel terrible about the other day. I'd like to get her a gift." I didn't understand what she felt terrible about; my mother was the one who'd been rude. "Flowers? Does she like flowers? Apricot cake? I make a great apricot cake."

"I don't know. Maybe."

"I'll bring by an apricot cake."

The sprinkler hit her feet and ankles each time it went around, wetting her shoes and the hem of her dress. She didn't seem to notice.

"Okay, sure. Thanks, Mrs. Becker."

"Your mother seems like such a nice lady. I want us to be friends. Does she like to go to the movies? Play cards?" Her smile looked unstable. The structure of her face couldn't sustain the weight.

"She likes to play mahjong," I said.

"I'm afraid I don't know that one."

"I'm sorry, Mrs. Becker, but I have to go."

"Oh! Sure. Is she waiting for you?" She looked in the direction of our house as if expecting to see my mother standing there.

"No, but . . ." I searched for something to say. "It's my turn to clean the house."

"Do you need any help? I have an hour or two. I could come over and help you."

I balked. "No, thank you."

"I'm sorry. That was inappropriate of me. I'm so sorry."

"I've gotta go," I repeated. I ran down the street.

Inside our dim house, I gave my eyes a minute to adjust to the light. Standing in the kitchen, I took off my pants, underwear, and shirt and pulled my scrunched socks up to my knees. I took out the apron, put one loop around my head and another around my waist, the pinched sateen catching on my sparse body hair. It felt like a second skin — a better one.

I turned on the television, knowing there would be three episodes of Giovetta in a row. A jaunty trumpet played the theme song over close-ups of gourmet dishes, intercut with Giovetta dancing. She only swayed her hips and snapped her fingers, her huge body pushing the borders of our nine-inch TV. I imitated her movements, sliding on my socks. At the end, with the show title under her round face, she bit an empty fork while staring right into the camera. She was pleasure incarnate.

I continued to dance to her voice as though it were music, coming thick through the layers of fat over her throat. "Mmm," she said. "If only you could smell this. Truly incredible." I shimmied through the house, picking things up off the floor.

As I entered the living room, I caught a flash of white in my peripheral vision. I instinctively turned my bare back and buttocks away. Mrs. Becker was standing in our yard, staring through the window as frankly as a ghost.

I screeched and ran. I could hear her voice, muffled but penetrating the glass. "I'm sorry! I'm sorry!"

I hid in another room for almost two hours, stayed until I had to go back out to the kitchen to get my clothes before everyone else came home. It was dark by then. There was no sign of anyone outside.

Mrs. Becker followed Bonnie and a boy home from school. He was one of the boys she went to the bar with on Thursdays, gangly with a splatter pattern of acne across his chin, but — Bonnie explained — he had dark eyes and was good at pool. They went into the woods behind the supermarket. He sat down on a flat rock and she got down on her knees. The hard soil scraped her bare-skinned legs as she bobbed her head up and down.

"Have you done this before?" he asked.

"Yeah," she lied. "But never with a guy my own age."

The boy loved this answer, Bonnie told me. He idolized older boys, and putting his cock in Bonnie's mouth made him one of them. He closed his eyes, opened them, closed them, opened them. "Shit," he said.

"What?"

"Someone's watching us."

Bonnie stood up. A flag of red hair disappeared along the path.

Bonnie decided that if Mrs. Becker was going to spy on us, we might as well spy on her too. We watched Mrs. Becker leave her house at four in the afternoon, get in the car, and drive away. Bonnie, who by then had all kinds of skills, jimmied open the Beckers' living-room window, which faced their backyard and away from the road.

The house was laid out the same way as ours—three bedrooms, one floor—which gave us the eerie feeling of being in a parallel universe. Our mother favored spareness and unpainted wood; the Beckers liked animal ornaments and cartoon vegetables on the curtains. Bonnie flipped through the mail on their kitchen counter, took a bar of chocolate from the cupboard, peeked in the fridge. I went straight for the bedrooms.

The first bedroom I went into had pastel-blue wallpaper bordered with ducklings and furniture under plastic sheeting. I lifted the plastic off a chair. When I dropped it again, the chair started to rock back and forth. The other furniture turned out to be a crib and a changing table.

I passed Bonnie in the bathroom, spraying perfume on her wrist and then smelling it. The bed in the master bedroom had a pink duvet and pink chiffon curtains between the posts. Except for its size, it looked like the bed of a very young girl, not a middle-aged couple.

I sat on the bed and sank in deeply, the mattress sloping sharply down toward me. I picked up the photo of them on the nightstand. It had to be fairly recent, as Mrs. Becker looked the same as she did now. She was looking at the photographer, smiling in her unsteady way. Her husband, older than her with tufts of white hair only by his temples, seemed to be tenderly admiring her ear.

Bonnie walked in. She went to the armoire and opened a few drawers before finding the one she wanted. She pulled out a pink nightgown and slipped it over her head, on top of her clothes. The neckline cut so deep, it sat lower than Bonnie's chest, and it had transparent sleeves cuffed in fur. Bonnie posed in the vanity mirror. "Yowza, Mrs. Becker."

She pulled out something that looked like strips of elastic with clasps on the ends. Neither of us knew what it was, so she put it back. Then she rooted around in the nightstand drawer—Bonnie knew where to find the best stuff.

"Jackpot!" She waved around a leather-bound notebook. Seeing my face, she added, "When notebooks are kept in the bedroom, they're always good." She took a sleeping mask off the nightstand and put it on, snapping the elastic under her hair, blinding herself. She flopped backward onto the bed, still wearing Mrs. Becker's perfume and lingerie, and threw me the notebook. "Read it to me, Peter."

One page had the corner folded over, so I turned to that. I cleared my voice theatrically.

"'September nineteenth. Dr. Shultz says that I was never pregnant. He says I made the whole thing up. He says the night I spent bleeding in the bathroom was just a nightmare.'" I stopped. I looked at Bonnie, who continued to lie stiffly under her mask.

"'I remember holding the baby in my hand. A complete child. Eyelashes, toenails, knuckles. But the size of a pear. A perfect miniature child. Hard as plastic. It came out of me while I cupped my hand to catch it. A nightmare, he says. That's not what it would look like, he says.'" I skimmed the rest of the page in silence.

"Why did you stop? Keep going." Bonnie didn't move.

"I don't think we should be reading this."

"We already broke into her house, Peter. This is no time to develop a conscience."

"'I told him about the positive test. He said I should have come in to have it confirmed. He thinks I misread the test. He showed me a picture of my insides. He poked the picture with his finger and said there had never been anything there. He poked it and poked it. Each time, he got louder. I could feel him poking me on the inside.'" Bonnie looked like a different person on the bed, her eyes and their sockets hidden, her wrists poking out of pink fur.

"'Darren has agreed to tell people I miscarried. He says we shouldn't have told so many people about the pregnancy in the first place.'" My voice got higher as I read, started to flutter like Mrs. Becker's. "'But it doesn't matter whether it happened or not. I remember it. I am entitled to my memories. I had a baby and it died.'"

My eyes focused on the top edge of the page so that my legs and the floor were a blur. "I don't want to read any more," I said.

The whole room smelled like Mrs. Becker's perfume, a generic berry scent. "Okay," Bonnie replied. She took off the mask and the nightgown. "I think I'm going to try and catch my friends at the bar. Wanna come?"

Our eyes met: two animals waking up in a cage for the first time. I wanted to go home and bask in Giovetta's voice. With the blinds closed. "No, thanks." We put everything back. Bonnie returned the chocolate. We left through the window. Back then, the afternoons were long and forgiving.

A week later, my mother gambled secretly in loud Cantonese. A mahjong Thursday. Bonnie let boys and men buy her drinks, elevating her plainness with jokes. When I got home, I unlocked the front door with one hand and unbuttoned my jeans with the other.

"Peter."

My father sat on the living-room couch, his hands on his thighs. The television was off; the radio was off; no book, no magazine, no newspaper.

I stayed where I was. He walked past me and opened the cabinet above the stove. He took out the apron. It had none of its shine in his large hands. Instead, it looked like a skinned animal. I knew better than to speak.

"Follow me," he said. We walked out onto our driveway. I still hadn't buttoned up my pants. The flaps folded open like a book.

He held the apron out at arm's length. With his free hand, he took a lighter out of his pocket. A high-pitched cry came from somewhere. My throat.

A flick of the flint and our pupils reflected orange. It burned as only acrylic does, pockets of petroleum and air self-starting, self-perpetuating, a noxious and invasive smell. He dropped it on the gravel and it curled in the flames, twisting inward as though alive.

We watched it burn out. I wondered if Mrs. Becker was watching, if she had caught the signal, the pyre light, from our yard. How else could my father have known everything, if not from Mrs. Becker? A neighbor, a woman who was merely convenient. Not Marilyn Monroe, not a fresh arrival, just a jittery nobody, the human equivalent of onionskin paper.

The ashes were hard and heavy, unmoved by the wind. My father picked a chip, about the size of a small pebble, out of the pile. He pressed it into my hands.

"Swallow it," he said.

It was warm, like a dark rock in the sun.

Bonnie appeared at the end of the driveway. My eyes were wide with warning—a caught animal signaling to new prey. My father put his hand on my shoulder to stop me from moving. We waited through Bonnie's long, slow march.

She stopped and stood before him expectantly. He put his thumb and index finger on her chin, holding her face still, and leaned in. He inhaled so hard I could see his face flex with the effort. I wondered which smell was the strongest: sweet rum, the smoke of a bar, the sweat of other men on the girl he still owned?

It was decided that my mother would quit her job in order to properly control her children. We listened to my father's calm voice from the hallway. "And," he said to her, "you haven't been depositing your entire paycheck. Where's the money?"

My mother's response was too quiet to hear. We wanted her to call him out, but she didn't, and we were too afraid. My father stole all our secrets and kept his own.

As an adult, I learned that few people had affairs as I imagined them. Passing bodies sometimes collided, random and blameless as atoms, then returned to their original course. People developed second relationships as sexless and mundane as their first. Partners were willingly blind. None of the things I attached to the word *mistress* existed. But in those days, I hated them all: my father, my mother, Mrs. Becker, and even goofy, unknown Mr. Becker, the adoring fool in the photograph. Where was he? Where was Mr. Becker when my father clutched a fistful of red hair and she pretended it didn't hurt, pretended to like pain?

My mother found an apricot cake on our front steps that Saturday morning. She flipped it upside down over the trash and then handed me the pan. "Go return this," she said flatly.

Mrs. Becker was on her lawn again. She wore khaki shorts and a big hat. "Hello, Peter!"

"Hi. Thanks for the cake."

"You're welcome! Did you eat all of it already?"

"We put it on a plate."

"Was it too dry? I was worried it was a little dry." Even in the shadow of her hat, she had to squint at me; I was still standing at a distance and clutching the cake pan.

"I haven't had any yet."

"Oh. Let me know when you do. It might be too dry. Jam would help. I should have given you some jam to go with it."

"It's fine, Mrs. Becker."

"Let me get you some jam."

"No, I . . ."

"Come inside!" She turned and headed for the door. I had no choice.

I followed her into her kitchen and set down the pan. I felt uneasy that I had been there before. "Where's Mr. Becker?" I asked.

"He works on Saturdays." She dug out a jar of orange-tinted glass with a checked lid and a tied ribbon. "Here you go," she said, beaming. "Homemade."

"Thanks."

"Can I tell you a secret, Peter?" In the dim kitchen, her hat shadowed her eyes. Her grinning mouth became her whole face. "I'm just so happy. I have to tell someone."

I held the jar close, as though it could protect me.

"I'm pregnant," she said. She tilted her head to the side. "Oh, I hope the baby has dark hair, like you and your sister."

I dropped the jar. I wanted it to shatter, but it only made a dull clank and rolled away. "We're not family." That wasn't what I meant to say. I meant to call her a bitch, a home wrecker, a slut. None of those words came.

Her smile remained. I still couldn't see her eyes. "I didn't say we were."

I said, nonsensically, "Get out of my house." Then I turned and ran from hers.

Mr. Becker sold insurance in a mall in another town. He took the six-thirty bus home and arrived at precisely seven forty each day. Mrs. Becker had dinner ready at precisely seven forty-five. The bus was never late.

One evening, not long after I left the jam on the floor, a van hit a pickup truck and spun out into the oncoming cars. Mr. Becker's bus sat in traffic for an hour, behind another bus, behind a car, behind a wall of flares.

At seven thirty, Mrs. Becker went into the garage with an armful of sheets and towels. She rolled them up and stuffed them under the garage door. She got into the car they didn't use — their insurance had lapsed — and turned on the engine, leaving the driver's-side door hanging open.

"She wanted me to find her," Mr. Becker said in the bar that morning, staring into the drink I'd bought him. "I would have come home in time on any other day. You see? It was an accident."

I see her, sometimes, leaning back in her seat, clutching a pear-size baby in her hand, staring into its tiny, sloping eyes, its body hard as plastic, its crown of dark hair no larger than a fingerprint.

# 4

# *From Germany with Love*

ADELE WASN'T TAKING her premed requirements. I listened from around the corner, where Bonnie and I always hid. Father was on the phone in the hallway, talking in his dangerously calm voice, soft as wet concrete. "Transcript," he said.

Then: "Because I'm paying for it," he said.

Adele sent her transcript by mail without comment. I thought this was characteristically elegant — a written, impersonal confession that conveyed no regret. She had transferred into the arts department and was majoring in German language and literature. Her grades were high. My father waved the transcript around the kitchen, snapping the wad of paper as it wrinkled around his thumb. "Why?" He turned to Bonnie and me, silent at the breakfast table. "Why?"

Mother busied herself peeling a pear. "A boy."

And she was right. Adele sent us a picture. London, Ontario, where she went to school, was only a couple of hours away. She could easily have brought him home, just as easily as our parents could have gone to get her. They could have dragged her from her dorm room by her ankles, cut her hair, kept her in her room until she came around. I'm sure they talked about it. Instead, there was another flat, factual phone call. Was she going to go to med school? No. Then there would be no more money.

Bonnie and I managed to look at the picture before it was thrown away. His name was August and he was disappointingly unhandsome: he had blond, wilted hair and the overbite of a donkey. Large-bodied with sharp Nordic features. Yet he seduced my sister away from medicine and then away from the continent; she returned with him to Germany without finishing her degree.

Adele sent postcards addressed to Bonnie and me. We had to be quick and fish them out of the mail before our parents got to them. I couldn't understand why she had gone to this place full of dead buildings and gray waters. Even the postcard pictures were taken on overcast days, as though the sun never shone there.

At first, Bonnie and I stayed up late dissecting the postcards, constructing a life for Adele. The morning she left premed biology and just couldn't take it anymore—London, Ontario, like Fort Michel with a Costco and a Walmart. Maybe she filled her pockets with stones and walked into the Ontario Thames. We pictured her wasted and lovely with despair. Milky water closed over her head. Then blond, robust, life-loving August reached in and pulled her out. He laid her on the riverbank. He nursed her back to health. Through a fevered haze, she heard him speaking in German, telling her these small Canadian towns were killing her, she must go to Berlin to heal her soul.

Bonnie and I acted out this scene. She played August and

I played Adele, throwing myself backward onto the bed with my hand over my eyes. I read aloud from the postcards in my best imitation of Adele's voice, and Bonnie spoke in Germanic nonsense, hacking her *k*'s and *v*'s. Sometimes we had Adele save August's life: He got lost, was unprepared for the harsh Canadian winter, the long roads to nowhere. He passed out in a snow-filled ditch, aching for the dense, crowded Old World, where the snow was kicked up by millions of feet, where you were never so alone. And then Adele appeared in a white fur-lined parka, his angel of mercy.

I woke from a recurring nightmare: I had grown an extra head. It craned its neck to look back at me. It had scraggly hair on its chin and neck. Extra arms popped out of my armpits; hideous growths and tumors appeared on my back and inner thighs, weeping pus. The thing between my legs grew. It *grew.* The second head crowed with laughter, its voice deepening away from Adele's musical lilt with each laugh.

I sat up in bed and looked outside for the sound that had woken me. Bonnie was climbing out her window. She wore a denim miniskirt, and her thighs looked moon-white as she landed in a crouch in the front yard, testing the silence. Earlier that night, she hadn't been in the mood to go through the postcards again. "She's our sister, not a saint," she'd said, irritated. "Who says it's some big love story? Maybe he was just her ticket out. Maybe he just liked her tits."

I stared at Bonnie—her new breasts strapped into place, lacy bra straps showing through a diaphanous shirt, the abrupt, fleshy curve of her back—and was struck with envy so hot I could have killed her. She'd broken a promise, done something alone that we were supposed to do together.

• • •

I wrote dutifully to Adele, filling the blankness for all of us: news from Helen at school in Los Angeles, Bonnie's latest boyfriend. Eventually her postcards were replaced by letters addressed only to me. They grew longer and more intimate as Adele started to forget. She missed these in-between years, my nightmare years. When I read her letters, full of grown-up confidences, I felt the way Bonnie suddenly looked—Adele's glamorous, sparkling equal. Like the young boy she'd left behind was a different person.

One afternoon, I borrowed *Sabrina*—the Audrey Hepburn film Adele had taken us to see during her last summer at home—from the Fort Michel library. I renewed it twice and then never returned it. I told the librarian that I'd lost it and paid the fine. I was devastated by the jaunty advertising copy on the box, about Hepburn's *most hilarious* role. I remembered it as a serious drama, not a slapstick where William Holden's character is tricked into sitting on the champagne glasses in his pockets. I chose to watch only a few parts over and over again. Hepburn pacing in an organza Givenchy gown and pearl teardrop earrings. Hepburn in black slacks and a black shirt that plunges down her back. Soon I could remember Adele's features only in black-and-white. Sabrina goes to Europe to become even more sophisticated, even more perfect. She goes for love.

Adele and August moved into a house in Berlin that was occupied, though not owned, by a large group of friends. It had once been a single-family manor with two stairwells in the front hall that led to what might be called wings. A spray-painted mural dominated the hall, an abstract image of blue and orange cubes. Ordinary graffiti of names and tags was scribbled on top. Adele thought this was sad; August called it "living art."

These friends promised to find Adele work, but nothing materialized. They needed the jobs for themselves. They came and went in extreme numbers. Each morning when Adele woke up, there were more people than there'd been the night before—they must have been hiding in some unknown cavern of the house. With nothing to do, Adele became the den mother. She cleaned the red, foul-smelling mold that grew over the rice cooker. She washed people's clothes in the sink and hung them to dry all over the house. To walk around, one had to push aside the damp shirts and sheets suspended from every lamp, doorway, and surface, like parting overgrown plants in a jungle. She rolled their unconscious bodies into positions in which they were less likely to choke on tongues or vomit. She made food that could be reheated easily for large groups at strange hours: meatless stews and soups, beans cooked until gray and earthy as mulch.

A very young girl lived in the house. She had renamed herself Cherry and was the house pet. She spent most of her time sprawled on the furniture or the floor, reading magazines or sleeping. Adele had to clean around her. Adele thought Cherry looked like a baby, with her plump arms and legs and her flabby, shapeless breasts. She had bright red cheeks and a stoned-looking smile; she took whatever drugs were handed to her with the lazy entitlement of a queen.

August started sleeping with Cherry. Everyone but Adele showered rarely and briefly, and hot water in the house was scarce. (*They call me the jealous American,* she wrote. *The jealous American who takes long, wasteful showers.*) As a result, August smelled like Cherry when he returned to the bed he shared with Adele: sample perfumes from magazines covering the chalky, sour scent of teenage sweat. *He plays it off as the nature of the house. As though the house is to blame. A free exchange of bodies and love and ideas.*

And as Adele scrubbed a stain from one of Cherry's childish, printed dresses, she thought that that would not be so bad, if it were true. If everyone fucked everyone and they all slept in a heap like rats. She thought of a man with a narrow, sullen face she had seen pacing the hallways of the east wing; it would be all right if she could have him, as easy as she pleased, offer herself up as an exotic feast, a platter of mangoes and pineapple and near-poisonous fish.

But it wasn't true. It was just August and Cherry and August and Adele, a triangle with nothing profound or freeing about it.

August offered to marry Adele to simplify her immigration. She agreed. It was a matter of paperwork and translation in a *Standesamt.* Two women from the house witnessed with stoic disinterest.

After, they all went to an illegal nightclub in an abandoned building. Christmas lights were wound around the pipes and airshaft. A large hole in one wall near the ceiling showed a fragment of sky and let in a wintry draft. There was broken glass on the floor from an unknown source. The crowd did not smile as they danced, as though their pleasure ran too deep for such showy expression.

August and Adele danced together under a scattering blue laser. He gave her dramatic, over-the-top kisses, dipping her backward by the waist or lifting her into the air. They drank beer mixed with lemonade. In spite of herself, she felt bubbly and light, like something had happened worth celebrating. August yelled to a group of strangers, in German, "Hey, guys! We got married today!"

The men cheered, raised their glasses. One said something Adele couldn't catch over the music. "What did he say?" she asked August.

August and the man laughed meanly. "He said that you are very beautiful," August said, winking at his new friend.

(*It wasn't the wedding I was happy about. Ironically, being married to August meant I could finally leave him,* she wrote, much later. I don't think that's how she felt at the time. She married the man she loved. She and Cherry had new titles—wife and mistress—and while Cherry's was more exciting, hers had its own sweetness. Her body was now his home.)

August chastised Cherry for getting fat. After August and Adele had come home married, Cherry had continued to spend her days lolling on the sofas, only now she ate. She ate tiny oranges, almonds, chocolates, olives, slices of cheese— a steady stream of small indulgences rather than meals. She wouldn't eat Adele's mushy curries and soups. When she got up to find more treats, Cherry would graze through the house like a large, unhurried animal.

August's criticism came charged. He found her more erotic than ever. A stream of abuse accompanied their lovemaking and could be heard throughout the house. He called her a fat, ugly sow as he squeezed her expanding breasts with glee.

Willowy, gamine Adele, the dark and classic beauty, to be seen and not touched—she sensed that something else was happening, that the raging, barefoot, feminine fire in the next room was bigger than chocolates and almonds. She was the first to say it out loud, although it was obvious by then. Cherry wore leggings and August's shirts over her bulk. Adele said, "I think you're pregnant."

(I asked Adele endless questions about Cherry's pregnancy. I wanted the most intimate details. Adele's responses were scientific and tinged with disgust; I focused on the ones that surprised me. That her hair abruptly went curly. That she sweated so much she darkened the upholstery. That her pasty skin became mottled and brown over the cheekbones and elbows.)

August called a house meeting. House meetings happened from time to time and usually concerned a minor theft. The results were always the same. The known-but-unnamed thief was blamed for breaking the familial trust of the house, and the victim was blamed for leaving anything of value unsupervised.

This meeting concerned Cherry, who now resembled a ship at dock when she wedged herself onto the sofa. August claimed that because of the nature of the house, no one could be sure who the father was or whether or not he still lived there. Therefore, the baby should be the house's responsibility. Cherry, docile as a drugged kitten, did receive other lovers from time to time, but the odds were still a thousand to one in August's favor.

Everyone agreed, to preserve the image of the house as a mythic, orgiastic place: the baby had grown from a house full of love, not from any one man and woman. August drew up a schedule. House residents—mostly women—signed up for days and times. By vote, they decided on Skye for a boy and Hanah for a girl. After being jabbed by August, people threw crumpled bills into a shoebox to pay for a bassinet and diapers. It was important, August noted, that Cherry not get overburdened. It's not her baby. It's *our* baby.

August and Cherry planned a home birth in the bathtub. There would be dozens of familiar hands on her belly, easing the child into the world. What actually happened: Women clustered in the doorway, left, and came back. Their hands went nowhere near Cherry. A sudden rush of blood caught everyone off-guard. "Is that normal?" someone asked, backing away from the door. When Cherry's placid mewling turned into savage shrieks, someone ducked into the kitchen and called for an ambulance.

Cherry and Hanah returned a few days later. Cherry moved from the living room to a bedroom with a door. Hanah floated through the rotation on the schedule for a few weeks. (*A wrinkly, cone-headed monster,* Adele wrote.)

August—who worked at a bookstore that clandestinely sold hash—liked to greet the baby when he came home from work. He picked her up under the arms and danced around the room. He blew raspberries on her belly until she made a toothless, wide-mouthed expression; August insisted that she was practicing how to smile. Then he passed her off to the person whose turn it was to care for her. He was not officially on the roster.

One day, Adele returned from the Turkish market with powdered formula for Hanah and fresh vegetables for Cherry. She checked the schedule taped by the front door: a woman named Gudrun was supposed to be watching Hanah, but no one had seen Gudrun for weeks. Adele checked Cherry's room; the girl was in a dead midafternoon sleep. The birth, according to the one woman who accompanied Cherry to the hospital, had been as swift and routine as one would expect from a seventeen-year-old in her prime. Yet Cherry had come home limping and miserable. She moaned in her sleep and whimpered as she plodded to the bathroom at night.

Adele found the baby alone in the connected garage. She lay on her back on a blanket once used to cover a car that had since gone missing, happily sucking on a paintbrush. Someone must have carried her there — she wasn't crawling yet — so the garage walls would insulate the house from her cries. Adele picked up Hanah and brought her inside. She moved the bassinet into her room.

"She's your daughter," Adele said.

"She is *everyone's* daughter," August said.

"Bullshit," Adele said.

The baby had August's silver-blue eyes when she was born, but they darkened toward Cherry's dull brown over time. In the end, Hanah's eyes were more striking than those of either of her parents, an unusual gunmetal gray. She stared at Adele in wide-eyed silence and Adele realized, not without sadness, that she was falling in love again. Not as an immediate, maternal rush; Hanah won her over by degrees, through small offerings. By learning to kick, by clutching Adele's long hair like it was the overhead railing of a subway car as they walked around the house, by crying when she was handed to anyone else.

Hanah's strange eyes and round face meant she could pass for half Asian. An old woman in a kaleidoscope-patterned headscarf stopped Adele on the street to tell her how beautiful they were. She grabbed on to Adele's arm with both hands. *"Schönen Mutter und Tochter!"* she said, as though begging.

(*That's great news about Helen,* Adele wrote when I told her Helen had gotten into UCLA Law. *Congratulate her for me.*)

The illegal club where they'd gone after Adele and August's marriage ceremony turned into a legal club, and then a furniture store. Hanah grew six teeth and could eat the same boiled vegetable mush as everyone else, if Adele blew on it first and spooned it into her mouth.

Cherry recovered. She vanished one night and returned around dawn high as a kite, singing loudly on the front steps. She couldn't figure out how to open the unlocked door. She spent the rest of the day in bed with August and a hairy Bulgarian boy who had just moved in and who loved August's body with jovial, manly aggression.

Adele rolled Hanah to the park in a stroller from the flea market. It didn't fold or have a protective roof, as all the new ones did—it might even have been intended for a doll. They both wore straw sun hats—Hanah's had a chin strap—and cotton dresses in pale rose. They were a vision.

She put Hanah in a swing and pushed her listlessly. She was thinking of the Bulgarian, his enthusiasm and his great big arms, fleshy as dough. When they'd met, he'd shaken her hand so hard she thought he'd dislocate her shoulder.

A small boy and his sister kicked a soccer ball back and forth nearby while their mother watched. The mother came to chat with Adele. "What an adorable baby," she said. "Is she yours?"

"No, I'm the nanny." Adele wasn't sure why she'd said that or why it had come out caustic as lye.

"Really? I'm looking for a nanny." The woman looked a bit old to have such young children, and she was wearing a royal-blue suit with gold buttons in a park in the middle of the day. She was dressed like a small, newly prosperous nation's head of state. "A live-in nanny. How long are you with your current family?"

"Actually," Adele said, thinking of Cherry's renewed sexual energy, "they won't need me much longer."

Hanah seemed bewildered but not displeased by the ride. She stuck her fingers in the holes of the swing's chain, and the wind lifted her wisp of hair. She had no idea what was coming.

On her last day, Adele dressed Hanah in a tiny sweater and pinafore, the first clothes Hanah had ever worn that were not from the flea market. She tied her hair into pigtails with velvet ribbons. She cleaned out Hanah's nose and trimmed her fingernails.

Adele strapped Hanah into the brand-new bouncy chair she'd bought with August's hash money. It was expensive; it lit up and played music when Hanah bashed the plastic buttons with her fists. She carried the chair to Cherry's room. "Cherry," she announced, "I'm leaving. You have to watch Hanah."

Cherry, who assumed Adele was going to the store, looked up from her magazine only briefly. "Get some gum and chocolate milk."

As Adele shut the bedroom door, she saw Cherry bouncing the chair with her toe. Hanah clapped and giggled. That was good enough.

(An epilogue: *I'm no good with children, Peter. I don't care about educating them or disciplining them. I just want them to like me. It's easier to clean up after them than to force them to do it. I make them chocolate-and-cream-cheese sandwiches and eat the veggies their mother left. I know that they're manipulative little monsters, but I love them so.)*

# 5

# *The Secret World of Men*

FROM MY DOORSTEP, I WATCHED the football team run laps around the neighborhood, their legs pumping in matching gray shorts and blue singlets, their breath visible in the cold hours between dawn and school. The coach chased after them in an open-chassis Jeep, screaming with his head out the window. His jowls flapped and exposed his teeth; he looked like a dog on a car ride. He had a face of burst capillaries and said "faggot" every time he exhaled. His wide arms and neck were sunburned even in winter, his nose bulbous and pockmarked as a tumor.

Ollie was noticeably the smallest on the team. The punter, compact and lithe as a featherweight boxer. He stared straight ahead as they ran past. I wondered if he remembered me and our days under Roger. If he remembered throwing stones and pissing in a bottle. After elementary school, he tried to get people to call him Oliver, but Ollie was ingrained in his face. When you looked at him, that's all you saw.

My father stood on the step and watched with me. It was

the fall of my senior year. He held a mug of coffee, looking as slick as he did in the mornings—the comb marks in his gelled hair like rows in a cornfield, shirt and jacket freshly pressed. His very presence was an accusation, but a mild one; we'd both accepted certain limitations of mine by that point. I was not going to join the football team, and it was enough that I should admire them.

The Jeep vanished down Brock Road, toward the high school named after the street, for the team's final laps around the parking lot. My father left his mug on the step for Mother to pick up. We walked to his car.

Father drove me the short distance to school. He saw me looking back at the house, where Mother would be waking Bonnie by ripping the blanket from the bed. She wouldn't comment on Bonnie still being dressed from the night before or on the imprint of makeup and sparkles on her pillow. She wouldn't respond to Bonnie screaming to be left alone. She would throw open the windows and draw in the sound of the neighbor's weed whacker, start up the vacuum and the rickety washing machine. Bonnie would slam the front door when she left, cursing and still pulling on her jacket.

"That's how women are together," Father said. Compared to the peace of these drives: down our road, past the houses' end, the empty pits, the failed condo development. A faded billboard showed the space-age skyline it was meant to have, uneven blocks of steel and glass, swooping neon. I noticed something had changed. There was a new sidewalk in front of the dead section, freshly poured and smoothed.

We stopped at the edge of the school parking lot. Father put out his hand to keep me from getting out of the car and gestured forward with his chin.

The football players were finishing their run, trickling

into formation around the Jeep. One of the first boys to arrive veered sharply to vomit in the bushes. The next boy fell where he stood, down on his back between cars. Father nodded thoughtfully, as though the whole thing were a show for his consideration.

The coach jumped down from the Jeep, his stream of insults dissolving into nonsense: You goddamn motherfucking weakling slaggerwit pansyfucker pantser twats! Ollie jogged up last. He'd taken the final lap — without the Jeep after them — at an easy pace and didn't even look winded. He was the only one standing up straight.

"You used to be friends with that one," Father said. I shrugged and reached for the door handle. He stuck his hand out again, level with the seat belt. Something bad was going to happen. I wanted to run from it; he wanted to stay and watch.

The coach pointed at Ollie and started to imitate him, taking high, mincing steps on his toes, like a baby deer startled out of the bushes. He flapped his wrists limply and hissed into Ollie's face. Ollie drew back and punched the coach in the stomach. He didn't even need to look to hit the wide target.

The coach doubled over. When he straightened up, his face was even pinker than before, his eyes tiny dots of fury.

Ollie's teammates said they'd throw him a goodbye party on the field that night. "We'll get the beer," they said. "We'll get the girls." When he arrived, they were standing around the goalpost, directly in the beam of the security light that hung off the gutter of the school. He recognized the way they stood in a half circle, heads close together. Ollie and I used to form part of that same half circle, back when we ganged up on smaller kids. He saw that there was no beer, no girls. Still he didn't run.

The quarterback—also smaller than the other boys, speedy, though not as small as Ollie—demanded Ollie's team jacket. Ollie handed it over without complaint. They asked for his shirt, and he gave them that too, feeling like there was something karmic about this turn of events, some kind of justice. "Now your pants," the QB said. His larger teammates loomed like mountains.

Ollie shook his head. Someone grabbed his arms and held them behind his back. Another boy lunged at his ankles, underestimating Ollie because of his size and earning a swift kick to the jaw. It took four of them to get Ollie's shoes, pants, and boxers off while he fought savagely. His elbow broke someone's nose. He sank his teeth into a linebacker's arm and had to be dragged off him, leaving scraped skin rolling up like cigarette paper.

Two boys dropped him hard onto the ground, naked. Stars behind his eyelids blurred into actual stars as he opened his eyes. He could hear his pulse sloshing in his skull. He weighed his options. There weren't many. The moment to charge after them and try to get his clothes back was rapidly passing. He flattened his hands and tried to push himself up, and various scrapes and bruises made themselves known. He let himself lie in the wet grass a little longer. His teammates weren't laughing—they were running silently through the weeds, like predators. He heard car doors slamming and then the sound of an engine turning over.

The smell of manure, of cut grass. All the fat on his body was freezing to the touch, his cock shrunken to an acorn. He sensed he would be colder when he stood. He accepted the only thing there was to do. He rose to his feet and began the walk home.

He followed the road from school, careful of his bare feet. After a few blocks, a cop car pulled up behind him, flashing its blue and red lights. Someone must have called in to report a teenage boy wandering naked through town. It would have been too much of a coincidence for the cop car to just show up there at this time of night.

He refused to press charges or name names. His teammates would do him the same favor when he cornered the quarterback in the locker room after hours, made him raise his foot onto the bench, and then slashed the tendon at the back of his ankle with a switchblade.

On the new sidewalk, I lined up with all of the unemployed youth of Fort Michel. White tents shielded the line from the spitting rain. Ollie's story was being passed around, abridged to nudity and blood. In spite of the weather, the air was festive.

We stood in the shadow of the new restaurant. It was alone on the dead strip, surrounded by abandoned construction sites and untended grass fields, as out of place as a crashed UFO. It was a promise, an act of faith: people started to believe the condo development would be resurrected, the sidewalk would widen into a boulevard, a modern city would grow from chainlink fences and dust. It was the kind of restaurant that had never existed in Fort Michel, and, after it failed, never would again. We would forever return to to-the-point diners with names like Billy's.

We were divided into Floor and Kitchen applicants, pretty girls in Sunday dresses splitting off from gruff-looking older men in sturdy shoes. I nervously turned over years of PBS cooking shows in my head. I was the youngest and the least white.

At the front of the line, I was ushered into a tent with a flap that closed. A man in an unbuttoned chef's jacket sat at a table, puffing on a cigarette. The smoke filled the small tent and clouded around him. I sat across from him. He wore a black undershirt beneath the chef's jacket, and an elaborate tattoo filled his chest above its neckline. I found myself staring at it. Two mangled birds carrying an empty circle between their beaks. The birds' tails were on fire, and they were twisted as though in great pain.

"Up here, Ling Ling."

I met his gaze. "My name is Peter," I said dumbly.

"Peter what?" He had his feet against one leg of the table and pushed against it to make the chair sway back and forth. He made me feel insignificant. An insect he was too lazy to squash. "Can I guess? Wing? Wang? Wong?"

"Huang," I said, the *H* nearly silent.

"Wong," he repeated, satisfied. Around his cigarette, his long fingers called attention to their joints. I thought they were beautiful. He could probably crack an egg, work his fingers inside the shell, and empty it with one hand, one flick of the wrist. "What are you applying for?"

"Line cook?" It came out as a question. I couldn't place his age. Anywhere between thirty and sixty. He had a streak of gray in his short, square haircut, and the bushy eyebrows I associated with older men. His face was young but hardened.

"Have you worked in restaurants before, Wong?" The pectoral muscles under his tattoo flexed, making the birds twitch. I wanted to touch them, to soothe their tortured faces.

Water beaded on my eyelashes as I blinked away the smoke. "No. But I cook for my family."

"Then you're applying to be a dishwasher." His chair continued to rock. "You look like a delicate sort of kid to me, Wong."

I was wearing a shirt of my father's. The sleeves were too long. "I'm not." I said the boldest thing I could think of: "Give me a chance. I'll show you."

He let his chair fall forward so the front legs struck the dirt floor loudly. He stubbed out his cigarette on the table, leaving a mark, and then leaned across the table and grabbed my hands. A jolt flew through me. His hands were large enough to eclipse mine completely. I felt his calluses on my smooth knuckles.

"You'll work nights," he said. "You'll steam your skin off. You'll smell like shit all the time."

I nodded as though these were instructions.

He let go of my hands. I left them on the table where he dropped them, feeling suddenly rejected. "I like you, Wong. I don't know why. I feel like I could whip you into shape. Like you're not anything yet." I nodded again, afraid to ruin the moment.

That evening, my father and I washed the car. The light rain had driven mud up onto the sides and into the tire wells. He lathered up the body while I scrubbed inside the tires with a stiff brush, squatting over the gravel. Breaking the silence, I said, "I got a job."

I listened for pride, suspicion, anything. He threw his rag into the soapy bucket and walked to the side of the house, where I couldn't see him, and began unraveling the hose. "What kind of job?"

"Dishwasher, at the new restaurant."

Water coursed over the roof of the car without warning. I jumped out of the way a moment too late. A few minutes passed as he sprayed back and forth, and I thought the conversation was over.

"I did that once," he said. "When I first came to Canada. It was hard to find work. My English was good enough, but nobody cared." I stood back, dripping. He glanced at the fresh shine of the hubcaps. "Good job."

The air hovered around freezing, so we had to dry the car quickly with old towels before the night—and the ice—set in. We worked side by side in short, muscular motions, a little too rough, risking the paint. A physical rhythm. My arms started to ache. Father seemed at peace.

When I first entered the restaurant kitchen, I had to squint away from the light. The dining room had been dim, with inoffensive jazz at low volume, tinted windows, black and red leather. The kitchen was bright as an operating room, and with the same urgent efficiency. Men ran back and forth, shouting. Metal flashed. The air went wavy for an instant when someone opened an oven. The cook at the broiler casually doused a fire with a bottle of water. I stood in the archway. No one paid me any attention, and I couldn't bring myself to interrupt them.

Hands clamped down on my shoulders so suddenly that I jumped. "Why are you just standing around, Wong?" It was the chef who'd interviewed me. His thumbs touched the back of my bare neck. Like everyone else, he was wearing his jacket buttoned with an apron on top, checked pants, and a black cap. Mine was the smallest size jacket they had. It hung flat off my bones the same way it had hung on the coat hanger. I cinched the pants tightly, and the legs ballooned around me like I was a wasting old man.

"I'm . . . new."

"We're all new, but you're the only one doing nothing. Let's go." He led me through the kitchen. "You have three basic tasks: dishes, cleaning, and fetching stuff for the cooks. Voilà, the walk-in cooler." He grunted as he pulled the heavy metal latch to release the door. The freezer was inside, past another door; a room within a room, about the size of a closet. "There's no light in the freezer part, so you have to hold the door open as you root around," he explained. I stuck my head in. Some faint alarm rang at how close together the walls were, at the rush of cold, the dark, the stout icicles lining the walls.

We walked back to the dish pit and he pointed out its parts. The high-pressure hot-water hose hanging over the double sink. The industrial dishwasher with its vertical steel doors that came down sharp as a guillotine. "All the dishes go through twice. First you wash 'em, then you bleach the fuck outta them. Any questions?" he asked.

I pictured his tattoo underneath the apron, underneath the jacket. The birds moving with each breath. "What's your name?"

"You call me Chef." He tilted his head. "Your jacket is buttoned wrong." His fingers settled on my chest. He undid the buttons, pulled the jacket straight, and rebuttoned it on the other side. It took a long time. I could smell his hair, a sharp, cold scent, like the air before it snows. Like the walk-in freezer. He ended by patting the jacket smooth. "Men button it on the left. Women on the right."

"Oh. Thank you."

A voice called down the line, "A waitress wants you, Chef."

I started an hour later than the rest of the night shift, at six. Dishes were already stacked high enough to form precarious towers. I put on the rubber gloves that floated with the detritus and patches of grease in the sink. The gloves were filled with hot water, which ran into my sleeves.

Chef talked to the waitress through the pass window. She was large and curvy, crushed into the uniform white button-up shirt and black pants, her coppery hair pulled into a high ponytail that exposed her forehead.

"Birthday at table twenty-three," she said. "The birthday girl doesn't like any of the desserts on the menu, and she wants to know if you can make her a fruit plate."

"Tell the bitch to go fuck her grandmother," Chef said.

She waited.

"I'm on it. Tell her it'll be a few minutes."

The waitress nodded and disappeared back into the din and artful leather of the dining room. I blasted food off the plates with the hose and loaded them into the dishwasher. The skin on my forearms was already breaking out in a rash. Chef went into the walk-in cooler and came out with an apron full of fruit.

Watching him work, I found it hard to reconcile his hands with the way he talked. He cut segments from a grapefruit, raw and pink as a baby's flesh, so that the membranes hung off the discarded peel like pages off a book's spine. He fanned out paper-thin slices of apple and peach, made spirals from out-of-season strawberries, cut the kiwis into stars, everything stacked toward a single citadel carved from a pineapple and drizzled with honey.

He placed his sculpture on a square, white plate and flung

it through the pass window. As the waitress moved it to her tray, he said, "Stick a candle in it and charge the bitch fifteen dollars."

Ollie found me eating lunch alone at my locker. He sat beside me and unwrapped what appeared to be a T-bone steak in tinfoil. I didn't mention that we hadn't talked since elementary school. We didn't talk about what he'd done or what had been done to him, though everyone knew. The buzz was fading. We were coming up on the anniversary of a car accident that killed four students the year before, and the retelling of that story had taken over. Ollie acted like we had always been friends. "You work out?" he asked.

I almost laughed.

"I need a new gym buddy," he said. *Because you knifed your last one,* I thought. He held the foil-wrapped bottom of the steak and ate it out of his hand, like it was a banana. "I can sneak you in for free. Nobody mans the desk at night."

"I work nights," I said.

"Get out. Where?"

"The new restaurant."

"Every night?"

"Three nights a week."

He drank a carton of milk with his steak. "Tell your parents it's five nights. We'll go lift weights, have some beers, and you can just say you were at work."

It was a good trick. In spite of everything, I wasn't afraid of Ollie. I felt pleased that he had thought of me. "Yeah, okay."

His head jerked backward as he ripped the meat off the bone with his teeth. "I'm going to get huge. Then small-dicked assholes like the coach won't be able to pick on me. He calls me a fag just 'cause I'm skinny." Ollie watched me peel the crust from my white-bread-and-strawberry-jam sandwich. "You aren't a fag, are you?"

I was supposed to shake my head, deny it up and down. He looked so cheery and simple, his cheeks stuffed with beef. I said, "I don't know."

Ollie took a hard-boiled egg from his bag. It gave off a strong, sulfurous smell when he rolled it on the floor and cracked the shell. I watched him pick the shell off and drop the shards back into the paper bag. "Well, do you want guys to suck your dick?"

I felt a revulsion so strong it was closer to hatred. *"No."*

He ate half of the egg in one bite. "Do you want girls to suck your dick?"

The revulsion didn't change. "No."

Ollie shrugged and swallowed the rest of the egg. "Then I don't know what you are." Perhaps from the way I sat there staring at the floor, he added quickly, "I'm not queer. I've got a girl up in Innisfil." I kept staring at the floor. "Hey, you okay?"

"I just don't like thinking about it."

"What?"

"Sex."

"Jeez." He chewed thoughtfully. "What's that like? I can't stop thinking about it."

It wasn't true. I loved the way the cooks at the restaurant talked about sex. Mapping out women's bodies for one another like explorers who've returned home. Their jokes with animals, old women, and babies as the punch lines. It was over-the-top enough, absurd enough, that it didn't feel real.

The sauté cook had graduated from Brock Road the year before. His name was Simon Hughman, and I remembered

him only because he had a notoriously squeaky voice, as im-
mortalized on the boys'-room wall:

*Simon Hymen*
*forever a virgin*
*voice so high*
*the girls won't screw him.*

On our third night, Simon's board had filled up with orders while everyone else was still going at an easy pace. Chef
came up behind him and surveyed the chits. Simon tossed
one pan and then another like he was juggling clubs. I had already noticed that the people who moved the fastest seemed
to get the least done. "What's the problem here?" Chef asked.

"Just got really busy." His voice cracked on *busy*. He tried
to elbow Chef out of his way, but Chef stood his ground.

"You jerking off on my time, Simon?" Chef mimed it with
an empty fist. He grabbed Lyle, the garde-manger at the next
station, from behind and started thrusting. "Having a good
time with Lyle over here?"

The other men, including Lyle, laughed. Simon continued
to flip his pans unnecessarily, as though it would make the
mushrooms cook faster. "No. Just busy. Fuck off."

The cooks hooted. I banged two pots together to join in
the noise. Chef put one hand on the range hood to cut off
Simon's path. "You telling *me* to fuck off, Simon? Is that what
just happened?"

"Sorry," Simon muttered, squeaking. "I'm just trying to
work." He tried to push past Chef again. "I need more onions."

Chef held him by the collar of his jacket. His voice
changed. "Stop being such a macho fuckup and ask for help

when you need it. That's my fucking job, to help you. Don't go running off to the cooler when your station looks like this —send someone. You hear me?"

I slipped away from the pit. The dishes were almost cleared. The rashes on my arms had begun to peel and weep pus. Inside the cooler, I filled a new insert of chopped onions and brought it over to where Chef and Simon were now cooking elbow to elbow, working to finish all the sauté orders.

"Thanks," Chef said, surprised. He nodded at Simon. "Maybe we should give Wong your job."

Simon pretended to laugh in his high, wounded voice.

In the front seat of Ollie's truck, I changed from the work clothes that my parents saw into a T-shirt and sweatpants. Ollie ate handfuls of raw almonds out of a bag on the dashboard while he drove. My unstrapped body flung around with each sharp turn. "What are you going to do after graduation?" he asked.

"Culinary school." It was the nearest approximation to what was expected of me that I could handle. My parents might be able to understand. It had the word *school* in it.

"My brother went to university," Ollie offered. This was still unusual in Fort Michel.

"So did both of my sisters."

"I know. We have that in common." He gave me a moment to digest that. "I'm going to follow him after I graduate. He lives in Montreal."

Ollie's gym was a storefront in one of the strip malls at the edge of town, its emptiness visible through the windows. We parked right in front of the door. "My brother says it's, like, the best city on earth," he continued. "The hottest women. The craziest parties."

We hopped out of the truck. He unlocked the door to the gym with his member's key. Though there was no one around, it still smelled powerfully of sweat and bodies at close quarters. A poster by the door showed a woman doing some kind of twist, one foot in the air. She wore red spandex shorts and a halter bra, her defined abs and cleavage oiled. "How do you look like *that?*" I said aloud.

Ollie took the question at face value. "Diet and exercise. I'm doing a bulk. If you want to look like her, you'll have to keep your body fat quite low." He didn't seem to think there was anything strange about my wanting to look like her — like it was as legitimate as his desire to be hulking and large. Another thing we had in common: we wanted different bodies than our own.

He called on me to watch and learn as he started loading weight onto a bar. My eyes kept drifting back to the poster of the girl. When I looked at it again, I couldn't tell if was in fact oil or if she was just that slick with sweat. Droplets clouded the air around her ponytail. "What about her legs? How do you get legs like hers?"

Ollie hoisted the bar behind his neck and started doing squats. He talked only on the exhale. "Your legs are already . . . as thin as hers. You just need to build . . . muscle on your ass." He lifted the bar back onto the rack.

I searched his face, looking for judgment. His expression was as resolute and unemotional as when I'd watched him running with his former teammates. He had me try squatting the empty bar. My knees bowed outward after only three, and he pulled it off me quickly.

I continued to scrutinize her legs as Ollie did his second set. The hair on my legs grew long but relatively sparse, compared to my sisters', and mostly on my shins. This girl was hairless as a seal. I imagined running my hands down my thighs and feeling no friction. I imagined the curve of my ass popping straight out in short shorts as hers did. Ollie made it seem achievable in the most matter-of-fact way.

Simon dumped a pile of sauté pans into my sink. I had begun to think of it as my sink, even though the middle-aged Sri Lankan dishwasher worked fifty hours a week to my eight-een. "I need these right now," Simon said. He hurried back to his station before I could say anything. I still hadn't gotten used to his voice that grated like nails on a window; it made me wince each time.

I kept on filling the glass rack; the bar had been reduced to serving wine in water glasses. Simon came back after only a couple of minutes. "Hey. I said I need these right now."

"I'll get to it in a second." I slid the rack into the dish-washer and went to lower the doors. "Move your hands." *Or they'll get chopped off,* I thought.

"You should have done it when I asked you to. Now I'm completely out of pans."

I left the door dangling dangerously. I gave one of his pans a quick pass with the steel wool, a blast from the hose, and then held it out for Simon to take.

"I don't need *one.* I need all of them."

"Take one for now."

"Then you won't do the rest of them for hours. Wash my pans right now."

At this point in the night, the scabs on my forearms were on fire, and my toes were numb from standing. "Wash them yourself. You don't seem to have anything better to do."

"It's your fucking job." *Fucking* sounded like a squawk.

Chef yelled for Simon. "What are you doing off the line? We're getting slaughtered up here!"

"I'm out of pans!" Simon yelled back. "Peter fucked up!"

Chef came over, tossing shrimp in a large silver bowl. They hovered in midair at the top of their arc, spices falling around them like snow. "Get out of the pit. You piss off the dishwasher and the whole kitchen falls apart. Take the pan and get back onto the line." It occurred to me that Chef looked the way Ollie wanted to: Nobody would fuck with him. And not merely because of the muscles and the tattoos.

In spite of what he'd just said, Chef hung around the dish pit after Simon left. He continued to lazily coat the shrimp. That same redheaded waitress appeared at the pass to gather plates. Chef gestured at her with his chin. "Hey, Wong, would you fuck her?"

They played this game all the time. I repeated one of the most common responses. "Too fat and too old."

Chef laughed. "She's barely thirty. Women don't know their shit until then. And did you see those tits? You could hide your head between those."

These conversations sometimes sent heat into my hips, just below my stomach and above my crotch. I used another one of their stock lines: "You wouldn't know what to do with her."

"I'd squeeze her tits together and fuck 'em with my balls in her face," he said, like it was a challenge. He held the bowl against his body with one hand and squeezed the back of my neck with the other, brushing the bottom of my hair. My lips curled in. I resisted the shudder. "Come on, haven't you always wanted to fuck a redhead?"

The question struck me as somehow ungrammatical, subject and object reversed. Like Ollie's question: *Do you want girls to suck your dick?* I realized what I had been picturing. Large breasts sliding sideways on my chest, his hands—those hands—stopping their momentum. Men squeezed each other's necks. "Sure."

I'd assumed Ollie's girl from Innisfil was an invention—who *didn't* have an out-of-town girlfriend?—but she materialized at our fourth workout. She looked enough like Ollie to be a sister or cousin, the same small eyes squashed under her eyebrow ridge, the same scrawny frame topped by thick, oak-colored hair. The effect, on a girl, was even more rodent-like.

She was in the center seat of the truck. She chewed a wad of bubblegum and knocked her knees against the gearshift between them. "This is Jeanine," Ollie said. She might have smiled. The movement was too lazy to tell for sure, dominated by the gum stretching behind her teeth.

Our routine didn't change. Jeanine ran slowly on a treadmill that had a bump where the belt had kinked, taking an extra leaping step each time it came around. Ollie started back at the bar. I sat on an empty bench. "She seems nice," I said.

"I'm thinking of breaking up with her," he said. She was only a few feet away. She continued to snap her gum and jog.

"Why?"

Ollie gestured at the room, like what was wrong with Jeanine was all around us. He lifted the loaded bar from the floor to his waist with a grunt, then from his waist to over his head with another. I was still trying to puzzle out the gesture. Maybe he meant Fort Michel, and Innisfil, and our provincial lives.

As though reading my mind, he asked, "Where are you planning to go to cooking school?" He dropped the bar and started the motion over again. I was struck once more by the focus and intent of his expression, probably the same one he'd had when he sliced through the Achilles tendon of a former friend as easily as through taut string.

"Not sure."

"You should come to Montreal with me. My brother will let us stay with him." His arms trembled from the shoulders. I could tell he wasn't sure about that second part.

"So you're quitting this year?" Most kids at Brock stayed on for the full five years, some for six. A couple of the football players who attacked Ollie were on their second victory lap, barrel-chested men with full beards. They filled the width of the hallway like overgrown trees: in need of pruning, trimming back. I'd stacked my schedule to get out in four years, as Adele and Helen had before me.

Two reps, and sweat beaded up on his nose and forehead, wet the collar of his gray T-shirt. "Yes," he panted. This time he moaned as he dropped the bar.

"Maybe you should use less weight," I said, like a child pointing out the obvious.

He shook his head. "The plan I'm on, you have to add weight every time. It's the same one Schwarzenegger uses." He did one more, making a long, low, guttural sound. The weights clanged onto the floor. "It'll be great. We'll party every night. Meet hot French chicks."

We left the loaded bar where it fell and went to another rack so I could do squats. Ollie didn't bother to spot me this time. He just sat dripping on the bench. Ollie wanted me to face the mirror to see my form, but I refused, facing the treadmills instead. The girl in the poster with her prodigious spandex-covered breasts and ass. Jeanine's upper thighs, skinny as

Ollie's, jiggling on the bone as she ran and chewed. "What will you do for money?" I asked.

"I'll get a job. I'll work construction or some shit," Ollie said.

I thought about living with Ollie. I imagined the kind of apartment I'd seen on TV, with a big living-room window framing a cityscape. I thought about having Ollie on my side. My loyal monster. "Ollie," I said, "when . . . when you . . . in the locker room . . ."

"I told him I'd cut his throat or his ankle. He chose. He bled a fuck-ton." Ollie was watching my knees in a protective way, making sure they were steady. "It made a loud noise. It was weird. Like when you pluck a guitar string and then stop it really fast against the wood."

I wanted to be horrified. I felt nothing. I looked at Jeanine, chewing away; Ollie would never tell her what it sounded like when a tendon snapped. I racked the empty bar myself after five squats. Ollie said, "You're getting stronger."

I don't know why any of us like or dislike people based on so little. Why I might love Chef as zealously as a supplicant loves a god, why Ollie would be my friend and Simon my enemy when they were both small-hearted, dangerous men. Why I felt like Jeanine was an intruder on a world I had barely entered, glimpsed through a doorway, seen through the steam of a high-pressure hose.

On a quieter Thursday night, before the quiet nights started to worry the management, Chef asked if I would come work for him full-time after I graduated. I told him what I planned to do—maybe culinary school, maybe Montreal with Ollie.

He objected to the first option. "Nah, nah. Don't do that. You'll have debt up to your ass and no one will respect you any more than they did before. You gotta pay your dues."

He yelled his life story at me from a distance, turning steaks for the broiler cook. At the end of the night, the arm he used to hold the tongs would be completely smooth, all the hair burned off.

Chef started in the dish pit when he was thirteen. At sixteen, he hitchhiked through the farmlands of southern Quebec, offering to cook and work the fields in exchange for food and a bed. He went to Europe without a visa and hopped from one cook job to another, learning that most countries don't refrigerate eggs and will scoop ants from the cooking oil and flies from the red-wine silo with a pool skimmer. He stayed in Budapest the longest because of a girl. She worked as both a bank manager and a nude model—he described the process of her undoing the buttons of her double-breasted suit at great length while the broiler cook and the two hot-appetizer cooks hollered—and then died in a car accident, her red Citroën AX crushed like a ladybug by a delivery truck. The girl's mother came and shooed Chef out of the apartment they'd shared, and he came home to Canada.

"To Fort Michel," Simon chimed in, his painful contralto appropriate for once.

No, there were a lot of years in between, so his dead Hungarian love had had time to become just another flicker in an erotic slideshow. There were a lot of kitchens before he was a head chef, and many more before the investors in this restaurant asked him to lead their new property. Culinary school was not a shortcut to Chef's life.

"But Montreal," he said, abruptly turning back to me, though I hadn't spoken in nearly half an hour. "You should definitely go. It's like . . . Paris, only lamer. Great food, good wine, beautiful women, and no one sleeps."

"My friend said the same thing." But when Chef said something, it carried more weight. I had discounted culinary school in an instant.

"I fucked a guy in Montreal." He plated a steak that had been resting, the juices flowing back to its center, and passed it to Simon. Simon fumbled for the plate. He was behind on the vegetables that were supposed to go with it, and a hard look passed between them.

The expeditor tapped his fingers on the pass window, glowering at the servers about the finished meals that were waiting there. "You tell this story all the time."

"Wong hasn't heard it," Chef said. He leaned over and put a cover over one of Simon's pans. "Speed it up, Squeaky."

"Tell me," I called feebly. The dish pit was larger than the rest of the stations, at the very end of the line, hidden in a web of hoses and pipes. Standing there made me feel disconnected.

"Not that much to tell. I met a girl, I fucked her, and she turned out to be a he."

Simon had had enough of being humiliated for rock-hard carrots and green beans. "Okay, wait just a minute. How the fuck does that happen? How did you not know?"

Chef shrugged. He watched the blood and clear juices beading up on the slab of meat, knowing the color inside as clearly as if he had cut into it. "She was gorgeous. I was wasted."

"No. I want more details than that." Part of me was glad that Simon was pursuing this line of questioning. "How *exactly* did you manage to start fucking him without noticing that *he didn't have a cunt?*"

"We went to her place. She went into the bathroom and came out in this short, sexy kimono thing." Chef made a round shape in the air with his tongs that could have meant any number of things. "I was so drunk I could barely stand. She lay down on the bed on her stomach, pulled her kimono up, and told me to fuck her in the ass."

"Her hairy *man* ass," Simon said.

"Nope. Smooth as a baby's. Greased up. Like perfect, firm pillows and round as peaches."

"Squats," I offered. The broiler guy laughed.

"And then what?" Simon pressed. He lifted the lid of the pan, slid the vegetables onto the plate, and passed the dish to the expeditor behind him.

"If they complain that the steak is cold, comp their drinks," Chef said. The expeditor nodded, wiping the edge of the plate with a cloth. "And then I fucked her, Squeaky. What do you think?"

"And he leaped up afterward and waved his cock in your face," Simon guessed. He grabbed his crotch. "'Ha-ha! Got-cha!'"

"No, she rolled over to yell at me for getting cum on her kimono, and I realized something was off."

"What did you do?" I asked.

Chef's muscular shoulders rolled under his jacket as he put more steaks and chicken breasts on the grill. The alcohol in the marinade dripped off and flared up on the coals. "What do you mean? Nothing to do. A good fuck's a good fuck. Didn't change that."

We went on chopping, frying, washing, stirring, but for a few moments, no one spoke, absorbing Chef's words: *A good fuck's a good fuck.* Simon took a peeled clove of garlic from his station and whacked the side of a knife against it, crushing it, then threw it into a pan. "I would've cut his fucking balls off," he said. He smacked another clove. "Wants to be a woman that bad, enough to trick *normal*, God-fearing, pussy-loving men into having sex with him—I'd fucking help him out."

Unrattled, Chef said, "Just focus on my side dishes, Squeaky."

One morning, a Saturday, I awoke with a fever. For a couple of years in my teens, I sometimes got fevers, with no other symptoms, that lasted a day and a half—thirty-six hours, like clockwork. My mother said it was related to growing; my father said it was a sign of weakness, of a delicate constitution. Some people, he said, mostly women, got sick whenever they were needed, when there was work to be done—vague, mild illnesses that let them continue to do things they enjoyed, like lying under fresh, cool sheets and complaining. "Sick in their heads," he said.

In the afternoon that Saturday, I called into work and told the waitress who answered the phone that I wasn't coming in. She passed the phone off to Chef. My father walked into the hallway. When he saw that I was on the phone, he came and stood stonily nearby. Chef shouted over the clamor in the kitchen, so my father was able to hear both ends of the conversation.

"We need you, Wong."

"Sorry, Chef. I'm really sick."

"Well, get better, kid. Hope you'll be in tomorrow."

I hung up. I shivered as I padded back to bed, my father following close behind. The hot, dizzying exhaustion let me ignore him as I crawled under the covers. I would normally have stood straight and waited for him to speak.

The curtains were closed, but the bright afternoon leaked

in, murky and mustard-colored. My father appeared as a dusty shadow. "Why aren't you going to work?"

"Because I'm sleeping," I murmured. I wasn't thinking about what I was saying.

"Have you ever seen me miss work?"

I didn't answer. The bed felt good. Firm but lulling, like strong arms lifting my back.

"This job doesn't mean much to you now because you're a kid, and I feed you and clothe you and put a roof over your head. When you have a wife and kids, you won't be able to laze around in bed whenever you feel like it. They'll all starve." His shadow stayed the same: a defined head and shoulders, everything lost to darkness below. My father did not gesture with his hands.

He left the room. I got up about half an hour later. I leaned on the wall as I dialed. I told the waitress that I felt better and was coming in for my shift after all.

That night, the surgical lights and gleaming surfaces assaulted my senses. Sweat soaked through my shirt and my jacket, poured down my face and back. The sound of the dishes clicking against each other, of a knife's *shink* against the sharpening steel, embedded itself in my forehead like shrapnel. I could imagine reaching up and digging the shards of noise out of my skin.

Chef kept looking at me. He didn't ask if I wanted to go home. He came by once with a bottle of water from the bar cooler and pressed it to the back of my neck. My spine arched like a stroked cat's. The cold came in a rising wave, engulfing, a strange, fevered ecstasy. He held it there for a solid minute, and then left it on my station for me to drink.

. . .

A few weeks into my routine with Ollie, I started to notice a change in my legs. It was most noticeable in the backs of my thighs, where rounded muscle had grown. There'd been nothing there before.

Ollie and I talked a lot about Montreal, spinning fantasies. We'd work in the day, party at night, sleep on his brother's floor, drown in money and freedom. Learn French. Take up smoking. Take up cocaine. We'd never be sober again. I'd become a world-renowned chef and he'd fuck supermodels. We'd leave my father and the ruined football stars in the Fort Michel dust.

Jeanine came with us half the time. Sometimes they were late to pick me up, and when they arrived, Jeanine's hair was stringy with sweat, and there'd be a foul smell in the cab of the truck. (Later, when I worked in a combined restaurant and bakery, I figured out what Jeanine smelled like: sourdough bread as it rose, homey but tainted.)

One night, Jeanine fondled Ollie in front of me, with her hand in his lap, cupping as though jangling the change in his pocket. He sank deeper into his seat, fingers resting lightly on the steering wheel. Without comment, he pulled over just before the bridge. He turned off the engine at the side of the road, the headlights dying with the key turn.

"Peter," he said, as Jeanine climbed on top of him, her bony fingers locking behind his neck, the three of us sitting there in the dark, "do you mind getting out for a bit?"

"Are you kidding me?"

He gathered her body in his arms as he looked me straight in the eye, conveying that we were part of a brotherhood: *Help me out, man.*

I got out of the truck. I slammed the door. I heard

Jeanine's hand smack against the window as I walked down to the river. When the dirt became worn rocks, I took off my socks and shoes and held them in one hand. I buried my feet in the water, focusing on its icy, alert flow. The truck rocked on its shocks. I glanced back now and then, not able to make out anything through the windows. I started to wonder how I would know when it was safe to go back. Would they come get me? Honk the horn?

At some point, maybe sooner than I'd expected, the passenger door of the truck opened. Jeanine's legs swung out. She threw her sneakers on the ground, stepped into them, and started to retie them. The cab light came on behind her. I took that as my signal and ascended the riverbank. I stayed barefoot, feeling the change from rock to dirt to craggy asphalt.

As I climbed back into the truck, thinking about what was probably soaked into the upholstery, Ollie said, "We're going to drive her back to Innisfil." They were done with each other for the night. She pulled out a wrapped, already-chewed piece of gum and put it back in her mouth. She must've tucked it away at some point in the action.

During the half-hour drive, I could feel something radiating off their skin, something more than heat and smell. Ollie and I didn't speak, and Jeanine gave sparse directions.

We watched her going up the steps of a small house with a screen door and beige siding. In the front yard, visible in the porch light, was a Halloween decoration—a stuffed witch that had survived many seasons outdoors. Stuffing oozed out between the seams.

After the screen door banged behind Jeanine, Ollie didn't start the engine right away. I sensed he was going to apologize or tell me about it in detail, and either way, I didn't want to hear it. I looked straight ahead through the windshield. "Dump her," I said. "And let's go to Montreal."

The weekend after Ollie and Jeanine left me on the riverbank, Chef asked if I wanted to train at sauté. Some of the guys applauded and gestured to suggest I had sucked Chef's dick, tongue bulging in cheek. "Simon's switching to daytime next week," Chef said, "so we'll get a new dishwasher, and you can take his station."

The garde-manger, Lyle, yelled while balancing shrimp tails on the rim of a martini glass, "Hey! I asked you if I could switch to daytime and you said there was no way. Why does Simon get the hours?"

"You're too good. I need you on nights," Chef said. Simon smiled grimly.

The night progressed as usual. The novelty of the restaurant had worn off on Fort Michel. Most families could afford to go only once or twice a year. During the brief dinner rush, Simon dropped off some pans at the pit. "Would you get me some more frozen carrots? I'm not supposed to leave the line." He spoke softly, so the high pitch was less noticeable.

"Sure." I left my light workload and headed into the cooler. I spent a few minutes searching the freezer shelves for carrots, holding the door open with my foot. I heard someone come into the cooler and pushed the door wider. It was Simon. "I can't find the carrots."

Simon didn't say anything. He pushed on the freezer door. I pulled my foot back so it wouldn't get crushed. It wasn't sinking in yet. "Hey! What are you—"

The heavy door fit into the frame. The darkness was complete except for a yellow line underneath the door. I heard something scratching against the floor just outside, in the cooler. Probably a stack of crates, milk or eggs or vegetables. I realized what he was doing just a moment too late, and I slammed my shoulder against a blocked door.

I banged on the door with my fists. "Simon! Simon!"

The cooler door clicked open and shut. The line of light vanished and the darkness became whole.

I beat on the door. I yelled. I listened. I couldn't hear the sounds of the kitchen—voices—so they probably couldn't hear me. All I could hear was the sound of coolants and condensed water passing through the walls, gurgling in the lines. I heard the fans whipping and clacking. The cold felt good on my wet, steamed skin for only a few moments, and then a chill set in.

I wrapped my arms around myself, glad of the heavy chef's jacket for once. In the dark, I felt for the edges of the door. The crack was too narrow to fit my fingers. Maybe I could back up and gain enough momentum to push the door and the crates. I took a step backward. A shelf struck me in the spine. There was no room to move at all.

I charged the door anyway. Maybe I could do it in increments. The impact reverberated from my shoulder through my skeleton. I hoped for a telltale scraping on the ground, so I'd know that I had moved the crates an inch. Nothing. I kept going. Bang. Bang. Bang. I switched sides when my shoulder got sore. The exertion kept me warm. Sweat started to run down my back and pool in the waistband of my underwear.

I didn't have a watch. Wouldn't they wonder where I'd gone? If they didn't notice my absence, they'd notice the dishes piling up. They'd notice they had nowhere to put their meals.

Simon might have given some kind of explanation. "Peter? Oh, he was feeling lousy and I told him to go home."

Or more likely: "Peter? I saw him go outside. I thought he was just getting some air, but I guess he's fucking off for the night." They'd call in the other dishwasher, or take someone off the line to do it, or Chef would do it. Chef was not above washing dishes.

We didn't use frozen carrots, I realized. Only fresh.

I sank down where I stood, thinking I'd lose less heat if I curled into a small ball. Stillness made me shiver. My fingers were already going numb. I flexed them in and out of fists, trying to keep the blood flowing. My best bet was to just wait until someone came into the cooler and then restart the banging and yelling.

I found that thought more comforting than I logically should have. Almost warming. Panic drained away. My toes pricked as though asleep. I wiggled them inside my shoes. I leaned my head against the wall behind me, my whole body fitting under a shelf. After a while, in the darkness, sleep became a strange, demanding force, like a rip tide. I was tired from working nights and going to school a few hours later. I was tired. More tired than cold.

I woke to muffled yelling. "What the fuck is this?" It was Chef. My mouth was dry, pasted shut. The crates were dragged away and the door was flung open before I could think to stand.

Chef stood over me. "Wong. Jesus. How long have you been in there?"

I blinked up at him. My arms and legs felt stiff as he pried them apart. I stumbled out into the cooler with his arm around me. As I woke more fully, I leaned on him harder, letting myself enjoy the firmness of his body, his smell of smoke and cooking meat and burned hair and spices and something more delicious besides. My body checked itself, decided it was fine. Numbness opened into uncomfortable heat. I buried my face in Chef's armpit, trying to go limp, to seem as pathetic as possible. My eyes watered from the strong light. I let the tears flow. He moved me into the kitchen, then bellowed down the line, "Who did this?" All the kitchen noises, crude jokes and clanging dishware, stopped.

Chef gingerly released himself from my grip, held me up by the shoulders. "Wong? Do you know who locked you in there?"

I considered what Simon could do to me. Fort Michel wasn't large enough to hide if someone was looking. I saw him cornering me in an alleyway between shuttered businesses, behind the Luther or the laundromat. I looked up. Chef's eyes, brown irises made warmer with rage, made me invincible. I saw my future there. I would leave with Ollie; I'd live a life as rich and exotic as Chef's, and Simon would stay here forever. "Simon."

Everyone turned to look. Simon Hymen, forever a virgin, voice so high the girls won't screw him. He looked convincingly astonished. "I didn't. I don't know what he's talking about." Still in the blast line of the Chef's rage, he tried a different tack. "It was just a joke."

I clutched at the Chef again, hugging his torso as though I'd collapse. He touched my cold cheek. "You're fired," he said to Simon.

Simon stared, uncomprehending.

"You're fired! Get the fuck out of my kitchen!"

Simon's mouth opened. His eyebrows knit slowly in confusion as he tried to figure out what had just happened. He looked to me. I smiled. I smiled with only my cold-cracked lips, so that it could have been a grimace of shock and hurt. I smiled so that only Simon saw.

The next morning in the shower, I had to shave. I'd put it off as long as possible. My father would mock the results—a notched-out teenage mustache, tufts of hair permanently under my lower lip and nostrils.

I watched the water bouncing off the blades. I considered. I stepped out of the stream of the shower, toward the back of the tub. I sprayed more shaving cream into my hands and spread it over my legs. Just running my palms up my legs and smoothing down the foam felt good. The razor felt even better as it slid up my shinbone. Clumps of hair washed away. I kept going. Stripping free the contours of my knee, then the scanter hair of my thighs. Water struck the skin with a new intensity.

I went over each leg twice, redoing missed spots, more fastidious than I'd ever been with my face. I shaved the invisible, downy hair off my buttocks. The water went cold and I let it. When I stepped out, I couldn't believe how sensitive my bare legs were; the towel felt too rough but raised goose bumps of pleasure.

I put on my bathrobe, made of slate-blue terrycloth, inherited from my father. Our bathroom had a narrow full-length mirror hanging on the back of the door that I always had to avoid. I turned my back to the mirror and looked over my shoulder. Those legs! Coming out of the bottom of my bathrobe, a little pale, but so slim, so shapely. Legs made for high heels. Legs made for short skirts. Legs made to be seen.

My robe became a silk kimono, black with a red sash, tied loosely. I pulled it slowly up, clutching what I needed to at the front, lifting it high. *Round as peaches,* Chef said, squeezing each one, testing for ripeness.

That night, Ollie drove up to my house. He sat in his truck on the street with the engine off. Eventually I went outside.

I had to knock on the driver's-side window before he noticed me. Even then he seemed to stare right through me, to the street. I knocked again and motioned for him to roll down the window. "Ollie, what are you doing here? I have work tonight."

"Get in for a sec."

I climbed in. "I only have a minute."

He nodded. He didn't seem to see anything around him. The cab of the truck was strewn with garbage, as it often was —food containers, condom wrappers, empty bottles. A wad of bubblegum was stuck to the dashboard on the passenger side. "Jeanine is pregnant," he said, almost to himself. "We're going to get married."

I inhaled the stale smell of the dirty truck. I shut my eyes. All around us, Fort Michel came home from work, sat down to supper, watched the daylight vanish behind the low bumps that were the closest we had to mountains, to texture in the landscape. Turned on their TVs, raised a hand to their children, raised them to leave each other naked in a field or leave a snaking trail of blood from the locker room to the front door. Ollie and I were seventeen. Still believing that life was different in cities where the condos had been built, the pits had been filled, the buildings were tall—where you weren't assaulted on all sides by failure and empty sky.

Ollie's voice and posture were leaden. "There're three girls in our year who are pregnant. None of them will ever leave Fort Michel. Nobody ever leaves Fort Michel."

His brother, my sisters. We were supposed to follow them. Ollie finally turned to me. I was going to be late for work, for Quebec farmlands, European lovers. Ollie waited. I said what needed to be said. What everyone would say, as useless as consolations to the grieving: "It's the right thing to do."

I left Ollie behind. His truck was still parked against the curb when I got to the front door. I went to my bedroom to change. I still hadn't heard his engine starting up.

I put on my uniform, and the pants chafed wonderfully on my legs. I would go alone to Montreal. I buttoned my chef's jacket with the buttons to the right. Maybe Chef wouldn't notice. Maybe he could make that mistake with me.

# 6

# *Margie*

FATHER DROVE ME to Montreal with Mother in the back seat. I sat in the front, a suitcase in my lap and a hundred dollars in my wallet, at the start of a grim experiment. Bonnie was on a plane to Los Angeles, to get her diploma at an "alternative" school that Helen had found. "Helen will straighten her out," Mother had said.

"What do you think you'll find there?" Mother said now. I turned in my seat. She had overtightened the seat belt and was struggling to loosen it; she looked strangled. "Your French is garbage. You'll be a second-class citizen. Believe me, I know something about that." Father flinched each time she spoke, unaccustomed to the sound of her voice.

Miles of scrub rolled past, sprouted grass and grubby trees like those I'd seen all my life. I wondered when we'd cross the line, when the signs would change language and beautiful things would start to grow. Mother leaned forward to address Father. "Where are we going to leave him? Just dump him in the middle of the street with nowhere to live?"

Father didn't answer, so I didn't either. "Your hair is getting long," he said instead. "You should cut it before you start looking for work."

"Hmm," I said.

We settled into a long silence. Mother stared out her window. The highway curved to follow the train tracks. Sprawling strip malls, RV parks, flat-roofed chicken restaurants, gravel roads that vanished into the flat horizon: the ugliness persisted even deep into Quebec. Bonnie, at that moment, was flying for the first time — her hand pressed to the frosty plastic window, the Nevada desert red as the fires of hell.

"I want to drive," Mother said suddenly. The quiet persisted. She corrected herself: "I want to learn to drive."

Father continued to squint out at the horizon, the midday sun looming overhead. His hand slipped from the wheel but he regained his grip before the car could drift.

Father stopped at the end of a pedestrian strip in downtown Montreal, where the asphalt intersected with the cobblestones. People and patio tables filled the corridor from end to end. Strings of light connected the buildings, forming a makeshift roof. It seemed like every window had an *À Louer* or an *Aide Demandé* sign, all of them calling to me.

Father pulled up the parking brake with a squeak that made my stomach clench. If I stayed in my seat, they'd drive me home again. Father turned off the car.

I got out slowly, suitcase in hand. Mother's eyes were distant; she was retreating into herself. As soon as I shut the car door, Father restarted the engine. He rolled down the window. Glaring sunlight made the car's interior seem dark by comparison, and his face floated in the shadows. "Give it a year," he said. He pulled away without closing the window. My mother was still in the back seat.

I turned at a corner, off the cobblestones. The street sign was bent, and another sign with a double-headed arrow indicated that the traffic changed direction in the middle. An old man sat on the steps of a building painted a bright, uniform blue. He gestured me over, suitcase and all. "You're looking for an apartment."

I nodded. "I have an apartment," he said. He stood, turned, and walked inside without saying anything more. Not knowing what else to do, I followed.

He talked over his shoulder as he opened an inner door and looped around a staircase. He had olive skin and a vague, trilling accent, and he wore brown canvas shorts with no shirt. "I like Asians," he said. "Quiet, pay on time."

With that, he flung open an apartment door. It was small as a coffin and mostly obscured by the door. "Full kitchen, full bathroom," he said, proudly. I stuck my head in: How was that possible? A bar fridge and a two-element stove took up most of main room, and an inner door revealed a bathroom where only the boniest legs could fit between the toilet and the bathtub; most people would have to balance their calves on the edge of the tub.

"Everybody wants to live alone for cheap, but there's nowhere else in the whole city, I swear to you. If you stay for one year, I give you the best price. One year! No bullshit!"

It sounded like a promise, an incantation: One year, no bullshit. What was space to me, with my silly little suitcase and hundred dollars? "I'll take it," I said.

· · ·

The year began: I found an apartment and two jobs in one day. I walked the street in my kitchen shoes, clutching resumés typed on my father's typewriter. Less than two blocks away, I walked into a café seeking an *aide-cuisinier.*

The owner, potbellied and skittish, came out when the cashier called him. He shook my hand and introduced himself as Buddy. We sat under tall windows at a table that had yet to be cleared of cups and plates and balled-up napkins. He sniffed through his clogged nose every few seconds as he looked over my resumé, which boasted only my single job and my high-school diploma. "Come back on Wednesday and we'll try you out," he said.

"How about tomorrow?"

"No, Wednesday. We're trying someone else out tomorrow."

I went across the street to a Japanese restaurant with decorative steel doors. I interrupted the four Japanese cooks' preshift meal with a harsh wedge of sunlight; they'd been sitting in the dark. We had the same conversation I'd had with Buddy.

"Come back on Wednesday and we'll try you out."

"I'm busy on Wednesday. Thursday?"

"Fine."

One year. I took both jobs. The cooks at the Japanese restaurant spoke Arabic and Japanese and ignored me as much as possible in their two-story kitchen that reeked paradoxically of both fish and vinegar. One of the two *cuisiniers* at the café quit and I got his job, working alone in the tiny, open kitchen behind the counter while the cashiers tittered lazily in a gutter slur of French and English. They faced the customers and I faced the wall.

• • •

I had not planned for the loneliness of being an adult in a new city. My landlord invited me to sit on the steps with him and watch the "kids" go by—university students my age and older who lived in the surrounding walkups. Our building was full of older immigrants, bachelors and widowers who played Iranian radio at five in the morning or left the smell of pickled herring in the grease vents. I kept my place as neat and spare as a monk's quarters. My clothes were folded in a suitcase like those of an overly polite houseguest for months before I caved and bought a small chest of drawers.

The kids wore brand-new clothes, whites not yellowed and blacks not grayed, bold reds and blues. The human traffic was so dense at eight in the morning and three in the afternoon that for a while I assumed the university kept the rigid hours of an elementary school. The students sat on their balconies as though on display, playing guitar, drinking beer from bottles, eating fruit or cake. And they were beautiful—a cultivated beauty, beauty of stiff hair and finger waves, highlighted cheekbones.

I looked for Chef everywhere. The beautiful university boys on the steps were too young, too lean, too well groomed. Shirtless in the sunlight, they revealed gym muscles that lacked his brutality. Our one hug grew into a love affair in my mind. There were days when I felt that his story about the kimono had happened between us.

I visited home just once. Father picked me up from the bus station and shook my hand as though we had just met. I could hear his thoughts as he took me in: his approval at my torn, dirty fingernails and scars—a workingman's hands— and his displeasure that I still hadn't cut my hair. I stared back at him openly for the first time in my life. His hair had become a flatter, one-dimensional black, all traces of brown and gray dyed out.

The house smelled strange to me when we walked in, akin to the smell of my apartment building, its ethnic mishmash of cooking food and outdated colognes. I couldn't remember what the house had smelled like before.

Mother served us broiled pork chops and vegetable soup from a can. We sat in three chairs huddled around one end of the table. The spare chairs were stacked against the far wall. "Have you heard from Bonnie?" I asked.

Father's knife scratched the plate as it finally broke through his pork chop. Mother had started to say something when Father interrupted. "Helen called," he said. "She bought a house."

"Wow," I said.

"Alone," he added. "All by herself. Without a husband, or even a boyfriend." He frowned at his plate, like the leathery meat puzzled him. I remembered sitting at this same table as Father waved around Adele's transcript, his voice choked: *Why?*

Mother finished first. Without a word, she got up from the table, put her dishes in the sink, sat down on the couch a few feet away, and turned on the television. The news was on. She turned the volume up loud, that absent, defeated expression on her face.

"How's Mother?" I asked softly.

Father's frown deepened. "She's learning to drive."

Back in Montreal, I got a letter from Ollie. A cursory mention of Jeanine and the baby, of being married by a municipal clerk, then eating Jell-O and drinking sweetened coffee in her parents' backyard in Innisfil. Everyone had gotten drunk.

Jeanine's older sister slapped Ollie in the face and yanked down the paper lanterns that someone had put up in an attempt at decoration. I tried to picture Ollie writing a letter. Perhaps at night, in his father-in-law's den, while Jeanine and the baby slept. But I couldn't even put him at a desk, sitting down, with a pen in his hand. His letter didn't ask any questions beyond *I guess Montreal is pretty great, huh?*

He still worked in Fort Michel, driving out from Innisfil each morning. He manned the service desk at the garage near our old elementary school. The mechanics had been used to ringing up their own customers and were wary of Ollie. They couldn't see why his job was necessary. I could imagine him there, wanting to tell the little boys on the way to school that these vicious, filthy days were the best they'd ever have.

The night that I read it, Ollie's letter sent me out into the street. I watched the end of an outdoor concert that had shut down avenue du Parc: an avant-garde jazz piece, a combination of wind chimes and slow picks at an electric guitar that silenced the street. The song was deeply unsettling. People stood with their arms crossed, mouths slightly open. I was too far back to see the musicians clearly. All six were dressed in black and barely moved as they played their instruments, appearing as thin stick figures from a distance.

I went alone to a nightclub; I picked the one with no line outside and a sign advertising no cover charge. Inside, the walls were painted pink, with low sconces that threw vertical lines of light upward. A group of girls who looked too young to be there—maybe fourteen—danced on a platform with one skinny boy, shell-shocked at his luck. I liked the music. It jolted, waking you up. I found a spot to lean on the wall near two older men. They had matching salt-and-pepper beards, and both wore full white suits. They pointed out girls to each other, talking with their heads close.

We watched the girls. Straps falling off their shoulders, their nascent breasts jiggling, short skirts riding up their thighs, spilling their sticky-colored drinks onto the boy in the middle, who didn't seem to care. What would turn me into them? Could I peel it all off their faces and bodies with a paint trowel and spread it over my surface?

Through the thudding beat, I could still hear the haunting, lonely jazz melody that had echoed down Parc. I left without dancing. Outside, I realized it was only a quarter to eleven. I bought a bottle of red wine at the corner *dépanneur*. I sucked it dry on the floor of my apartment, walls closing in, small as death. For this I had come.

Spring came. Fallen petals blanketed cars and gathered in the gutters. A man sold bikes in the parking lot of the music department of the university—an old, cathedral-style building with Gothic railings and dormer windows and weeping limestone. The bikes were chained together against a rack. He looked like Chef for an instant, in that sea of steel and aluminum. He had veiny forearms streaked with black grease, an expression indicating he was content to wait.

I had no real need for a bicycle—both my jobs so near to home and each other—but I imagined that my world would grow because I had one. That the person I had come to Montreal to be was just a little farther from the city center. I locked my bike to the front railing of my building, intending to go for a ride in the early morning before work.

In the humid, fly-crusted dawn, I saw what had become

of my bicycle. Any Montrealer would have told me I was a fool to leave my bike on the street, on that street, overnight. My first thought was that the front wheel had been stolen and could be replaced. Then I looked closer. The front of the bike had been cut off, around the wheel. They'd sliced right through the frame.

I didn't know much about bicycles, but I was sure there had to be an easier way to get the wheel off. A few cables to snip. I tried to imagine the time and tools involved in this task. A hacksaw and enormous patience. Just to be sure that the bike was truly mangled, truly unsalvageable.

A thought appeared in my mind, unbidden, as a fully formed sentence: *This is the most unhappy I have ever been.*

My hair grew to my shoulders, had to be tied back at work. I bought a pair of women's shoes. I'd spent an hour circling the block of rue Sainte-Catherine that contained the shoe store, sweating into my wool coat and willing myself onward. When I went in, I picked up the shoes I had been looking at and announced in an awful, loud, artificial voice, "I'd like to buy these for my girlfriend!"

They were platform sandals, straw-colored with a four-inch wedge and a strap that wrapped around the ankle. Every day, I came home, took off my kitchen shoes and socks, and put on the sandals. I wore them whenever I was in my apartment. As I made meals, washed the floor on my knees. At first I loved looking down at my still meticulously hairless legs — all the muscles extended and activated by the shoes, which tilted at the same sharp angle as a Barbie doll's feet — and then it was routine, it was the first mouthful after numbing starvation, the one that gives your stomach a voice. Painfully *not enough.* And I still could not pin down what would be *enough,* other than resetting time, going back to before my birth, before my conception, and finding a way to choose.

The man who sold me the bicycle gave me his number. He looked me dead in the eye. "I do repairs, tune-ups. Or if you know anybody else who needs a bike."

I couldn't work out the steps in between. Seduction. Disguises. I could imagine the endpoint. The lifted kimono, the thing tucked away, heels on, my hair long across my shoulders. I could even decorate the scene: my apartment punctuated by candles, a dress hanging on the bathroom door, disarming flowery scents, throw pillows and tassels. My apartment all my own.

But suppose that wasn't the endpoint. Suppose he turned out to be like Simon. A moment of confusion, a stray hand. The bike mechanic, strong hands like Chef, forcing me by the shoulder to roll over. Simon's high voice like a power drill through the bones of my inner ear: *Wants to be a woman that bad—I'd fucking help him out.*

I tried to hang myself. That was something I told people later in life—*I tried to hang myself when I was nineteen*—when I was trying to explain how I'd felt. That there could be misery in families where no one drank, no one hit anyone, no one had a diagnosed mental illness, where there was nothing so recognizable and lurid as murder or incest. I could tell them about the burned apron, about swallowing that hot shard of a thing I had loved. It often made people laugh. There was no clean word to use, like *alcoholic.* That's what most of my friends were, later on: alcoholics born of alcoholics, abusers born of abusers.

But even that story, the hanging, is not strictly true. I got a book from the library on knots. It turned out to be extremely difficult to tie a hangman's knot in a wide, knit scarf, but I managed. I tied the other end to some exposed piping near the ceiling of my apartment. I put the loop around my neck. I stood on a chair.

If I had jumped, one of two things would have happened: the scarf would have torn, or I would have ripped the water pipe out of the wall and sprayed sewage all over my ascetically white furniture. I didn't jump. I kept my hands inside the loose loop of the noose, between my neck and the rope. I leaned forward until I felt pressure, strain in the rope, the scarf straightening sharply, like a schoolboy who's been cracked with a ruler.

I realized that no one was going to stop me. No one would even know. Servers and cooks at both restaurants regularly just stopped showing up for work and were promptly replaced. The kind thing, I thought, would be to do it near the end of the month, so that the landlord would come for the rent soon after and find me before the smell became a problem.

Considerate and well-behaved to the end. I got down off the chair. I left the scarf there, swinging from the momentum.

There was a deep-down, physical ache. The opposite of a phantom limb: pain because *that thing,* that thing I loathed, was always there. I had to use it and look at it every day. But more than that, pain because I wanted to be seen. I wanted to be noticed, in a way that both men and cooks were not. The hostesses at the Japanese restaurant wore makeup that made their eyes cartoonishly large and dresses in oriental prints that were slit to the upper thigh. They were required to wear their hair in high, old-fashioned buns. They were art. They were there to be looked at and admired and worshipped. I was there to serve a purpose, to make things. A workhorse. A man.

One year, and then Bonnie came.

Bonnie stood in my doorway with a freshly razed head and a duffle bag slung across her body. The front door of my building was propped open for the summer and coated in flies. She held her arms out for a hug. I stared at her. She dropped her arms and pushed past me, into my apartment, her chandelier earrings and the coin tassels of her skirt jingling.

She threw down her bag and went straight to the fridge, bent her knees to rummage. "You have any beer?"

I closed the door and leaned back against it. There wasn't anywhere else for me to stand. The apartment felt even smaller with someone else there. "No."

She found a takeout box, opened it, and sniffed at it. "Oh, this is good. Where's it from?"

"The shish taouk around the corner." Her skirt went down to her ankles, several layers of fabric in hot colors, red over orange over yellow. She wore a white wifebeater with no bra, the material so thin that even the areolae of her dark nipples were visible. Lines of red and gold glitter were streaked across her chest and cheeks. "What are you doing here, Bonnie? Does Helen know you're here?"

Bonnie started shoveling the rice and kebab into her mouth with her bare hands. "Oh yeah, sure. She thought it was a great idea. She helped me pack and find an apartment and everything."

I crossed my arms across my chest. "So you're not living with me." I couldn't tell if I was relieved or disappointed.

"Nah. I think I've learned not to shack up with family." She politely made no mention of the fact that two people could barely stand in my apartment, let alone sleep. Closing the empty takeout box and tossing it on top of the fridge, she added, "Aren't you going to ask where I got the money?"

"Should I?"

"Helen would. She asked me all the time. God forbid I try to pull my own weight." Bonnie put one hand on her hip, dropping all her weight onto one side in exaggerated exasperation. The muscles in her face tightened and hardened as she scowled. It was startling; she really did look like Helen. She made her voice hoarse and judgmental. "'Where did you get that? Have you been stealing? Selling drugs? Turning tricks?'"

"Were you?"

"Yes." She didn't specify which; maybe all of the above. She relaxed into herself again. Her cheeks were plump and flush. Her shoulders and arms were more muscular than I remembered.

"You look happy," I said. I meant to say *healthy*.

"As a horse," she said, as though she'd heard *healthy*. Her imitation of Helen had made me feel slightly giddy and superior, like we were speaking in a secret language in a crowd. "LA agreed with me."

"I hope Montreal does too."

Bonnie laughed and took a step toward me. We were almost nose to nose. "That's what I love about you, Peter. No questions, no complaints. Everything is just fine by you." She put her hand against my forehead, as though checking for a fever. Her skin was cool.

"That's not true," I murmured, pressing into her touch like a cat.

Bonnie had a housewarming party a week later. I brought a six-pack of fancy beer as a gift, chosen because the girl in the label art reminded me of Bonnie. It was a raspberry beer in opaque glass bottles, the last of the summer stock. The girl had flowers for hair, the flowers' vines creeping down her neck.

Bonnie lived in a shared eight-bedroom apartment in the lower Plateau — essentially a house built atop a coffee shop. As I came up the outside steps, the front door was thrown open by a man in a tie, sweatpants, and no shirt.

"Hey!" he cried, as though I were a long-lost friend. "Here for the party?"

I stopped walking, though I was still a few steps down. I had to look up at him. "Yes. I'm Bonnie's brother." I held the beer up over my head like an offering.

"Cool. Get in here."

Inside, I went up a second staircase, lined by one brick wall. Photos of people I didn't recognize were mounted onto the brick, in mismatching frames that climbed with the stairs. Near the top was a decorative white frame that I had seen sold in dollar stores around Mother's Day. You were supposed to put a picture of your mother inside; there was raised black lettering underneath that read MOTHER ★ HERO ★ FRIEND. Instead of a photo of Mother, there was a picture of Helen, Adele, and me, lined up left to right, taken when Helen and Adele were teenagers and I was an alarmed-looking child clutching Adele's hand. I couldn't believe Bonnie would put up something so personal so quickly.

I found Bonnie right away. She wore a black lace full-length bodysuit that went from ankle to wrist to a turtleneck collar, the lace only slightly thicker over her breasts and crotch. She hugged me and kissed me on both cheeks. "Peter! I'm so glad you're here. Isn't this a great space?"

In addition to the one brick wall, there were ceilings that were cavernously high and floors made of scratched, stained hardwood. The living room was huge, crammed with people of a wide range of ages. A toddler sat on her father's shoulders, higher than the crowd, staring with naked curiosity.

"It is." I meant it. "I brought beer."

"Great! Put it in the kitchen!" She returned to the conversation she'd been having and then, noticing that I hadn't moved, added, "It's over there."

The kitchen was relatively empty, only one woman inside, her back to the archway that I walked through. The noise seemed to fall away into a flat hum. Her hands were busy; I assumed she was making a drink. In the narrow passageway, I couldn't get past her to the fridge. "Pardon me. Can I just— get in here . . ."

She didn't move.

I flattened myself against the cabinets and slid by. The acidic smell of rotten garlic—in my line of work, I could identify the scents of specific foods rotting—emerged as I opened the fridge door and put the beer inside. I glanced over. The woman was peeling apples. "Oh," I said, with relief, "you're cooking."

"Yes."

"Can I help?" I didn't know what to do at a party. I knew how to peel apples.

She took so long to reply that I searched her face. She was older than I had thought from her high-pitched voice, her singsong *yes* that had seemed teenage in its disdain. Deep lines followed the shape of her mouth down to the loose skin of her neck. Her hair was bleached white and cut short, flat to her head, her bangs slicing a severe diagonal across her face.

"Absolutely," she said finally. "Take an apple."

I went through all the drawers until I found another usable peeler in the mishmash of tools and rust. I kept coming across utensils mangled beyond recognition. The kitchen had a hanging, charred smell—burned popcorn, dirty stove elements, the ruined bottoms of pots and pans.

We stood peeling in silence. Press of the peeler on my thumb, smooth run of green skin. "I'm Peter," I said, feeling like I had to say something.

She put down her half-naked apple and faced me, slamming her hand on the cabinet behind my head, all in one swift motion. I realized she was taller than me. The details of her face flooded my field of vision. Her eyebrows were plucked into straight lines that slanted down toward her nose with no arch, and she had light crow's-feet, like dough imprinted by a fork. Flecked granite eyes. I could feel her breath as her nostrils flared.

"God, you're pretty," she said.

I jolted. The thing twitched. I felt like she had said a word that only I knew, that I had made up. Her eyes flicked down, staring at my mouth. I looked at hers. Thin lips coated in a dark plum. Pretty!

Someone entered the kitchen, singing to himself. It was the man who had greeted me at the door, his tie now undone and hanging over his neck, one end in each hand. He walked to the syncopated rhythm of his song, his left and right steps distinct from each other. "Hey, Margie! Hey, Bonnie's brother. How goes the salad?" He didn't seem to find anything unusual about the position we were in.

Margie relaxed, picked up her apple and peeler again. "Hi, Dave. Still working on the dressing."

I went back to my apple as well. I pressed down hard to stop the shaking.

The door greeter patted his naked belly in an exaggerated way. "Well, hurry up. Lots of hungry people out there!" He lumbered back into the living room.

We finished our apples. She handed hers to me and told me to mince them both, then started pouring juice and oil into a blender.

"What are we making?" I asked, rooting through the cupboards for a cutting board.

She started the blender and talked loudly over the noise. "Salad. Nuts and dried berries and spinach. That's all Dave eats."

"Do you live here?"

"No. Dave does." She stuck her hands in an open bag of pistachios on the counter. "He's my son."

"Oh." She glanced sideways at me. I hadn't meant to sound so surprised. "Why does he call you Margie, then?"

She shrugged. One of the pistachios opened with a gunshot crack. "What do you call your mother?"

"Mother."

"Why? Why not Mom?"

"I don't know. It sounds wrong."

"Well, the only thing that sounds right to Dave is Margie." Another crack. I was looking at her hands while I chopped, watching her thumbs ripping open the shells, breaking their backs. I felt a sting and dropped the knife on the cutting board.

"Oh shit," I said. I had glanced my knuckles with the knife, shearing off a thin layer of skin. My eyes welled up.

Margie grabbed a paper towel and wrapped it around my hand. It was hardly bleeding, but it stung. "Are you crying? Oh Lord. You pathetic little girl." She pulled me violently into her arms. I clutched my cut hand with my good hand behind her back. She pushed the back of my head to mash my face into the crook of her neck. "There, there, pretty darling," she said.

I wanted overwhelmingly for her to kiss me. I had been looking for Chef everywhere. His gruff masculinity and crude hands. How had I found him in a woman in her fifties, wearing silk trousers and dark lipstick, whose neck smelled like the spray of fake roses?

Bonnie told me later, when it was too late, to stay away from Margie. That she was insane, cruel, bigoted, twisted. "And *old,*" Bonnie added at the end, as though that were the worst part, the part that she found the most bewildering.

Margie had brought most of the alcohol at the party, perhaps two dozen bottles, and everyone toasted her with glasses filled with her wine. The salad was unpopular. I took a big bowl when it became clear no one else was interested and sat munching on it slowly in a corner. I sat on the floor. Many people did.

Margie came and sat beside me, folding her legs carefully. She held a bottle of wine in one hand and two glasses, crossed at the stems, in the other. "I notice you're not drinking," she said, pouring.

"Not much of a drinker," I said.

"That's rather rude," she said, "considering my generosity."

"It must have been very expensive," I agreed.

"Money doesn't mean much to me," she said. She handed me the glass. "Are you looking at my bracelet?"

I hadn't been. It was a diamond tennis bracelet, whiter than white. "Very nice," I said.

"Try it on," she said. She unsnapped the clasp and then yanked my arm straight. She slid on the bracelet. It was cold. Her skin hadn't warmed it.

We both admired how it looked on my thin wrist. The bold piece of jewelry went well with the arm I had waxed clean with a drugstore kit. Margie stared me up and down, her top teeth exposed in a sneer. Blunted, penetrating. Women did not look at men this way. Grown men looked at young girls this way, sometimes, men who could take and possess from a distance.

I went to unclasp the bracelet and Margie reached to stop me. "Keep it," she said. I smiled unsteadily at her, feigning protest. But I wanted the bracelet.

"I've always wanted a little China boy," she said. "I've never had one before."

I opened my mouth, trying to find a sentence, something I had been taught to say. The stranger offers you candy and you say no. The anthem begins and you rise from your seat. The fire alarm rings and you file quietly with the others outside. Someone calls you little China boy and you rage, you lecture, you gook, you chink, you traitor. I wanted the way she looked at me, into me, pushed inside of me. I wanted the bracelet. I said nothing. I drank.

Bonnie said she'd looked for me when the party was thinning, and Dave told her I had left with Margie. I remembered getting into the cab and out of it, not the ride in between. I remembered sitting at the foot of Margie's bed, swaying, my spine softened to a reed by alcohol. I watched her take off all her clothes. I had lived my life in children's beds. Her sturdy, king-size bed felt palatial.

Still completely dressed, I rested my head against her belly as she stood in front of me. I kissed her navel — a round, surprised mouth — with a joking smack, the way you'd kiss a baby's stomach. My navel was an indented line, as though I had been stabbed in the stomach with a boning knife. *Bonnie has an outie,* I thought, *the tied end of a balloon.* Even my thoughts slurred, sloshing left and right through my mind.

The idea that I was supposed to pleasure Margie hadn't really taken root. I squeezed one of her breasts experimentally. It didn't feel the way I had expected it to — I was surprised that the skin gave so much, that it changed shape in my hand. I thought breasts would be harder and more resilient, with just the suggestion of softness underneath, like a tomato. I pushed one to the side and watched it spring back.

I traced the line of pigment down her abdomen — from having Dave. It was fucking beautiful, that border. It put her on one side as a mother and me on the other.

"Oh, you're so gentle, my poor little boy. Probably never seen a woman, right? Not supposed to look at women? Got beaten for it? Don't worry, little Peter Huang, little Huang, little wang, Margie will show you what to do."

Where was she getting this? Who had led her to expect these things? When did I tell her my full name? Peter should have protested, punched her on behalf of Asian men everywhere. But I was — I was — drunk. The name that had never fit slipped completely out of my grasp.

Margie pushed me down. She pulled my shirt over my head, unbuckled my pants, pulled them down with my underpants, tossed it all aside. I did nothing to help or resist.

"Oh!" she said, delighted. "You're hairless, like a little boy. So pretty and delicate. Just like I hoped." She took the thing in her hands, cupped it like a caught butterfly. "And your cock is so cute."

"Don't call it that," I said.

"Cute?"

"No. The other thing."

"What? Cock?"

"Yes."

"What do you want me to call it?"

"Don't call it anything," I said.

My only other memory of that night: Margie lying on top of me, both of us facing up, her weight nearly crushing me. I shut my eyes to the overhead light. I ran my hands over her body, spending a long time on her breasts, lifting them, tweaking the nipples, pretending they were mine. Then even longer between her legs, both hands tracing the folds, the stiff hair, the slick walls. From this angle, it was perfect, it was just where it was supposed to be. It was between my legs. I rubbed her and could almost feel it myself.

She felt me against her back and remarked, "Ah, so it does get hard! What else does it do? Does it fuck?"

"No," I said, irritated at being interrupted, "it doesn't do that."

I went to Margie's house every night after work. I sat in her bathtub with its jet streams while she knelt against the edge and washed the fish smell and bits of food out of my long black hair. She let me rest my wet body on her sheets as she plucked the hair from my stomach and chest. The first time was a long, exquisitely painful process, each pinch of the tweezers a kind of release. At the end, Margie squirted lotion onto her hands. She cooed as she rubbed her hands together and then slid them across my torso, telling me how smooth and soft and pale I was.

Then the games began. She liked to pamper me and then beat me with her hands or a crop. She liked to sit on my face, not requiring me to do much—it was the idea of suffocating me that appealed to her. She made me wear a brocade hat with a braid built into it from a novelty store; she made me fake an accent, a cruel mimicry of my father. I spoke in random, halting, lisping sentences, swapping *l*'s and *r*'s. She wasn't offended that the thing didn't respond to her overtures; she seemed to like sucking on it flaccid, liked it small, batted at it like a toy. I had to look away. She knew the only thing I liked—that position where our bodies lined up, became indistinguishable to my hands. She dangled the possibility of it in front of me and I would do anything.

The best thing, though it happened only once, was when she forced me to wear her panties and stockings. We were in her bathroom. I was careful not to ruin it by seeming too eager, my eyes cast downward as she rolled the nylons up my legs, clipped them to a garter belt.

She sat me down on the closed toilet seat, across from her queenly bathtub centerpiece. I watched her red-painted fingernails spider across the wall and flick on the vanity lights that bordered the mirror. She applied the plum lipstick first, making a shape wider than my lips, like a clown mouth. But with odd care, deliberate motions. She lined my eyes heavily inside the rims. I could feel the point of the pencil against my eyeball.

She peered close, stroke for stroke and impersonal, as though she saw only a canvas. She left the liner pencil rolling sideways on the counter. My chin pinched between her fingers, she turned my face back and forth in the light, examining it. She looked satisfied.

I took the pencil and touched her cheek to keep her still. She let me draw a quick, thick mustache under her nose, silly and Chaplinesque.

She motioned for me to stand. As soon as I did, she shoved me down to kneeling, facing away from her. Our eyes met in the mirror. She took off the violet feather boa that had hung over her bare breasts and coiled it around my neck. The same color as the lipstick. She pulled the ends of the boa tight. Choked me from behind. Knees on the bathroom tile in front of the mirror, so I could watch my own blissful face white out slowly, glowing like an angel's, until I passed out.

At the height of our affair, Margie sent me to the twenty-four-hour grocery store at three in the morning to buy more lotion. She wouldn't let me clean the kiss-shaped lipstick stains from my face. I had a vivid half-moon bite mark visible above the collar of my T-shirt.

I stumbled through the narrow aisle drunk on pleasure and lack of sleep. As I rounded a corner, I saw Bonnie, dressed in a silver sheath dress and heels, her eyelids painted. She was peering into the frozen-foods case with her arms full of chips and instant-noodle packages.

"Hi," I called.

She blinked at me, equally dazed. "Hi." Her hair had grown into something like a pixie cut; I realized how much time must have passed since I'd seen her.

"Just came from a bar?"

"Stayed until closing time, when the lights went on. Everyone looked awful." Bonnie stared at my neck. She raised her hand as if to touch the spot where Margie had bitten me. Only one tooth had broken the skin. Margie had pressed a cold cloth to my neck, lifting it at intervals to check to see if the bleeding had stopped, while we watched TV, my head curled into her shoulder. "How have you been? I haven't heard from you since the party."

I could only smile.

Bonnie put her hand down. "You look happy," she said. She didn't mean *healthy*.

Mother called me on a Monday night, a rare evening that I was home. She might have called a dozen times before; I would have missed them all. As soon as I answered, without saying hello, she said, "Does Bonnie really not have a phone?"

I barely thought of Bonnie. "I don't know."

After a pause, Mother said, "I want to see her. I'm coming tomorrow."

Mother left home at six in the morning and drove the five hours to Montreal, alone. Bonnie eluded her completely. I got the restaurant to give me a two-hour, unpaid lunch. When I realized Father wasn't with her, I took her to a dim sum place inside a mall in Chinatown.

The entrance was at the top of a tall, curving staircase with a plastic chandelier that threw pink and green splinters of light. A small crowd waited for tables dusted with sparkles. My mother was wearing a blouse that had once belonged to Bonnie and a skirt that had been Helen's.

Mother went to the hostess behind the podium to get a number. A flash of pleasure passed over her face as she spoke the few words in Cantonese, then again when our number was called. "*Sei-sup-yut.* Forty-one."

We were seated far from the main path of the carts. We watched the food from a distance and had little to say to each other. After a long silence, my mother said, "Is Bonnie a whore?"

"What?"

"A prostitute. Does she sell herself to men?"

"No," I said.

"What does she do here, then? How does she make a living?"

"I don't know. I haven't seen her much." I started playing idly with my teacup, spinning it on its bottom rim. My mother took the teacup out of my hand and put it back on the table. I could hear the women pushing the carts shouting the names of their dishes, could smell the breading and garlic, feel the wet heat, but they never seemed to come any closer.

Mother tried again. "So! Do you have a girlfriend?"

"Yes." We both seemed surprised by my response.

"Is she Chinese?"

"No."

Her gaze fixed on the ponytail tossed over my shoulder. "Your father will be pleased," she said. All around us, the cart-pushers continued to call out, trailing the sounds and smells of what my mother had lost. This was supposed to mean something to her, the idea of a girlfriend. The conversation between them after Adele and Helen were born, the need to try again for a son—my father must have told her about this day, when I would have a girlfriend, and then I would have a wife, then a son, and we would be a real family, an endless line.

She stared at my ponytail, at another of her strange, disappointing children. She remembered holding newborn Adele, searching her blank heart for the joy she'd been promised. She imagined me offering her a male grandchild, a baby clothed in her married name, another greedy mouth. She didn't care. Mother, a pilgrim who walked a thousand miles only to find the sacred grove was just a clump of trees.

Bonnie called from someone else's phone, someone who was doing something in the background that made her giggle and gasp. She said, "I finally caught you. You're never home. Want to have breakfast with me tomorrow?" I told her that I had to work. "The next day?" I had work then too. "What, do you work seven days a week?" Yes. "Days and nights?"

"Mondays I only work days. Tuesdays I only work nights."

"Jesus. Why do you do that to yourself?"

"I need the money."

"For what?"

My rent was paid after only a few days of work. I ate most of my meals at the restaurants. I had no debt. I had endless energy, even — or especially — once I started seeing Margie. I kept thinking that this was only the prelude, that my body was a starter home. I would need money when I decided to start my real life. "The future," I said.

A man's distant voice. Bonnie let out a satisfied groan, like a splinter had been pulled out of her thumb. "Whatever," she said, returning to our conversation. "Then let's have breakfast on Tuesday, when you only work nights."

When I didn't reply right away, she added, "I miss you." She yelped. "Stop that!" she called, her mouth farther from the receiver, her hand perhaps covering it. "You still there?"

The diner advertised its $1.99 breakfast special in paint on the window, orange letters with green outlines and a sharp-

edged explosion around it. *Wow!* it said. The flat-roofed building also housed a tire store and an entrance to the Métro station. A bell over the door rang as I walked in.

Bonnie sat at a four-top with Margie and her son, Dave.
Between them, cups of oily coffee and a crusty ketchup bottle and a saltshaker with a dead bug inside; the only other customer ate alone at the counter. A saxophone version of "The
Girl from Ipanema" played at low volume. The free chair
scraped loudly across the floor as I pulled it out and sat down
next to Dave.

"Hi, Peter," Bonnie said. "I thought it'd be fun if we all
had breakfast together. Hope you don't mind." She wore a
child's sweatshirt with the neckline cut out so that the sweatshirt slid over her narrow shoulders. Her eyes blazed, tense in
their sockets.

I nodded. I tried to catch Margie's eye. She stared stonily
into the distance. I had never seen her in full daylight, without makeup. The colors of her skin and eyes and hair were
dulled, and her expensive clothes—a cream-colored satin
blouse with a bow tied at the neck, more tailored slacks—
seemed sad and out of place. I wanted her to sit in my lap and
let me reach under her clothes, to feel the body I coveted, en-
vied, knew better than my own.

"We were just talking about Dave's birthday party last
year. Margie took him and a bunch of friends on a cruise. For
Dave's *twenty-fifth* birthday." *Older than you,* Bonnie meant,
her voice cheery.

"It was awesome," Dave said.

"What did you do for your birthday, Bonnie? I'm sorry I
missed it. When you were in California. With Helen." *Helen
who judged you,* I meant, *as you're judging me.*

"Nothing special," Bonnie hedged, keeping the conversation on her track. She put her hand on Dave's arm. "Tell Peter about Akhil."

"Oh, yeah. This is hilarious. Margie fucked a maintenance guy on the cruise and got him fired. It was, like, in the boiler room or something. Whatever that's called on a ship. And they got caught by—what are they called? One of the sailor dudes? The important ones? Sorry, I'm not very good at telling stories. But it was fucking hilarious."

Bonnie gave a fake, sparkling laugh. Excited, like it was all a game, she squeezed Dave's arm again. "Tell him about the rainbow."

"Oh, yeah. We used to joke that Margie was aiming for a rainbow. 'Cause she always fucked a guy of a new color, yeah? Like Akhil was the Indian band of the rainbow. Bonus points if they don't speak English."

Bonnie kept flicking her eyes sideways to Margie—who cradled her coffee cup vacantly, as though there were nothing strange in a son talking about his mother this way, in front of his mother's new lover—and then back to me. I'm sure Bonnie's imagined scenes were dead-on. The humiliation, the racial stereotypes so old or specific I had never encountered them before. Bonnie thought she was saving me. But Margie had saved me. This was the only way I could do it. This was the closest I could get.

"How far into the rainbow are you?" Bonnie asked Margie. Dave laughed earnestly, like he couldn't feel the shift in the air.

"Just a joke," Margie said, her words slow and stiff.

"Peter must be slowing you down." Pretending to choke on her mirth, pretending it was that funny! "You've been stuck on yellow for so long."

Margie looked at me. I could tell she was startled by my

expression. I was trying to tell her that I loved her, that I worshipped her, that nothing Bonnie said could change that. Margie leaned away from me, away from my radiant love, like I was a slobbering, mangy dog with shit-mottled hair ready to jump up on her clean slacks. "Just a joke," she repeated.

I went to Margie's house after work, as always. She usually led me straight to her bedroom or its connecting bath, and I never thought about the rest of her house. That night, we walked through her dark front hall to the living room. She turned on a couple of gloomy, shaded lamps. "Drink?"

"No, thanks."

We sat on the couch. Old-fashioned, stuffed green leather, with button studs in the back. It squeaked. I smelled like fish. I wanted Margie to make me pretty in the bath, for her to stand in front of me in the mirror, wanted to squint my head onto her body.

Margie kissed me. We kissed longer than we ever had. I opened my eyes. I could see her scowling, her eyes shut aggressively tight as she mashed her mouth against mine. She shoved me backward. "Do something!"

"What?"

She leaped up from the couch and went to the window. Thick, diamond-patterned glass, the same as in the sideboard that ran along the wall. She pushed aside a heavy curtain. Her house was at the top of two flights of concrete steps, strip lawns on either side. Chemin de la Côte-Sainte-Catherine, a busy but uninteresting street, ran below. The only things she would be able to see were car lights heading up the mountain, their white heads and red tails, and the tops of trees. She watched the traffic for so long that it made me nervous.

"What do you want me to do, Margie? Tell me. I'll do anything."

It was hard to see her where she stood, some distance from the lamps. A flash rain had just started, one that would last for only an hour. "I'm getting bored with you."

All over the city, people were crowding under awnings and inside bars and restaurants, waiting out the storm. She must have been watching the rain flood the gutterless streets, race sideways with the wind. "I knew you guys were, you know, shy and effeminate. I didn't know you don't even fuck."

"They do," I said. Admitting that I wasn't one of them, what she wanted me to be. Her yellow man. "Just not me."

"I want to be fucked."

"So go get fucked," I said. "By someone else. And then come back to me."

"I don't do that. I'm an old-fashioned, one-man kind of girl."

I thought this was a joke and I laughed. I caught the glint of her eyes in the dark. She wasn't joking. "I'm sorry. Let's go to bed. Please." She turned back to the window. "We'll play our games. I'll be your little darling. You can dress me up. Bathe me. Beat me. Order me around." I watched her solid back and realized that I was doing this wrong. I wasn't offering her anything; I was begging for what I wanted.

The rain continued to fall in unbroken sheets, loud on her balconies. She came back. Sat beside me. Her white blouse radiant in the lamplight. "Stay the night," she whispered.

I mistook the look in her eyes for tenderness.

I woke up choking, out of a dream in which someone was trying to crush my windpipe from above. The feeling was the same: that too-much shock, the need to escape. Tightness closing in. Only not in my throat.

I felt her weight pinning me down. Margie's weight. Margie on top of me, her shirt gaping open, her hands on my abdomen. Her pubic bone cutting into mine.

The thing was inside her.

I shoved her off me, thrashing to get free. I fell sideways from the bed. I ran in a half-standing lurch and heard her call something after me. I heard the word *enjoy*.

Her house—all its diamond-patterned glass and Old World, mocking strangeness—blurred past. I got to the front steps. I leaned over the railing, naked, looking down the dizzying height at the wet grass, murderous traffic, morning commuters, buzzing flies, no storm, no rain, everything so terribly normal. I threw up.

I straightened up. I bent all the way back, chin to the sky. Margie watched me from the window. She looked the way the bile tasted in my mouth.

Later, I could barely remember walking down Côte-Sainte-Catherine in my kitchen clothes from the day before. Asphalt with no shade. I did remember going back into Margie's house, forced by my nudity: Her voice coaxed, the words meaningless, when I refused to go farther than the front hall. I remembered being handed my bag, wincing when our hands touched. I remembered the newness of a room I'd seen only in the dark. Dusty wind chimes hung far from the door, so they never made a sound. Pictures of Dave as a child.

Bonnie's bedroom shared a false wall with the room next door. The only natural light came through the narrow glass at the top of the partition; she had no real windows. Two of her roommates, neither of them Dave, were having a fight on the other side of the wall.

We lay in her bed, on top of the covers, far from each other. Like regretful lovers. Space enough between us for another person. I had cried myself inside out. We listened to the bickering from next door. The woman did most of the talking, too shrill for us to make out any words. The man kept saying, "Easy, easy," as though his girlfriend were a horse.

I turned onto my side. "Has this ever happened to you?"

Bonnie was silent. And I felt a terrible, unexpected pride. A kind of sisterhood. A womanly rite of passage. What happens when you paint your eyes large, proffer glimpses of thigh: the assault the world thinks you deserve.

"Tell me about Helen's house," I said.

Bonnie stared into the middle distance as she spoke, at the space between her face and the ceiling, as though she saw something there. "It's big. Bigger than Mom and Dad's house. She has a wooden deck with a wooden roof made of slats, so you can see the sky through the gaps. There's a garden box, though it was empty while I was there. And a barbecue, but Helen never used that either. A real backyard, not like that crappy little strip we had."

"Is she still mad at you?" I asked.

Bonnie didn't answer, a way of answering. "Helen is a lot older than me. Us."

"Someday she won't be."

Bonnie smiled at that. I looked at the same spot, the same speck of dust, where her eyes were focused. We looked at it together. It was Helen's deck. A hot day in California, sun breaking through the slats. Helen stands over the barbecue, cloaked in hickory smoke. Tomato plants in the garden box, some of the fruits a shy, blushing orange, some of them explosively red. Adele plucks one and slices it into a salad. Bonnie hands me a drink in a glass overwhelmed by limes. Mother, hero, friend.

# 7

# *Hair*

F OR MOST MEN, I suppose, it can be slow agony. They watch their tonsured crowns grow or their peaks recede as if they were watching the tide go out and never return. My fanatical avoidance of mirrors allowed me to tie my ponytail lower and lower on my head without dwelling on it too much. I thought I was too young; it came on sudden and swift.

I caught the bus home to Fort Michel before dawn on a winter morning. I tried to sleep leaning on the window. There was nothing outside but pitch-black scrub and highway ditches filled with melting snow. The window reflected back the palest parts of my face, the whites of my eyes and the socket bones, while the dark centers were replaced with the blackness outside. The top of my head shone as though polished.

I was no longer balding. It would have been vain to keep using the word. I was bald.

The bus station in Fort Michel was in the middle of a row

of Victorian houses on small lots. It had one counter, one bench of beige leather seats, and a vending machine that looked gap-toothed from empty slots. Slush and gravel had been dragged across the linoleum floor by passengers' boots. I sat down before I remembered that no one was coming to pick me up.

Though it was eleven on a weekday, the streets were empty. The garage where Ollie worked was closed. New gas pumps sat out front. I peered through its window with my hand over my eyes. The waiting area for customers looked just like the bus station, down to the connected beige seats.

My mother answered the door wearing a bathrobe and a pearl necklace. On the shelf by the front door were three ivory statuettes I had never seen before. One was fat, bald, and cheery, like a laughing Buddha, leaning on a staff. The other two were old men with crowns and long beards.

Mother caught me staring at them. "Household gods. They're good luck," she said. "Don't tell your father." I realized Father must not leave the house anymore.

She opened their bedroom door and motioned for me to go in ahead of her. My father was sitting upright in bed with his back against the headboard and his hands in his lap. He wore crisp, brand-new pajamas. My mother had just combed his hair the way he used to do it for work, leaving the comb marks. But she'd used water instead of gel, and it softened as it dried.

"Hello, Peter."

"Hello, Father." I came close to the edge of the bed. "What did the doctor say?"

My parents looked at each other. I lowered my head to retract my question, to find a pose of respect and shame. My father lifted his hand and signaled that Mother should leave.

I stared at the bedspread. The half-open blinds left a barcode of shadows on my father's legs. I could tell, even through the blanket, that his calves were thin as broomsticks.

"Do you know what kills Chinese men, Peter?"

I shook my head.

"Tuberculosis and suicide."

Even now, my father seemed robust and ageless, like he could crush me with his fists at will. His hair had gone white as rapidly as my hair had fallen out; there were no transitional salt-and-pepper years. "Do you know what kills Chinese women, Peter?"

I waited.

"Chinese men."

I looked up. It sounded simultaneously like a joke and a threat.

"They carry China in their hearts and their lungs and eventually it kills them all. My father, on the other hand, died like a real man. A Western man. In a mine explosion."

In sixth grade, we had to make a family tree. Our teacher handed each of us a worksheet of empty boxes connected by lines. Your own name went in the middle. The kids around me started filling in the boxes immediately.

I didn't even know my parents' first names.

The sound of scratching pencils made me self-conscious. The teacher tapped me with her pen and told me to stop dawdling.

You would think that my father's rigorous scrubbing of heritage and the unavoidable fact of race in central Ontario would have made me more curious, but it hadn't. The other children, who knew the names of their aunts and uncles and cousins, hadn't been curious either. The information had been forced upon them at weddings and funerals and on Sundays at their grandparents' homes. Children of the wrong age they'd been forced to play with. Houseguests who'd overstayed their welcome. Crude calculations of wealth: who would die, how much they would leave and to whom.

I made it up. I invented whole families. I gave my grandfather my own Chinese name, Juan Chaun. Everyone else got arbitrary Western names—Bob and Mary and Sue. China was known then as conformist, polluted, censorious. I thought for the first time about my parents' childhoods. I imagined their schools had been vast and orderly, straight lines of genderless children in black shorts and white shirts, eating government lunches of rice and choy under a foul, snot-colored sky. I imagined they escaped together by sea. For Canada! For the cold, clean, empty wilderness. But I didn't ask. None of us asked.

Died in a mine explosion, Father said, like a point of pride. "That was forty years ago," he said. He paused, and then he said it again. "He died forty years ago. Still, I'm careful, every day, not to shame him. Not to do anything that would make him ashamed. I know he's watching."

Father's eyes were alight, glowing like coals. It might have been fever. "I want to tell you that I'm proud of you. I've known men like you. Men with . . . weaknesses." I closed my eyes. His voice grew stronger in the darkness. "They were weaker than you. They always gave in, and let it destroy them. I want to thank you," he said, "for not shaming me."

I opened my eyes. He was reaching out as though he wanted to hold my hand. I let his clawed hand rest in mine. I remembered, as I held my breath, how disgusted my father got when he saw me cry. *You cry more than your sisters,* he'd said, and it was true.

We released our hands. He settled back into the blankets. "You don't have to visit me again until I die," he said. There was no malice or irony in his voice. He meant it. "Just know that I will be watching you from the other side."

It was only around four o'clock when I got back to Montreal. I went to the club on south Saint-Laurent where Bonnie worked. On the sign above the door, neon hands touched neon breasts in two-state animation.

Past the first door, there was a buffer hallway and then a second door, as in a photographic darkroom, to ensure that no daylight got inside. A sign under a UV light reminded patrons that there was no cover before 11:00 P.M. but you had to buy a new drink every twenty minutes.

In the perpetual midnight, a few guys sat far away from one another. A handful were scattered along the bar that surrounded three sides of the stage, and another sat in one of the stained, upholstered armchairs at the back. Bonnie sat in the far corner, eating a meatball sub. She paused to wipe off orange grease that had dripped all over her hands, up to the wrists. Her feet were up on a second chair in front of her. I went to join her.

"Doesn't it ruin the magic if customers see you wolfing down a sandwich?" I asked.

She opened her mouth to show me the balled mulch of bread and beef and sauce inside. "I don't go on for an hour."

As a kid, Bonnie had always been plain and pug-nosed, but she was so popular and beloved then that I hadn't really noticed. The first time I saw her dance, the first time I tried to see her as the audience might—men who had come just to look at her, who had never and would never hear her speak —I realized that she was ugly. Her nostrils pointed outward instead of down, her eyes were tiny, deep-set beads, and her forehead and lips were flat and wide. Her face looked like it was being pressed against an invisible pane of glass. But I saw the appeal: she was the only Asian dancer, and she had hard, ice-cream-scoop tits on the frame of a little girl.

The naked beat of the music stopped long enough for a radio-announcer voice to say, "Coming to the stage . . . say hello to Brand-eeee!"

The girl stepped out from between the curtains wearing a translucent blue baby-doll slip over a matching blue bra and thong. She took off all three items of clothing right away, without ceremony, as though undressing for bed. She walked the perimeter of the stage. She took big, deliberate steps in her see-through plastic heels.

"Are you even allowed to eat in here?" I asked.

Bonnie licked her fingers as she stuffed the napkins and wrapper back in the bag they'd come from. She gestured at a sign over the bar with a picture of scrambled eggs. "On weekends, there's a breakfast buffet. To encourage guys to stay all night."

Onstage, Brandy went down to her knees and leaned back so her vulva was directly in the beam of the footlights. The outer lips were wavy around the round, silver stud that pierced the hood of her clit.

"Oh shit," Bonnie said, noticing a greasy spot on her white T-shirt. She held the fabric toward her and squinted at it in the dark.

The girl onstage put her hand over her mound, the index

and middle finger spread in a V, catching the piercing between them. Her hand flitted left and right. I'd tried to masturbate the same way: the *thing* held between my two longest fingers, wagging it side to side, my head turned away, my other hand pressed so hard into the edge of my desk that it left a red, imprinted slice. It worked for a while. I had to end clutching the thing in a fist, feeling its whole, disgusting, senseless mass.

"I have to go get ready," Bonnie said. "Want to come backstage with me?"

"Won't that make the other dancers uncomfortable?"

"There's no one else back there at this time of day."

*Backstage* was actually the women's washroom. There weren't enough female customers for that to be a problem, except in September, when co-ed groups of freshmen came in squealing and laughing before falling into a silent stupor. At night, girls in matching sets of lingerie would sit on the sinks to smoke and gossip. They peed with the stall doors hanging open, rolls of fat and track scars from needles all exposed in the regular lights.

Now it was empty. A pair of beige underwear was wadded up in a pair of shoes, and an overturned bottle of glue was stuck to the floor where it had landed. "You hear from Helen lately?" I asked.

Bonnie opened a locker. The waxy, nutty smell of dirty hair poured out. The lockers weren't attached to the wall and were severely dented; they'd clearly come from somewhere else. "She sent a card for my birthday. Just a signature. You?"

"Never," I said.

Bonnie pulled out two wigs. "You hear from Adele?"

The letters from Adele had petered out after I moved to Montreal. We sent unlabeled photographs instead, a few per

year. Hers stopped being of churches and Reichstag buildings
—or of the often cute, often severe-looking children who
were in her charge as she went from job to job as a nanny
—and started to be of her empty breakfast plate, the broken
spine of a book she was reading, a shape that may have been
a man's back. At first I sent her pictures of the lit cross on the
mountain, the steps of my apartment building, the Old Port,
the café and the Japanese restaurant where I worked. Then
they were of my salt-eaten boots, a kettle I'd found on the
street, an old sweater of hers that I still wore to bed. I started
carrying a pocket point-and-shoot with me all the time, just
in case.

"She sent a picture of a cat. I assume it's hers. You?" I said.

"Never," Bonnie said. Her body went still for just a moment. I could see her snuffing out the sadness before she
even felt it, like a match that lights, flickers, and dies in the
wind before it has a chance to flare. I wanted to tell her that
these allegiances weren't intentional—Bonnie had a second
mother in Helen, who clung to her failure to reform Bonnie
in LA, and Adele and I had our cryptic, epistolary relationship
—but I didn't have the words to abridge our whole lives. Bonnie held out her hands with a wig balanced on each. "Okay.
Pick one."

Her left hand wore a metallic blue bob with straight-cut
bangs. Neon pink curls flowed off her right. "They're both
very pretty," I said. Reverence had crept into my voice.

"Some help you are." She put on the pink wig. She tucked
her pixie-cut black hair underneath at the edges, and then
tossed her head back and shook out the curls.

"I'm losing my hair," I blurted out. "Not losing. Lost."

Bonnie turned to the unmounted, full-length mirror that

leaned against the lockers. "Have you checked the couch cushions?" She adjusted the wig. "I still don't know." She came up behind me and plopped the blue wig onto my head, tugging it into position.

"What are you doing?"

She twisted me by the shoulders so we both faced the mirror. "Let's get a side-by-side comparison."

We stared at our reflections for what seemed like a long time. Bonnie didn't rush me. The bangs hung in my eyes and added a blue glimmer to the top of my field of vision. When I moved my head, everything sparkled.

"Can I take a picture of us?" I asked.

I arrived at the café just before six the next morning. The opening server, Marisa, stood shivering on the front step in a red miniskirt and red leather jacket. No hat or scarf. I stepped past her glare, picked up the newspapers, and unlocked the door.

Marisa and I didn't speak to each other for the first hour. The sun rose in the tall café windows as I painted long, tight curves of diluted bleach on the floor with a mop. Most days I liked mopping—the full muscular motions, pushing the bucket on its wheels in backward donkey kicks of my heel. One corner to another.

Marisa leaned on the counter, squashing her breasts in their low-cut sweater, ate a day-old pastry, and sucked down some coffee. The servers chose the music, and Marisa always chose something slow and depressing, to suit her scowling and slouching. If I looked like her, I would stand with my back straight and my chest thrust out, smiling with my white teeth and puffy lips. Male customers flirted with her with varying degrees of desperation. They promised her the world; they trembled and sweated. And Marisa just sighed. "Pathetic," she'd say.

That morning, the boss rolled in on his Rollerblades at seven, the same time as the first customer. He usually didn't come in until ten or eleven, if at all. Buddy muttered "Fuck, fuck, fuck" under his breath, his eyes bugged out, fried: he was coming down from something. He sat at the bar and yelled in my direction, taking off his skates.

"I bladed all the way from Laval," he said. I had no concept of how long it would take to Rollerblade from Laval to downtown Montreal before dawn with your drugged heart racing at highway speeds. "The health inspector is coming in today."

"Shit," Marisa said, sidling up next to Buddy with a cup of coffee. "Man or woman?"

"Woman. They're always the worst. Peter!"

"Yeah, Buddy?"

"Don't lay out the inserts today. Keep them all in the fridge. Or, uh, in a carboy full of ice. But change the ice. All the time. No, keep them in the fridge. No—fuck. I don't know. Just don't leave them out like usual. And whatever she says, no matter how fucking crazy or impossible, you just say, '*Oui, madame. Oui, madame,*' and *nothing else.* Got it?"

The customer stayed by the front door, quietly removing his gloves and tucking them in his pocket. Marisa ignored him and remained where she was. "Yeah, Peter," she said. "Don't fuck it up."

"Pretty girls shouldn't talk that way," Buddy said, squeezing Marisa on the side of the stomach. He reached down and pulled something out of his bag. "Oh, and wear this." It landed by my feet in the open kitchen. A hairnet and a black cloth hat.

"But I don't have any hair."

"Doesn't matter."

"But I can't get hair in the food when I don't have anything. See?" I ran my hand over my head. "Smooth. Smooth as an egg."

"Still have to wear them. And if she asks, pretend you do every day."

The hairnet scratched at my scalp, sunburned in the piercing blue-skied winter. Once I had secured the little hat on top, Marisa said, "You should wear it every day, Peter. It's a good look for you."

The customer coughed but didn't speak, and neither did I.

I left that afternoon with the health inspector's voice ringing in my ears. She'd called me into the walk-in cooler to point out a dripping box of meat above a shelf of vegetables. She waved a thermometer in my face to show how warm it was near the door. We climbed into the attic storage. She was a fast-talking, diminutive woman who could stand up straight under the low ceiling. When she saw the dead weevils in the sack of grain, I thought she was going to hit me. *Oui, madame. Oui, madame.*

I had the night off from the Japanese restaurant. I took my latest roll of film to get printed at the one-hour lab. I sat sucking on a soda on the curb outside while I waited, rubbing and rubbing my head, feeling its raindrop shape and unfamiliar lumps.

I took the pictures home. As soon as I was inside, I flipped straight to the end. One of the last pictures on the roll was of two girls standing shoulder to shoulder, taken in a mirror. The flash whites out their faces. Their reflections are softened by grease and dents, and the tilted glass makes both of them look taller and leaner. They have solid, brightly colored hair. The one in the pink wig has her arm around the one in the blue, and their heads lean together. Their bodies are straight lines, feminine but fashionably athletic, petite.

I went into the bathroom, which housed the only mirror, on the medicine cabinet above the sink. I would brush my teeth walking around the apartment to avoid it.

I pulled the chain on the bare bulb, setting it swinging, causing the light to bounce around the room, hide and reveal. I tilted my head down so I could see the whole thing, whole continents of skin flashing when the light swung by.

I got a black Sharpie from the main room, the kind I had used to draw on Adele's back as a kid. Without looking, I wrote HELP ME across the back of my head. I held the camera behind me to take a picture.

Marisa and a counter girl whose name I couldn't remember worked with me in the tiny corridor that constituted both the kitchen and the espresso bar. We had to slide around one another during the lunch rush. We held things above one another's heads and sucked in our stomachs. Then Marisa turned suddenly from the milk shake machine. We collided. She dropped the shake in her hand, and the parfait glass shattered. Glass and a thick puddle covered the floor from end to end.

"Oh, fuck you, Peter!" Marisa said.

"Fuck you," I mumbled, already getting a mop from the supply closet. The closet doubled as Buddy's office; he was sitting on a box of syrup pumps, talking frantically into his cell phone. *"Oui, oui. Merci beaucoup. Pas aujourd'hui, si possible."* I shut the door behind me.

"Six burgers!" the other girl shouted, even though she was right next to us.

I would have to cook the burgers one by one in a pan on an electric hot plate. I leaned the mop against my side of the counter and bent down to pick the big pieces of glass out of the mess. "Who comes to a coffee shop for burgers?" I said.

"They're on the menu," the girl said. She sounded hurt, as though I had insulted her personally.

Marisa tried to get past with a tray full of water glasses. She let out a shriek of frustration. "Get this mop out of here!"

"Just step over it!" I yelled.

"There's no room for it in here!"

"Are you going to start on those burgers?" the girl asked.

Buddy burst out of the supply closet. He ran up to the counter. "The health inspector is coming back this afternoon for our follow-up. They're going to let us off the hook if we've got our shit together this time. Ice! Hairnets!" He looked down. The vanilla milk shake had started to turn gray as it mixed with the dirt on the floor and the bottoms of our shoes. "What the fuck is this?"

We ignored him. I dumped the glass I was holding into one of the dish carboys and washed my hands. I put the first burger in a pan and laid out six plates with six open buns.

Marisa came back from delivering the waters. "You're taking up the whole counter!"

"How else am I supposed to do it?"

"Hairnet!" Buddy repeated.

"In a second!"

"Peter," the other girl said, "you have a phone call."

I hadn't even heard it ring. I ran along the line of buns, throwing down tomato slices. "Must be a mistake. Nobody has this number."

The girl spoke into the phone. The customer she should have been helping let out a dramatic sigh. She held her hand over the mouthpiece and shouted at me, "It's your mom!"

I grabbed the wireless phone from her and tucked it between my ear and shoulder, still moving along the line. Lettuce, lettuce, lettuce, lettuce, lettuce, lettuce. "Mother?" I said.

"Peter."

Pause.

"When?" I asked.

"This morning."

"Helen?"

"I called her. She booked a flight."

"I'll tell Bonnie and Adele."

"No. Your father didn't want them there."

Pause.

"Okay," I said.

"When can you come home?"

"I can leave now—"

"Do you have work tomorrow?"

"Yes."

"When is your next day off?"

"Monday."

"Come then."

"I will."

Pause.

"I love you," I said.

"Okay," she said. "See you Monday."

Adele had gone on vacation somewhere. The pictures she sent were inscrutable: blue curtains over a train window, a photo someone had taken of her as a blurry wisp on a beach. Wherever she'd gone, the wind was strong and the sand was white. Enclosed with the pictures was a thin glass vial with a plain silver top filled with seawater. She'd attached a white label that said *The Mediterranean* in her tender cursive.

I told Bonnie that our father was dead and that Mother didn't want to see her or Adele. We walked down to the Old Port together, looking for a place where you could reach the water. We poured out the vial. It vanished right away, indistinguishable from the St. Lawrence River. Bonnie knelt and refilled the vial. She gave it to me. I had that same Sharpie in my pocket. She stopped me before I could cross out *The Mediterranean* and write *The Atlantic*.

"It's all one ocean," she said. I passed her the pen and the vial. She wrote COME HOME in big, shaky, childish letters. *We even have the same handwriting,* I thought, remembering how HELP ME had come out in the photograph.

I sent everything to Adele's address in Berlin: the cry for help from the back of my head, the vial of the St. Lawrence, two of her younger siblings in stripper wigs. I imagined her, still in some warm, sunny place, slowly pouring out the bottle onto a hot rock. The briny water forms shapes that quiver but retain their surface tension. It spells out a message. COME HOME.

On the bus to Fort Michel that Monday, the driver turned off the overhead lights to let the early-morning passengers sleep. There were no reflections in the windows.

The woman in front of me tilted her seat back as far as it would go, nearly touching my knees. She slept for the first couple of hours with her baby on her chest, her arms locked around it even in her sleep, like a bird's talons.

The baby started to cry. It was a plaintive sound, like whimpering, searching for something lost. The woman undid a panel on her shirt and slipped out one of her large breasts.

She was pale enough to catch the little light from the oncoming traffic. Her wide hips and buttocks squished by the seat armrests, she shifted around, trying to find a comfortable angle. Her nipple brushed the baby's cheek. Still the baby's face groped, nosing, a blind mole.

I watched her feed.

There was no funeral. Helen, Mother, and I watched as two men broke through the frost with jackhammers. The backhoe driver got upset that we were standing there in the cold with our red noses dripping. He shouted for us to come back later, after the hole was finished. Helen went over to talk to him. She wore a black pantsuit and a wool coat. Mother wore a white long-sleeved dress under her parka. The skirt trailed in the mud. It could have been a wedding dress. She had pinned a loop of black ribbon to each of our breasts and tucked white chrysanthemum blossoms into Helen's hair.

The jackhammers vibrated on the frozen ground. It seemed loud and industrial, the cart beeping as it backed up to the grave, machines of all kinds churning; I had always thought of the Fort Michel Cemetery as a solemn, silent place, but every death turned it into a construction site.

Helen came back, her high-heeled boots crunching in the old, thin layer of snow. "They'll let us stay." No one refused Helen anything.

When we got home, Mother went straight to the bedroom. The skirt of her dress left a thin trail of dirt on the linoleum and the gray carpet. Helen and I waited by the door without taking our shoes off. The household gods had been moved to the kitchen table.

Mother came out holding a bunch of porcelain picture frames, her hands awkwardly full. She set them down on the table with the gods. She took a moment to arrange them. When she moved away, I saw that most of them were black-and-white pictures of people I had never seen before. The largest one was a family portrait. An old man with small, round glasses sat on a stool in the center. On each side of him was a woman, both women younger than him, each with big, circular curls pinned to her head, each wearing a high-necked cheongsam, each with one hand on his shoulder. Only their faces differed. About a dozen children were lined up in front of them. One girl, in overalls, had my mother's features, even the same face-length haircut she had now, as an adult.

Here was the family I had invented. Our unknown aunts and uncles. Our grandfather with two wives, who would not have fit into the boxes on a worksheet. Mother added a photo of our father to the table, a recent picture in a cheaper frame than the others. She stepped back to examine her arrangement. Without looking at us, she said, "Come here."

Helen and I took our time. I untied my boots. Helen unzipped hers. We kept our coats on. We came into the kitchen and stood together before the table of photographs — dozens of unsmiling faces; faint, implacable reflections of ourselves. Mother stepped back.

"Bow," she said.

I lowered my head. I glanced sideways at Helen. Her back stayed straight.

"Bow to your ancestors," Mother repeated.

Helen started pulling the flowers out of her hair. "This is ridiculous. Father wouldn't have wanted this."

"Bow!"

"No."

Mother grabbed the back of Helen's neck and yanked downward. Helen fell into a bow, catching herself just before she toppled forward. She snapped upright. She took a step backward and massaged her neck as if to make sure it was still there. They stared at each other.

I hadn't seen Helen in a long time. She looked the way my mother did in my memories, the image I held of her when I was away. My mother looked like a stranger, leathery and wasted, face tightened around her mouth.

"Death is special," Mother said. "Your father understood that."

Helen unpinned the ribbon and let it fall out of her hand. It fluttered softly to the ground. "We're supposed to be honoring *him*," she said. "Not you."

"Get out of my house."

"Mother . . . ," I began.

"Get out of my house. Both of you. I gave up everything for you. He made me give up everything *for you*, you ungrateful, useless children. You garbage. You faggots and whores."

Helen walked out, picking up her boots as she went, stepping onto the frozen front steps in just her socks. I turned to Mother, pleading with my eyes. She went back to the bedroom. Helen left the front door open. Winter blew in. I followed her out.

Helen drove me in her rental car back to Toronto, where I could take a shorter bus trip to Montreal. "I'll change my flight once I get to the airport" was about the only thing she said.

As Toronto started to grow along the highway, the CN Tower like a hypodermic needle breaking the skin of the sky, I said, "Dad knew. About me."

Helen looked over her shoulder as she went to change lanes. "Knew what?"

I stared at the back of my sister's head. Her hair was pulled into a tight bun with gray streaks.

"Nothing," I said.

Helen went back to Los Angeles, and we went back to not speaking.

When I got home, I pulled down the curtain over my one window. I put on the television. I had rescued it from the curb at the beginning of winter. After about eight hours passed, I called in sick to the café. After another six hours, I called in sick to the Japanese restaurant. I dozed. I called in sick to the café again; that time I talked to Buddy, who insinuated between sniffling inhales that I would be easy to replace. I hung up on him.

I lay on my side and watched TV. Late at night, there was a string of old sitcom reruns. It was just what I wanted. I wanted to see those actors when they were young.

The morning of the second day, my buzzer rang. I answered it without thinking. *"Livraison,"* the voice said.

I let the mailman into the building and opened the door when he knocked. My breath and body stank; my tongue was glued to the roof of my mouth. I'd been staring so long at the TV that spots in the air clouded my vision. The mailman said, *"Bonjour."* From my stony expression, he switched to English. "Uh, package for you."

I took it and shut the door. The box was stamped all over, had been opened and then resealed with tape somewhere along the way. I cut it open on the kitchen counter. Inside, I found a tied plastic bag and a photograph.

The roll of film must have sat, shelved, for a long time before it was developed. The photo had yellow starbursts from light leaks in three of the corners. It was a picture of Adele, a glamorous, posed photo with her head tilted back. She looked about nineteen or twenty and wore a cheongsam patterned with red and orange flowers, like the ones in the picture of our grandmothers. Her hair was a single shape that cut in a straight line down to her waist, like black, lacquered wood.

I untied the plastic bag and lifted the wig out slowly. It was surprisingly heavy, not as long or as shiny as Adele's hair, but styled the same way, all one length. I went to the bathroom holding the wig at a distance with both hands.

It scratched as I slid it on. It felt like hay. I still looked like Peter — in the narrow strip between the wings of hair, I could see the spotty five-o'clock shadow on my jaw, the Adam's apple popping from my thin neck. Peter in a bad wig, a witch costume. I turned to the three-quarter profile pose Adele held in the photo. I tilted back my head like her, making the hair seem longer, making it fall away from my face. I tried to smile like her: mysterious, sexy, the arch of an eyebrow disappearing into a dark, flowing river of hair.

I used my hands to hold the hair up in a ponytail, then shook the ponytail so a few strands scattered loose around my face. I pouted. I let it down again, turned around, and glanced over my shoulder so I could see my reflection only in the periphery of my vision. The hair stretched down my narrow back. It was better than my hair had been at its longest, in a way I could not describe. *Earrings,* I thought. Earrings and plucked eyebrows and bold lipstick, done in sincerity, not Margie's caricature. That's all it would take.

I stared into my eyes, pleased that I had the same eyes as Adele: brown in the sunlight, black in the dying incandescent bulb of my bathroom. We all had the same eyes. Helen, Bonnie. My father.

Father. I wondered about his father, the mine explosion. I supposed his eyes were the same color. And his father's father's, these purebred men.

I felt my father staring through my eyes, the grotesque image in the mirror, the halfsie freak. The grandfather I hadn't known, the great-grandfather, all watching as my father strove not to shame them, every day until he died. All of them watching me now.

I remembered visiting Helen when she'd volunteered at the nursing home in high school. Helen had done all kinds of things she wasn't qualified for. She'd mopped up the liquids that seeped out of the dying. I'd watched her chase a man wandering the hallway in nothing but an open-back gown. His broad white behind had been as huge and disconcerting as an owl's eyes lit up by headlights.

I went back to the main room. I dumped the wig into the sink and turned on the garbage disposal. I crammed it down with one of my platform sandals, running the tap. The shoe exploded into chunks of cork as it hit the blades. Stringy wet hair poked up from the drain as if I had tried to dispose of a human head.

The sink made the agonized sound of metal lodging in rubber. It stopped dead. I flicked the switch on and off and it stayed stuck. Later, when the landlord used a crowbar to dig out the remains and tried to get the wheelhouse moving again, I stayed in the bathroom with the door closed. I wanted to die like my father. Wearing crisp, new pajamas and issuing orders. Honored more than loved. A man.

# 8

## *Pathway to Glory*

FATHER TOOK US to church just once. In Fort Michel, the one Catholic church, the one Baptist church, and the one Unitarian church were lined up along one street. The street had a real name on its city sign, but everyone called it God's Highway. Behind the churches was a grassy rain ditch and a fence, and behind that, the real highway — the 400 — went roaring by our town.

I was five years old. I remember being dragged out of bed in the dark without explanation. My mother buttoned my shirt and tied a tie around my neck without turning on the lights. The tie hung almost to my knees. I batted it back and forth between my legs in the car. I liked how the black fabric shimmered when we passed a streetlight. Adele sat in the front seat, and Bonnie was strapped into a booster seat beside me. Helen and Mother walked there, heels in hand, like girls creeping back from the bars at dawn.

Father chose First Baptist — not that there was a Second or Third Baptist — because he preferred its down-home wooden exterior to the faux medieval stone and stained glass of the Sacred Heart. The storefront Unitarian church of Fort Michel, which could easily have been a 7–Eleven from a distance, wasn't a contender. First Baptist had the peaked roof and squat shape of most of the older houses in town. The cross sat at the apex of the roof without a spire, unassuming as a weathervane. It was the very picture of normality.

I don't remember much of the actual service. Hard pews, strangers in dour clothing, singing and standing and clapping. The pulpit was dead center with what I thought was a small, octagonal swimming pool off to the side. After a time, the preacher started pointing into the congregation. I hadn't been listening and I jumped in my seat. *You,* he said. *And you. And you!* Mother dutifully filled out one of the cards for new parishioners that were with the Bibles in the back of the pew in front of us and left the card in the collection plate as it came around.

A woman called the house the next morning and spoke to my mother. What good timing, she said. The church picnic is this Saturday! Surely you'll come?

A teenage girl called that evening and asked for Adele. You and your sister should come to youth group on Friday!

A man called the day after and asked for Father. Adult Bible study is a great way to network.

We went to the church picnic. Mother brought some horrific combination of marshmallows, potatoes, and mayonnaise in a casserole dish. It turned out not to be a matter of good timing at all—there was a picnic every three weeks. Some kids whom Bonnie knew from preschool seized on her. Adele vanished toward the rain ditch with the teenagers, one of whom had a guitar. The same woman who'd called my mother ambushed her to ask what was in her *delightful* potato salad. Father went to chat with the pastor. Helen and I sat on the grass in a corner. I ripped out blades of grass and tied the ends together.

The next morning, we got up early; Mother tied on my tie, Adele buckled Bonnie's dress shoes, everything the same as the week before. We stood in a line in the hallway, alert as soldiers, waiting for my father to be ready. He came out in his pajamas. "Go back to sleep," he said.

Just as he didn't discuss why we'd gone, he didn't discuss why we didn't go back. It seemed like the kind of ritual he'd enjoy: getting dressed up, shaking hands with less attractive versions of June and Ward Cleaver, drinking sour coffee and eating stale muffins. Was there anything more white-bread? Bonnie made a wry guess when I asked her about it many years later: "He didn't want there to be a higher authority than himself."

But I remembered watching my father and the pastor at the picnic. The pastor put his hand on my father's back. He pointed vigorously at the sky. I saw his lips form the word *heaven*. Or maybe, I thought later, *heathen*. Father looked up. Maybe Mother was right—death was special. And my father, the vainglorious, covetous adulterer, would be with his father, and his father's father. No one would tell him otherwise.

In 1881, Mark Twain gave a speech at the Windsor Hotel in Montreal. He commented that you couldn't throw a brick without hitting a church window in this city. I heard this story from the Japanese-speaking sushi chef, who directed it at his crew of Arabic-speaking underlings. He used English only to quote people and he attributed just about everything to Mark Twain, so I had no reason to believe Twain had really spoken these words. "It's like what Mark Twain said: 'A lie gets half-way around the world before the truth gets its pants on.'"

But no matter its source, it was true. On rue Prince-Arthur, near where I lived, a large church had been converted into loft apartments. Laundry was slung over once-sacred wrought iron. I passed several churches on my way to the grocery store: Notre-Dame de la Salette, St. John's Lutheran, Pathway to Glory, and the Chinese Baptist. I'd stopped to read the sign for services in Cantonese, English, and Mandarin. I sometimes saw the youth-fellowship group leaving, kids in their early teens getting picked up by their parents or walking to the Métro together. Their hair fell along a range of bleached colors. From watching Bonnie's hair under a transparent shower cap, I knew exactly how it worked. Black hair turns brown, then red, then brass, then a canary yellow that could only charitably be called blond.

God had never had a role in my life. If I thought about Him at all, I imagined Him as a small figure, something that could fit in your pocket or perch on your shoulder. A cheerleader for good, a kindly kindergarten teacher. The Chinese Baptist church called to me. I imagined its congregants could replace my father. I imagined they'd understand why I was ashamed. They'd understand guilt and silence. They'd use the same careful, euphemistic language that Father had—I was a man with *weaknesses*—and they'd guide me in the right direction without making me confess aloud. I assumed all kinds of things just because the people going in and out were Chinese. Because they looked like me.

And maybe that is what would've happened if I'd gone. Instead, one morning, I saw a poster taped to the side of a bus shelter.

*Are you seeking a better life?*
*Are you troubled by your own thoughts and desires?*
*Has modern decadence left you feeling empty and guilty?*
*You can change. We can help.*

*PATHWAY TO GLORY*

I'd seen the Pathway to Glory sign pointing down the external stairway of a brick building on rue Jeanne-Mance. I stood staring at this poster, reading the words over and over again. The cold morning bit through my spring jacket.

"Hits home, doesn't it?"

Only when she spoke did I realize that a woman had been sitting on the bench inside the shelter. Her cheeks and nose were red, like she'd been sitting there a long, long while. Her frizzy blond hair was dense as a topiary sculpture. "Hi. I'm Claire."

I shook her offered hand. "Peter." She held just my fingers, no higher than the knuckles, a ladylike gesture that I wanted to imitate.

"You should come to a meeting," she said.

"A meeting?"

"At Pathway."

Her face was sweetly plump; there were a few rolls over the waistband of her dress under her open coat. "Do you just sit by this poster all day?" I asked.

"Not every day," she said with a gruff laugh. "It's part of my ministry. I just came back from their residential camp, Pathway to Love. It was my second time there. I recommend it."

"Thank you, but I'm not very religious."

She took out a card to give me. "Why don't you have coffee with me? Maybe I can convince you."

I felt drawn to Claire immediately. The way she forced a smile was both endearing and familiar. Her black coat had powdery gray patches from dust or flour. Was she flirting? I took her card. "Maybe," I said.

When I went in to work that morning, Buddy was there, asking a table of girls how their service had been, calling for free Irish coffees from the bar. The café had survived its follow-up inspection; even coked up, Buddy had a certain charm. He came to collect the coffees personally.

"Buddy," I said.

His eyes stayed on the girls, a saucer balanced in each hand. "Hmm?"

I hesitated. I wanted to know how Buddy saw me, how Claire might have seen me. I deepened my voice. "Could you set me up with someone?"

"Like, a date?"

"Yes. With a woman," I added.

Buddy looked me up and down. His laugh was sudden and pointed. "I don't know anybody for *you,* man."

On our first date, I met Claire at a dessert shop on Saint-Denis. Claire got there first. She ordered us both coffee and a pot of chocolate fondue with bananas and strawberries. She poured five sugar packets into her mug. As we talked, she waved for coffee after coffee for us until I felt like my eyelids had been peeled back and pinned to my head.

Pathway to Love, the residential camp, was held on a small island where the church-owned boat was the only way on or off. "I learned that my disturbing desires were caused by a poor relationship with my mother and poor relationships with women in general," Claire said in the flat, arrhythmic voice that children use to recite poetry.

"I heard God twice." Claire speared a banana slice. "He spoke directly to me. Once during directed prayer, and once during the ice baths."

Claire described the baths — steel tubs left over from when the camp was a care facility. One of the camp leaders had helped her into the tub, naked, shoving her feet through the layers of melting ice into the cold water below. The leader put glossy, torn magazine pages into the bath, a mix of decades-old pornography and modern fashion magazines. A woman in a leopard-print bikini looking over her shoulder, showing a cheeky smile and just the side of her high, pointed breast. Two women in long T-shirts and no underwear, kissing — one woman's T-shirt was pulled up around her waist, and the other woman had slipped a finger inside her. Claire remembered the silky, natural pink of her nails, the color of the underside of an oyster shell.

The camp leader watched Claire from the corner. "Do you feel the Lord moving through you?" he asked.

Claire's skin stung. She felt like she was shrinking, like her arms were retracting into her shoulders and her legs into her hips, her head sinking into her neck like a turtle's. The sensation was not unpleasant; her whole life she'd felt overly large, somehow more solid and obvious than everyone else.

The stinging became real, fiery pain. Claire started to lift herself out of the tub. "No," the leader said. "God means for you to feel that. Look at the pictures."

The paper was starting to dissolve. The women's faces were coming apart, their spread legs, their arched backs. Only a few minutes had gone by. Her breathing quickened.

"Call to God," the leader said. His voice was soothing, far-away. "Ask Him for guidance. Can you feel Him? Can you see Him? Can you hear Him?" He asked the questions over and over again, in time with Claire's chattering teeth. "Can you feel Him? Can you see Him? Can you hear Him?"

Claire shut her eyes. She tilted her head back, submerging her hair and feeling a new jolt as the water touched her scalp. "I feel Him. I hear Him." She said it first, and then she did, she heard the voice, clear as day.

In the dessert shop, jittery with caffeine, I asked, "What did He say?"

Claire looked radiant. "He forgave me. He forgave all my sins. He said there was a wonderful man out there waiting for me, and one day soon, He would bless our love." She took my hand, stilled the shaking. "I know how you feel, Peter. You want one thing, but more than that, you want to want something else."

I could feel her bliss, her peace, through the warmth of her palm. "All things are possible in Christ," she said.

Claire lived in her late mother's house. In the airy, ramshackle kitchen, we baked several cakes at once, using all of her pans: a Bundt cake, a loaf cake, a round cake, a square cake, a cheesecake in the springform. Once the last of them was in the oven, we started on a batch of butter cookies. Claire had trained as a baker but quit to devote herself to Pathway. She kept tall bulk bins of sugar and flour under the sink.

We had our own, two-person version of Pathway. I told her about blissful dreams where I was a woman. Dreams where I would be running my hands down Margie's thighs and suddenly I would *be* Margie, that body mine all of the time. Dreams where I was a wife and mother in a shiny, prefab house. Dreams where I was a Jane Austen heroine, witty and demure in a hand-sewn housedress, fending off suitors.

Dreams where I was an ancient queen or a supermodel, admired by all—antiquated, hyperfeminine fantasies. Dreams where I was penetrated by men. Dreams where the thing snapped off as easily and painlessly as a tree branch. I told her about Father. I had never spoken so candidly with anyone.

We iced the cakes and decorated them with candy and fruits canned in syrup. "What you want and what your father wanted aren't so different," she said. "He wanted you to have a family. You want to have a family."

She told me about a recurring dream where she was at an orgy of women—every woman on earth was there, fields of pink and brown smoothing out toward the horizon. She told me about an ex-girlfriend. "A sinful, sinful woman," Claire said dreamily.

She led me into a small room off the kitchen. Intended as a pantry, it had walls with built-in shelves stocked floor to ceiling with animated Disney films on VHS. She picked a few —*The Little Mermaid, Sleeping Beauty,* and *Cinderella*—and we watched them on the couch. We ate all of the cookies and two whole cakes without noticing. The next cookie was in my hand before I had finished the last one so that there were no pauses in the pleasure.

Once we were too full to move, as Cinderella ran from the ball, her dress unraveling into sparkles and rags, Claire pulled a blanket over our laps and leaned her head on my shoulder. "Doesn't this feel nice?" she said. I felt starved for touch. I put my arm around her.

Prince kissed princess. The music swelled in choral voices. Claire sat up and turned to face me. I touched her cheek. Her breath smelled of icing, and I wanted to kiss her. She looked proud. Could it be this easy?

I touched my lips to hers, found her skin warm and dry.

She was the second person I had ever kissed. It wasn't bad. All things are possible.

Before me, Claire had dated a man she met at Pathway. After several tries, they successfully made love once. At a meeting, he confessed that he'd spent the whole time reliving the details of a homosexual encounter "just to get through it." The counselor asked Claire if she'd done the same. "No," she said.

Claire remembered turning her head while they were in bed and seeing his knuckles whitened from squeezing the pillow underneath her. She hadn't thought about much of anything. She had watched him — going through his frantic, stuttering motions and hawing like a donkey — in the same state of meditative peace that she evoked in me now. She didn't associate it at all with her previous liaisons with women, where she'd been possessed, where some malevolent force had caused her to pull at her own hair and scream frightfully, had given her hallucinations of falling and knots untying and angels descending. A man thrusting inside her had felt good, like voting or getting your teeth cleaned.

That's how sex is supposed to feel for a woman, Claire explained. Like civic pride, like virtue, like doing one's duty.

With me, she went slower. Firm, close-mouthed kisses, caresses on the inner forearms. On a long, contented afternoon of small touches, we lay on her bed together, fully clothed. She was on her back and I was on my stomach, stroking her hair. "We could get married," she said. "Someday."

I pulled apart two of her tight, frizzy curls. She closed her eyes, smiling. "We both want children. We'd be amicable roommates. It's more than most people have."

"I want that," I said. "More than what I want."

She nodded. She always knew what I meant. "We could fill this house with children," she murmured. I moved closer and kissed her. Her body tensed and she recoiled, then she obediently tilted up her face.

We fell asleep. When I woke, it was dark; she had turned onto her side and I had spooned against her back in my sleep. The thing was hard between us. I tried not to move, tried to pack down my disgust into something smaller and denser, into something small enough to swallow, something I could make disappear.

Dating Claire was like learning to meditate. Discipline consumed my life. All the clamor inside was silenced, replaced with static, white noise.

Claire's pastor told her she was neglecting her ministry, so we went to the Village on east Sainte-Catherine to hand out flyers for Pathway. Rainbow flags hung from every other balcony, rainbow stickers in the shop windows. Claire said one of the principles of Pathway was "reject temptation and accept the Lord." She said, "You need to approach the devil to defeat him."

We stood on the sidewalk between two bar patios. Claire thrust flyers into the hands of two girls walking together. "Do you want to know the path to happiness?" she asked. "The path to love?"

"I know the path to love, honey," the girl said, still heading for the bar. "It's right through those doors." She and her friend laughed.

I didn't say anything as I handed out the flyers. Most people took them. I watched some get thrown away at the first trash can. One man, younger than me, read it through and tucked it into his back pocket. Someone threw a beer at us. We jumped back and the plastic cup just splashed our feet.

A woman approached us. My first thought was that she was unusually tall. She wore a striped blue sundress and opaque tan nylons with white pumps. Her crooked, once-broken nose called up a strange memory: little boys beating each other on the playground.

She faced us directly, her hands on her hips. "I think you two better get out of here," she said.

"This is a public sidewalk," Claire said.

"Yes, but you're harassing my customers." Her voice was throaty, awkward. False. "You can go on handing out your hateful little flyers across the street."

"God loves you," Claire said. "Even when you do what is unnatural. Even when you disobey Him. He's always waiting for you."

"I can call you in for loitering." Thick-limbed, thick-shoul-dered. Square jaw smothered in orange-toned foundation, fake eyelashes in the daytime. Still somehow convincing. I felt a sinking sensation, like the sidewalk had gone soft under my feet. The white static in my brain crackled back into images. It's easy to have a phobia of water if you always stay inland, avoid the shimmering, inviting, treacherous depths.

Claire tugged me by the sleeve to the corner of the inter-section. Passing cars roared in my ears. She stroked my hand sympathetically as we waited for the light to change. "The devil conjured that demon just for you," she said.

I'd left Mother alone after Father died. When I thought of her, I imagined all but one of the chairs against the wall, Mother sitting alone at the kitchen table and mourning—her dead husband, and her children who had run to every corner of the earth.

Mother answered the phone in Cantonese. *"Wai?"*

"Mother?"

"Peter? What do you want? I'm busy."

I wanted her to meet Claire. I wanted to marry Claire, wanted the train of her wedding dress to trail behind us like a white flag of surrender, erasing *faggots and whores.* I'd thought Mother would be overjoyed to hear from me. Her voice was brisk and unfamiliar.

After a moment of dead air, Mother made an impatient noise. "Are you still there?"

"Yes." I hesitated. "How have you been?"

"Fine, fine. Are you coming home?"

"I can come visit."

"Good!" I could hear the TV in the background on Mother's end: someone cried out in high-pitched, whiny Cantonese, *"Aiyee!"* Canned laughter. "Can you bring a big car?"

I rented a van and drove it to Fort Michel on my next day off. The outside of the house was in need of repairs—the gutter had come loose, the paint on the sidings was chipped—but the inside was spotless and bare. She'd had the carpets ripped out and replaced by laminate, fake wood that broadcasted its fakeness: even, glossy, no knots. The new table in the kitchen sat only two.

Mother and I packed up all of my sisters' and my belongings; our father's things were already gone, down to the last sock. She threw open the windows, letting out the stirred dust and the smell of molding clothes.

Mother was like a different person. Silent except in rage all our lives, she'd blossomed at the mouth. She couldn't stop talking. Anecdotes about our childhoods burst out of her, grown strange or impossible from too much time in the dark of her closed throat: Adele taught herself to read. I brought a family of rats home in my backpack. Helen bit a wasp right out of the air and chewed it before it could sting.

"When we brought Helen home from the hospital," she said as we dragged garbage bags full of clothes and toys and books to the door, "she slept through the first night without crying. And the next, and the next, and almost every one after that. *Geng sei-a,* I kept checking to make sure she hadn't stopped breathing.

"At her vaccinations, she didn't cry when we handed her to the doctor. She watched the needle going into her fat little arm, then she turned to the wall. No tears. We thought maybe she was . . . what's the word? Broken-headed. Broken in the head."

I opened up the chest of drawers in the room that had belonged to Adele and Helen, then Helen and Bonnie, then just Bonnie. No one had touched it since Bonnie had moved out. "This too?"

"Everything," Mother said. She continued her story. "And Helen didn't talk. She didn't talk until she was three years old, when she said a complete sentence. 'Can I have a cookie?' Can you believe that, Peter? 'Can I have a cookie.' No jibber-jabber, no *mama, dada,* like the rest of you. I guess she just didn't feel like talking. Ha!"

I had to stop and stare. The *Ha!* threw me so completely, my mother laughing at her own joke. My mother laughing.

There were pictures of people I didn't know all over the house. Most of the photos were old—black-and-white, or the red sun and washed-out grays of the '60s and '70s—but one stood out as recent. My mother, as she looked now, stood with a young woman at a crowded picnic in the park. I picked it up as a way of changing the subject. "Who is this?"

"Oh, I met her at the Chinese Association." Mother's gaze held steady. "She's like the daughter I never had."

I put down the picture, turning my back. Mother's hair was thinning in a way that left visible strips of scalp, and her nails and skin were becoming that same fragile, rosy ivory.

Mother wrote down the address of the Salvation Army store in Barrie, Ontario. They were expecting me. I loaded all the bags and boxes into the van.

While I didn't believe in the devil literally, as Claire did, I did feel as though this temptation was somehow the result of a greater force. That the universe had conspired to send me down the bumpy local roads with a van full of women's clothes, shoes, and accessories. The teenage wardrobes of the women I had most idolized.

This was my chance, I thought, to prove my strength. I pictured each step in turn: Giving a firm handshake to the volunteers at the Barrie Salvation Army, helping them unload. One of the bags rips and a particularly coveted item peeks through the corner. Adele's prom dress, say, with its short flare and underlayers of tulle. And I just ignore it. I pictured the drive back to Montreal. The empty van like an empty mind, a clear and guiltless heart. I couldn't wait to tell Claire that I'd fought the devil and won. I could see her excited face. I could see us taking our clothes off and going to bed together.

I only realized where I was when I was already on the 401, halfway to Montreal.

The dress, with its tiny waist and stiff, sweetheart neckline — creating cleavage where there was none — zipped smoothly up my back. The silver high heels fit; the clasp on the silver pendant still worked.

Among the toys, I found a baby doll that I'd forgotten about. The body was filled with absorbent polymer beads. When you poured warm water into the hole in her back, she felt soft and responsive.

I propped her up in my lap and read to her from our old books. Another doll leaned against my side. I squeezed her hand, and a recording in her chest said, "Mom-my." The Zen static was completely gone; everything came crawling from the shadows, rejoicing in the light.

Claire might have forgiven me. I was sure Pathway had a ritual for it—I saw us sitting in Claire's kitchen and shredding the clothes with fabric shears, purposely nicking the skin between my fingers, dark drops of blood ruining the white collar on one of Helen's blouses. The dolls pulled apart, their dismembered bodies in sealed bags. She would have prayed for me, both of us down on our knees and our hands thrown up in the air: forgive us, Lord, our weakness.

I couldn't do it. I couldn't let her take it away.

One morning, Claire visited the café wearing a long, shapeless dress that appeared to be made out of burlap and that had sweat stains under the arms. It was an odd look, even for her. Marisa brought Claire her latte and chocolate croissant; she wore a black acrylic halter top and denim cutoffs at seven in the morning. Claire cracked her jaw to stuff the croissant inside.

I took a break and sat down with her. Her eyes were bloodshot and she slumped forward against the table as she ate. "Are you okay?"

"Yes, I just need my coffee." An avalanche of sugar. She peered at me over the rim of her cup. "I've decided to give up pants."

"Oh. Why?"

"Modesty," Claire said. Marisa was taking up her usual pose, bent over the counter, making her ragged shorts ride up her thighs. Sin on legs. She caught Claire's gaze and nodded at her, flashing a quick grin. In all my years at the café, I'd never seen Marisa smile. She sighed and rolled her eyes at every customer, like the requests were endlessly taxing.

"Why now?" I asked. Claire wasn't smiling back at Marisa. I couldn't imagine two people less alike than Marisa and Claire.

"Penance," she said distractedly.

These single-word answers made me nervous. "For what?"

"Everything." She looked at me like she'd just realized I was there. She reached out and touched my cheek. "You're so handsome, Peter."

I had a strange thought. "Do you know Marisa?"

Claire pulled back her hand. "Who?"

"The waitress."

Claire looked to the side, smiling with just her mouth, like she couldn't believe I would ask such an absurd question. "I do know her, yes."

"From where?"

She rubbed her chin, still looking sideways. "Some den of perversion."

Pathway talk. "A nightclub? A bar?" I asked. Almost unconsciously, Claire bit the knuckle of her index finger. I said, "A lesbian bar." I could see the skin caught between her top and bottom front teeth. "Have you slept with her?"

Claire's hand dropped from her mouth and smacked the

table. "It's not sex. Women can't have sex with each other. But it is . . . unclean." She finally looked straight at me. "It was a long time ago."

"How long ago?"

"Since Marisa? Years and years. Years and years ago."

Claire looked exhausted that morning. Claire worked for Pathway. "How long since you've—how long since any woman?" She shook her head. I asked again. "Claire, how long?"

"Yesterday," she said.

I stared at her. Claire looked a little embarrassed, a little agitated, but at the same time, I saw that this was how it had always been and how it would always be, and that she was just upset at getting caught. I thought of us proselytizing in the village. Had she come back that night as her other self? Her selves farther and farther apart, one in a sack dress eating cookies with me on the couch, converting sinners on the street, testifying at Pathway, and the other—what was she like? "I don't believe this," I said.

Claire took my hand. She spoke quickly. "I want us to go to the camp together. Pathway to Love. I wanted to ask you to do this for a long time, but I was afraid. We'll go together and make our vows to each other and it will be the end of all our wretchedness." She squeezed my fingers. "They can help us."

She waited for my confession. What was I doing yesterday? Wearing Adele's bikini, lounging beneath the heat of an imagined sun and the gaze of an imagined crowd, as I had seen her do in reality so many times. I would not give Claire that. "You cheated on me," I said.

Claire looked surprised. "I know," she said cautiously. Then something clicked, and she plunged into it. "I know! I'm weak. I'm disgusting. Disgusting!" She beat her hand on the table again, this time with a rhythm, lining up with her chant: "Disgusting! Disgusting! Disgusting!"

I became aware of the people at nearby tables. Claire was putting on a show. She collapsed forward with her head on her arms. After a moment of stunned silence all around us, she lifted her head slightly, one eye open, like a child peeking to see if she's been caught. Her one eye stared straight at me, as if to say, *And you?*

I wanted to dive in and denounce myself. I saw the cycle ahead of us, of Pathway meetings and alter egos, of sins and forgiveness, false promises. Sucking other people in. Telling them they could change. Angry tears started to well in my eyes. I heard Father, I heard Claire: You can change!

I pushed my chair back from the table and stood up. "You are disgusting," I said.

Claire clutched my arm as I passed. I jerked free and left her alone at her table.

Months later, walking home in the pit of another winter, I passed the basement steps leading down to Pathway. Singing came from below. One woman's voice rose high and clear above the others, tremulous, on the verge of tears. The conviction of someone who has heard the voice of God.

In my memory, I tried to change the look on Claire's face as I pulled away from her in the café, tried to make it calculating and cold. Tried to make her into someone who lied to me and the world for the sake of the church that paid her, who said, *See, I did it. You can too!* Who understood that we were both frauds, who was even happy to be free of me. I needed it to be that way, so I could forget her, so I could go on thinking of myself as a victim of the world.

I stopped and listened to her sing—Claire, or someone like her. I remembered the tightness of her grip on my arm, and in the well of her wide, pleading eyes, I saw the girl who had gone to Pathway the first time, who feared a hell of fire more than a hell of ice, who meant it every time she prayed for forgiveness. Maybe she saw me as I had seen her. Maybe she believed that she was weak and I had overcome.

# 9

# *Geography*

HELEN MOVED ABRUPTLY from Los Angeles to Washington, DC, to teach law at George Washington University. A few days later, she called my mother at four in the morning. Helen, who had built an impressive career from being articulate as a poet and immovable as stone, slurred into the mouthpiece, "I done bad, *Ma-ma*. I done bad."

Mother waited until Helen had cried herself out. "I'm coming to visit you," she said.

Helen sobered immediately. "No. No need to do that. I'm fine."

"Ha! Fine! You book the ticket. I'm doing nothing out here. So good to be old! I can come visit you whenever."

Helen, sitting on the floor between unpacked boxes in her new apartment, crossed her splayed legs. She dignified her posture as though being watched. I could imagine all of this, even the monstrous shadows of unarranged furniture, a pile of lamps on a couch like severed heads. Her voice became measured, business as usual. "I'm just having a bad day," she said. "Sorry to alarm you. A visit would be nice, but I'm very busy getting set up here." She had expected a silent, furious auditor, an abstract *ma-ma*—the way our mother used to be. She would've been as surprised as I was by the *Ha!*

"Busy? How much stuff could you have, what do you have to do? Just a young single girl."

Helen, forty years old, didn't comment on that.

"You wake me up crying and expect me not to visit? My favorite child? Ha!"

Helen resisted the urge to say *That's news to me.* Her instinct to bargain kicked in. "I'll buy you a bus ticket," she said, thinking she could wear my mother down.

"Great!" Mother said. "I want to go next week."

*Who is this woman,* Helen thought.

The bus pulled up to the border crossing just north of Buffalo, New York, shortly after midnight. It had weaved all afternoon through Ontario, and as the lights went on, a babel of tired voices tittered in German, French, Italian, Farsi, and Mandarin. The mix of languages reminded Mother of an orchestra tuning up. They passed from the overwarm bus to the overwarm Customs building with only a brief reprieve of cool night in between.

My mother wore sneakers and black dress pants that she had hemmed too short. Hers was the only bus being processed, and there were nearly as many agents as passengers. A middle-aged couple stood in line in front of my mother. They were huddled and stooped as though they were much older. The woman spoke frantically in Italian to her husband, gripping her headscarf, and the man shushed her with a backward motion of his hand.

My mother was called up. The agent at the counter was a

young man with a military haircut and muscular shoulders, though his gut pushed his belt down to his hips. His last name was sewn into his vest: Sosa. Like the baseball player, Mother thought. He swung his chair sideways, away from her, as he squinted at her passport photo. "So where you going?"

"Washington, DC."

"Uh-huh. And what's there?"

"My daughter."

He glanced at my mother then. An image flashed through Mother's mind, an image from when she was in primary school. The students had to stand at attention whenever they were asked a question. She remembered how, after you'd given the answer but before the teacher began her ritual of humiliation, before the ruler came down on your knuckles, you just knew, from the quality of the silence, what was coming.

"I see. And what's her visa status there? Does she have a green card?"

"Yes. I think so. Yes." The poster on the wall behind the border agent had three smiling young white people with their arms crossed, standing in front of an American flag. We are the face of the United States of America, it said. We welcome you to our country.

"You coming from China, ma'am?"

Mother glanced at her Canadian passport. The agent flipped it absent-mindedly between his middle and index fingers. "No. I'm Canadian. I've lived there for more than forty years."

The agent started typing something swiftly into his terminal. The old keyboard clacked as it sprang back against his fingers. "Forty years is a long time to keep that accent. May I see your return ticket to Canada, *ma'am?*"

"I don't have one." He stopped typing. "My daughter is going to buy me a plane ticket home."

"How long are you staying?"

"Until she feels better."

"Is she sick?"

"She's . . ." My mother strained after the word. Her accent had gotten worse since he had mentioned it. "She's . . . sad."

"Uh-huh." His victorious, almost private smile seemed familiar to Mother. "I'm going to have to deny you entry, ma'am."

"Why?"

A few windows over, an agent screamed, "I don't speak any fucking Italian!"

Sosa's eyes flitted left and then returned to Mother, unaffected. "Because you don't have a return ticket or an expected date of return. That counts as trying to immigrate without a visa." The agent spoke in a calm voice, one you could use to hypnotize an animal. Mother couldn't account for the rage that was building up inside of her.

"Isn't anyone going to do anything about that?" she said.

"About what?"

She gestured toward the agent who had screamed. "What she just said to those poor people."

He continued typing. "Would you like to file a complaint?"

"Yes!"

"You'll have to go to the Canadian consulate and provide an incident report. About something someone said to someone else." He stood up. "Now, I'm going to tell your bus driver that we're detaining you. Do you have a cell phone?"

The voice, the smile. It was my father. Mother saw him standing there now, in this agent's uniform, one hand on his pistol, running her life with a light touch, being so goddamned *reasonable,* never raising his voice or his hand. She wouldn't let another one tell her what to do. Another one of these men who make all the decisions, strip you of autonomy and disguise it as kindness.

"I don't want to live in your stupid country," she said, her accent worse than ever. "I have a house in Canada. I have children there. But one of my stupid children chose to move down there and she needs me!"

Still smiling. This, too, was familiar: hearing herself scream at a brick wall. "Are you yelling at me, ma'am?" he asked. As though it were a legitimate question and not a trick you use to patronize children.

"No."

"Put your bag up here, please."

He unzipped her small suitcase slowly, as you might undo a lover's coat. The way Father drew out a punishment. He picked through her underwear piece by piece, with the long line of her fellow passengers behind her. He went through her pockets. He held the clouded sandwich bag with her toothbrush inside up to the light. Everyone was watching them now. She heard someone ask, "What's happening?"

"May I see your arms?" he asked loudly.

Uncomprehending, she held out her arms.

"Roll up your sleeves past the elbow."

"Why?"

"Please do as I asked, ma'am."

Mother started to tremble. She had loved my father once. Loved his quiet authority, his impeccably shined shoes, the way he would order for her at restaurants and guide her by the small of her back. She had pitied other women her own age, with their husbands who drank, who were needy as babies and violent as teenage boys. She'd married a leader, a king. When he died, she'd felt abandoned, overwhelmed by the smallest choices.

One morning, she found herself staring at the carpet in the living room. How she hated it. The white that had turned to sooty gray almost immediately, stained by four drooling children and four careless teenagers, how much of her life had been spent vacuuming and scrubbing this ugly, impractical thing. She saw it gone. She touched her hair, still kept girlishly long, as Father had liked it, even though it was too thin and brittle to wind into a bun anymore. She saw it gone. An exposed neck, exposed floors, everything lean and light. She could eat whatever she wanted, go wherever she wanted, call old friends. She didn't need to ask permission and try to work out his web of leading, trapping questions.

She kept her eyes lowered as she rolled up the sleeves of her shirt. The agent examined the crooks of her elbows. She wanted to grab his pistol. No more. No more.

When he was done, Sosa leaned back in his chair and yawned, cracking his knuckles over his head. "Okay. Follow me. We'll get you printed and photographed, and we'll run you through the FBI database. Should only take a few hours. Thank you for being so cooperative."

Eventually two agents, one of them Sosa, accompanied Mother back to the Canadian side, where she could wait for the first morning bus. It was dark and moonless, any starlight drowned out by the overhead lights of the wide asphalt road. The two guards walked a few meters behind her and Sosa shouted directions. "Turn left here. Keep going straight."

She wondered why they didn't walk ahead and lead, or walk at her sides, and then remembered Sosa's hand on his gun. They were behind her in case she ran. They were behind her so they could shoot. The older you get, the more every trauma is the same trauma.

Helen said, "Go to the consulate. I'm a lawyer. I'll talk to someone who knows about this kind of stuff." Helen said, "I bought you a plane ticket, round-trip this time. They're nicer at the airport."

Mother said, "'Fucking Italian.'"

I used the plane ticket.

I arrived in DC on a Saturday in August. I was acting as my mother's spy, as the last child to whom she had access, so I could find out why the only good one, the only one of us with money and success, was so sad. "It was a boyfriend," Mother theorized. "I bet he promised to marry her and she waited and waited. Forty years old and still single, tsk-tsk."

Helen picked me up at the airport in a violet-gray Audi that looked brand-new. Rather than come to the gate, she waited leaning on her car in the passenger-loading area, daring someone to tell her she couldn't park there.

As soon as I stepped out of the air-conditioned airport, my shirt wilted and stuck to my chest. Mosquitoes swarmed my legs. Washington felt like the drained, paved swampland it was.

"Beautiful car," I remarked.

"It was a gift from my firm in LA," she said. She was wearing a wool pencil skirt and a long-sleeved shirt and hadn't broken a sweat. She was even thinner than I remembered. Her ropy calves looked squeezed dry, like she had no water left to give.

"They must have really liked you," I said. She skimmed

through her cell phone as I put my suitcase in the back unassisted.

We settled into the immaculate leather interior of the car. The air conditioning came on so strong it knocked me back in my seat. "Can I turn it down?"

"Knock yourself out," she said. I reached across. The knob was right beside the steering wheel. I noticed how pale my skin looked next to hers, with its mottled California brown.

I watched the highway and then the city streets. Memorials and government buildings seemed at war with the sky. Police cars were everywhere, sometimes four on one corner. Helen didn't seem to want to talk, so I didn't bother her.

We pulled into the parking lot of a strip mall. The car had turned rapidly into a freezer, and I welcomed the soupy heat outside. Helen didn't seem bothered by either. I trailed behind her as she bought a gigantic bottle of bourbon in the liquor store. The bourbon jug was made of cheap plastic and was the size of a large gas canister, with the same kind of built-in handle. Helen carried it to the register, holding it loosely by the handle with her bony fingers, as though it were weightless. As we waited in line, she idly plucked a can of insect repellent from between the chips and condoms in the impulse-purchase display.

The silence started to make me uncomfortable as we took off again in Helen's car. "Where are we going?"

"My townhouse. Then lunch. Then I'll show you around the capital." Helen made the whole thing sound nonnegotiable, more like a prison orientation than a vacation. I decided our mother must have exaggerated when she told me about the late-night phone call. I couldn't imagine Helen's brusque voice breaking, wailing, the *Ma-ma,* any of it. I planned to tell Mother that Helen was fine. She was the same as ever.

The front door of Helen's townhouse locked from the inside and the outside with a key. She locked us in. I put my bag down by the door because that seemed as good a place as any. Her unpacked boxes blocked the windows. A mattress leaned against an empty bookshelf. I wondered where she'd been sleeping.

"Where's the bathroom?"

Helen pointed as she disappeared down a hallway. I went in and threw cold water on my face and the insides of my arms. Her house was cool and dark, with stone tiles for flooring in every room. I opened the cabinet over the sink. Two neat rows of prescription pill bottles were inside. They varied in size and color, a rainbow of translucent plastic. The overall effect was cheery and efficient, like a well-run dispensary.

When I came out, Helen was drinking bourbon on ice in the kitchen. I asked, "Is it safe to drink that with your medication?"

She scowled. It was the expression I remembered best and, oddly, made her look young. "Snooping for Mother already, are we?" She took out a second glass and pressed a button on the fridge for ice. "I'm not on medication anymore, if you must know. Do you want one?" she asked, although she was already pouring the bourbon.

"Sure, I guess."

She handed me the glass. "We used to drink bourbon every afternoon at my firm."

"When you were on medication."

"Yes. If you must know." Helen didn't seem to be drinking quickly, but her glass was already empty. She poured herself another, knocking the cap to the floor in the process. It rolled under the fridge and she made no move to retrieve it.

The bourbon tasted as you'd expect bulk bourbon to

taste—cloying and medicinal as cough syrup. "What were you taking?"

She looked me up and down, sizing me up. "Antidepressants and antianxiety meds," she said finally. "I couldn't find any that didn't interfere with work."

"But you brought them all to Washington with you."

"Teaching doesn't require the same mental acuity," she said crisply. "I'm going to try them all again." With her free hand, she pressed her fingernail into a mosquito bite on the arm that held her glass.

"Do you have a doctor?"

"Not here, no. I don't need one." She lifted her nail without looking at it, freeing a small bubble of blood in the center of a pressed line.

"Is that why you left? The job was too stressful?"

Helen slammed down her glass, suddenly out of patience. "I left because LA is a hellhole. People wash up on the beach like garbage." She started pouring a third bourbon, and the motion of her arm caused the blood to streak. The ice in her glass hadn't melted. "Are we done with the interrogation? You want lunch?"

We sat on the patio of an Italian restaurant on the same block as her townhouse. It was part of a chain, decorated in an American's idea of Italy, with mass-produced paintings of vines and olive trees lining the walls. Helen looked out of place in her leaden work clothes; all the other women were wearing halter minidresses, hot pants, sarongs. My shorts and polo were soaked through with sweat. Imagine, I thought, wearing just breezy hollows and bare skin like the women were, all those smooth round stretches glowing in the sun.

Helen had three gin and tonics with her spaghetti, which

she'd sent back the first time for being overcooked. Helen had held up one noodle on her fork and waved it in front of the waitress, making it sway soddenly as she explained the term *al dente*. "'To the tooth,'" she'd translated. "As in, gives some resistance to the tooth."

The woman behind Helen had three children. The oldest played on a handheld game with the volume turned up high. The younger two, a boy and a girl, ran around the table in circles, giggling and poking each other. They bumped against Helen's chair and used it to swing around their own table faster, their small hands brushing against her legs.

Helen turned. "Excuse me. Can you control your children? I'm trying to eat."

The mother stood. She was enormously pregnant and red-faced from the sun. She had to steady herself on the chair. "Don't tell me how to raise my kids."

I sank back into my seat. I expected Helen to escalate the hostilities, but instead she looked stung. "Sorry," she said. She fumbled for her drink.

The woman sat down again, one hand on her belly. She seemed dissatisfied, like she'd wanted a fight. She ended up doing what Helen had asked. "You two!" she barked. "Sit the fuck down and eat!"

The kids stopped. Like their mother, they had red, sun-cooked faces. I leaned in close to Helen and murmured, "God. They're so burned."

Helen shrugged.

The kids pulled themselves into their chairs. The girl, maybe four, held her fork in her fist and stabbed it downward at her food. The boy stuck his hand experimentally into his macaroni. I felt the same way as their mother: sunstroked, ready for a fight. The height of the inland summer in Ontario, while just as hot, was very different. It made you apathetic and slothful, overwhelmed by the flat, endless sky. You wanted to lie down in a dark room. This Southern heat roiled the blood. Distorted by the light, everyone looked like an enemy. I could see why the crime rate went up with the temperature.

"I would be a great mother," I said.

Helen bumped her glass into her front teeth and then looked down at it in confusion. "I wouldn't," she said, not rising to the bait.

Helen and I spent the afternoon popping into free museums and government buildings. Helen moved through each as though she were ticking it off a list in her head, so quickly that it was unclear why we'd come. We spent less than ten minutes inside the Library of Congress. We went from one end of the National Air and Space Museum to the other without going into any of the exhibition halls, as if the clusters of upright rockets and hanging planes were trees and jungle canopy to be slashed out of our way.

We stopped only at security checkpoints. Helen was well practiced. She knew which ones would ask you to surrender phones, which ones needed to search your shoes, which ones banned pens and paper. Like Mother, I saw our dead father everywhere. In the way the guards held their mouths in disgust, their bland, shaming voices: How dare you bring a water bottle? Did you think we wouldn't know? That we can't hear the vile thoughts in your head? The twisted happiness you squeeze out of dresses and dolls when you think you're alone? We are watching you from the other side.

How Father would love the new America, its all-seeing, all-knowing eye.

In the evening, Helen and I walked for nearly an hour along a boulevard of baking concrete, looking for a bar. The sun was setting and we moved through visible clouds of insects, their buzzing drowned out by low-flying planes from Reagan National Airport.

We ended up at the W Hotel on Fifteenth Street. The lobby had black marble floors and dripped with crystal. A bouncer hovered by the elevator, roped off with red velvet. "Rooftop terrace," Helen explained to me. "It would help if you were better-looking."

The terrace was no cooler than the ground, made worse by the dense crowd of wet, steaming human meat. Helen ordered us both straight bourbons. I held the glass to my face as we leaned against the railing. The W Hotel was a squat building that managed to look out over all the other squat Romanesque buildings of the capital.

Helen pointed out a few landmarks in the distance and then said, "I love America. Land of new beginnings. It's like LA and DC are on different planets. Canada is so much bigger but there's nowhere to go." We could see the roof of the White House. Black silhouettes of men with long-barreled guns paced in circles, aimless as the flies and mosquitoes.

"Bonnie said you liked LA."

She held the drink to her mouth thoughtfully, statue-still. Her lower lip stuck to the glass.

"Why did you leave?" I pressed. I felt dizzy and argumentative. "That's why I'm here. Mother wants to know—why you left LA and your six-figure salary. Why you called her. She thinks it's because of a man."

Helen laughed. "What, like I'm Adele?" She bent in half over the railing, staring affectionately down at the city.

"I quit both of my jobs to be here, you know."

"Nobody asked you to do that." Her limp hands almost spilled her drink. She recovered it and took a sip. "Do you think Father's proud of me?" She turned, vindictive, channeling his ghost. "Do you think he's proud of you?"

"Father's dead."

A blast of wind threw both of us back a step; it was followed by a sound like an angry bellow. The planter trees of the terrace flattened in one direction as a square, military-gray helicopter appeared above the trees of the White House lawn. It lurched as though being yanked upward on strings. Everyone rushed to the balcony, squashing Helen and me against the railings. People watched until the dot vanished among the clouds.

"Can he see us?" Helen asked. The president, Father, God.

We got into the car, and Helen drove back and forth across state lines until she found a gas station that sold beer. I let her drive, squinting red-eyed at the dark, complex interchanges. She seemed to be doing fine.

We went back to her townhouse to drink more. I sat down on the rug in her living room, and the rough weave scratched my mosquito bites raw. She cleared a space for herself on the couch, tossing lamps and boxes aside.

She came across a box that gave her pause. It was full of labeled cassette tapes, carefully organized by date into smaller boxes. Her fingers danced across the top of the tapes as she sucked at the beer bottle. "Guess," she said.

"Guess what?" I said, itchy as hell.

"Why I left LA."

"You got your heart broken," I spat.

"Nope."

"You got fired."

"No, but you're getting closer."

"This is stupid." I crawled across the rug and came to the canister of bug repellent she'd bought at the pharmacy. "God, why didn't we use this?" I moaned.

"Let me show you something, little brother," Helen said, plucking the canister from my hand. She took a lighter from her pocket. She sprayed a mist of repellent and then lit it. A fireball exploded between us.

For a moment, a moment shorter than a blink, I saw Helen through flames. And she saw me. She allowed her face to open up, to be vulnerable, sisterly, small. And I could imagine her crying on the phone now, crying to me just as easily as to our mother. "I done bad, *Ma-ma*. I done bad."

All the tiny flames went out like a breath. Helen and I stayed kneeling on the rug across from each other. "I just wanted him to be normal," she said. "Like I wanted you to be normal."

"Who? What are you talking about?"

She pulled out one of the tapes and the personal recorder that was in the box with them. She slid the cassette inside and pressed Play. Her own voice came from the speaker. "Case notes," it said. "April twenty-sixth. *Reis versus Reis*."

I sat back on my knees. In my earliest memory of Helen, Father had tasked her to divide up a small cupcake between the four of us. We were all shouting: Adele deserved the whole cupcake because she was the oldest. Bonnie deserved it because she was the youngest. I deserved it because I liked cupcakes the most. Helen ignored us all. Her concentrated face, tongue poking from between her lips, focused just on steadying the knife, on making two perfect cuts, in half and half again.

Initial consultation: A father seeks to win custody of his son. Good afternoon, Mr. Reis, Helen says. Marcus, he says. His voice is calm. He wears a gold necklace, gold rings, and a gold watch. ("Note," the recording says. "Remind Marcus not to wear his jewelry to court.")

You seem very calm, she says.

I just want my son, he says.

They talk for an hour. They go through the papers. His case for custody is sound. The wife lives in a small apartment in Pasadena with the lover who ended their marriage. Mr. Reis kept the four-bedroom house. The wife is unemployed. Mr. Reis owns a construction company with significant government contracts.

The son is fourteen years old with severe autism and a fixation on maps. Mr. Reis argues that the wife is negligent. She lets the teenage boy wear diapers. She dresses him in wrap dresses, as they are easier to get on and off. Lets him eat alone and with his hands. Lets him sit all day surrounded by atlases and globes, memorizing, reciting, drawing maps, the same ones over and over again. The boy, however, cannot answer geography questions when asked directly and is not classified as a savant. The boy is obese. (All this said on Helen's recording in clipped, orderly sentences.)

Mr. Reis has drawn up a contract with a full-time ABA therapist, who will be with the boy eight hours a day, five days a week, if Mr. Reis is granted custody. Mr. Reis has consulted a psychiatrist, who will meet with the boy weekly. Mr. Reis has a plan.

Private negotiations between the parents fail. They go before a judge. Helen is confident. The therapists testify. Studies show, they say. Complex system of reward and punishment. Token economy. Alternative means of communication. Results, they say, and Helen smiles. In her youth, Mrs. Reis had a dropped charge for marijuana possession. Her housekeeper, whom they have quietly bribed through a third party, testifies to her continued use.

Mrs. Reis's lawyer attempts to restrain his client, but Mrs. Reis shouts out in court anyway. He's happy, she says. Look at him. He's never going to have a job. He's never going to be normal or productive. There's only one thing in this goddamn world he enjoys, so why not let him have it?

These experts would disagree, Mrs. Reis, Helen says.

Mr. Reis smiles. It just takes hard work and time. His son will learn to tie his shoes, button his shirt, hold conversations, look people in the eye, sit at the dinner table. ("A simple win," Helen says into the tape.)

I woke up on the floor. My ribs felt crushed from my sleeping on the tiles, and the throbbing in my head beat in time with the throbbing of my mosquito bites. My memory of the previous night faded out like a scene from a movie. I couldn't remember how the tape had ended.

I found Helen in the kitchen, already showered and dressed, leaning on the counter with a mug of coffee and reading the paper. Her wet hair dripped and left a trail down the back of her blouse. She wore more makeup than the day before. "Good morning, Peter. Coffee?"

"Can I shower first?"

"Extra towel hanging up for you."

The shower was enclosed by unfrosted glass. I watched a centipede crawling across my reflection in the mirror over the sink, lifting its iridescent body in waves. I thought about turning up the water temperature. It was still over a hundred degrees outside, but the steam would prevent me from having to see my shriveling male body.

I closed my eyes and opened my mouth. The water tasted milky and strange. I heard the door swing all the way open and hit the far wall. I was too tired to react or hide my nudity. I just stood there, naked in the shower stall, arms hanging down.

Helen raised her voice to be heard. "You haven't done anything."

Like it was that simple. Like we had talked about it in those stark terms, like I could have done the job with a pair of garden shears. "No."

She hesitated, and then added, "I don't think you should."

"I know."

I knew what Helen saw when she looked at my sunken chest and the thing clinging tight and shrunken between my legs: absolute, immutable truth. There is and there isn't. And look, there, there is.

Helen entered and leaned her back against the wall. "He's brain-dead."

"Who?"

"The Reis boy. He attacked the ABA therapist. He broke her collarbone and gave her a concussion. She quit." The voice on the tape started to come back to me. This was exactly what it had said, in the same loud, flat tone. "The psychologist put him on meds that kept the violence in check, at least most of the time. Then Marcus left him alone for a moment and the boy started ripping pages out of an atlas and cramming them down his own throat."

The lukewarm water, heated from the hot earth around

the pipes, finally started to run cold. "He had been without oxygen for too long when the paramedics arrived. He's a vegetable. His mother wants to pull the plug. His father doesn't. His father wanted me to get a court order preventing her from doing it."

I felt a sickly movement in my gut. Alcohol poisoning, or hope.

"He was happy," she said. "With his stupid fucking maps. He was happy. No amount of therapy was going to make him happier than that. I took it all away."

I turned off the water, stepped out, and grabbed the towel off the rack. I wrapped it around myself under the armpits. She must have seen much worse in LA, people who molest their children, beat them senseless, hand them off to strangers to do the same. She had won cases for bad people before, had stayed up all night researching arcane precedents for them. There were judgment calls where she'd made the wrong call. This wasn't such a call. She had known, without a doubt, that Mr. Reis was the better parent. Look at the documents. Anyone would agree. There is and there isn't.

Helen looked at my feet, my legs, and the shapeless rectangle of the thick white towel before she found my face. Possibility bloomed like a fireball. She shrugged. *I don't know,* it said. There is and there isn't, and there could be. She strode out of the bathroom. I heard ice hitting the bottom of a glass, the bourbon that had sat open all night glugging as it was poured. I couldn't believe it. Helen had shrugged and Father was dead.

# 10

## *Née Peter*

INTERVIEWED AT a French restaurant called Le Carré
sur le Carré—the Square on the Square—in Angrignon,
a wealthy Anglophone area of Montreal. They told me to
come in at nine in the morning. The doors were locked, but
I could see a waiter standing on a table scooping fly carcasses
out of a chandelier with his hands.

I knocked on the glass. He dumped the flies into a bucket
and let me in, then sent me to the kitchen. He was tall and
stick-thin with the wet, buggy eyes of a lizard, and I could feel
him watching me as I walked through the swinging doors.

"Hey! Whoa!"

I almost crashed into what appeared to be a child in a red
baseball cap. I realized he was wearing a chef's jacket and carrying a bag of garbage. "I'm sorry," I said. "I'm . . ."

He put the garbage on the floor, wiped his hand on his
jacket and extended it to me. He wore his chef's jacket with
the sleeves rolled all the way up to the elbow. His wide, red

straight-laced skater shoes were the same color as his hat. "You must be Peter. I'm John. I'll be trying you out."

John was short and stocky, with a classically handsome face that seemed more of an objective fact than a matter of attraction. Bonnie called these men "picture handsome" —they looked good in photographs but were somehow too clean-cut for desire. I shook his hand. "Hi."

He hefted the garbage bag again. "I read your resumé. I'd be surprised if we don't hire you. Have any questions before we get started?"

The blond fuzz on his cheeks suggested the early days of puberty. "Do you mind if I ask how old you are?"

"Nineteen."

"And what do you do here?"

"I'm the saucier. The saucy saucier." He gave me a horsy, long-toothed grin. The waiter beside us was laying out place settings and stemware that flared like diamonds under the clean chandelier. I could feel him listening. Perhaps sending this kid to train me was some kind of test. "Just let me dump this outside and we'll get started."

We walked through how to make their steak marinade. John stood close behind me as I grilled a bunch of halved lemons. I had to be careful not to elbow him in the stomach as I pulled the lemons off with tongs. He never stopped grinning and humming, sometimes tunelessly, sometimes recognizable as "Walking on Sunshine."

"You're doing awesome." He took off his cap and wiped the sweat with the back of his arm. I saw the waiter hovering by the pass window, folding napkins, carefully observing us. "How long have you been a cook again?"

"Fourteen years," I said. "Since you were in kindergarten."

He laughed—also equine, like a whinny. "I've been cooking since I was in kindergarten too. You couldn't pry me away from the play kitchen. I want to be a pastry chef." My brain filled in the end of his sentence: *when I grow up.* "It's the best job in the classical kitchen. You set your own hours, make almost as much as the head chef . . ."

"You need to go to culinary school, though," I said.

"I'm saving up for it. Did you go?"

"No."

"Or I want to own my own restaurant, with a fixed menu that changes every week. Five courses, set up kind of like a brasserie but with—"

His incessant rambling was starting to annoy me. "What next?"

John handed me the citrus reamer. He looked surprised when I juiced the lemons without waiting for them to cool. His hands probably hadn't had enough time to callus over. "What do you want to do?" he asked.

"Well, we could actually cook a steak so I can see how you plate them."

"No, I mean—long-term, what do you plan to do? You want to have your own restaurant? What's your dream?"

If I had other dreams, they stayed hidden behind the bulk of the one dream that consumed all my thoughts, dominated my existence. What else did I want? I couldn't see past it. I had no energy left for other fantasies. "My own restaurant. Sure."

"Okay, why don't you go ahead and slap a steak on the grill? I'll get the stuff for the sides."

I nodded. John bounced as he walked away, something between skipping and hip-hop swagger. When he was inside the cooler, he started singing, loud enough to be heard through the shut steel door. "On top of spa-*ghetti* . . . all covered with cheese . . ."

The waiter stuck his head in the pass window excitedly, like he'd been waiting for John to leave the room. "He's weird, isn't he? Don't you think he's weird?" Spittle flew off his lips when he talked. Flecks of white foam hit the metal pass.

I opened the plastic bin of already-marinated hanger steaks. I lifted one out with a pair of tongs. "He's just young."

"He's the boss's nephew. Used to be his niece."

My tongs came together empty, with a scratch of metal. The steak hit my shoe. I knelt down to pick it up and brought my face too close to the grill. I shot upright, smacked my head on the counter edge, and fell backward.

John came out of the cooler, using his apron to hold vegetables. He saw me sitting on the floor and cradling my skull. "What's going on?"

The waiter had vanished, leaving his spit on the pass.

"I dropped the steak." I stood.

John put down the vegetables. He took a wide-legged stance and clapped his hands between his legs, like a soccer goalie. "Kick it here!"

I kicked the steak and it slid over to John, leaving a red streak on the floor. He flipped it onto the top of his foot like it was a Hacky Sack.

The waiter popped through the pass window again. He looked disappointed. "That's a thirty-dollar piece of meat."

"Not anymore," John said. "Don't worry about it, Peter. It happens. I'm still going to recommend you for hiring."

I thought of the bar employee who had sent me and Claire across the street while we were preaching, her artificial falsetto, the way the pavement had melted. John's voice was deep and rich, and his veiny forearms had visible seams of muscle. The waiter struck me as shifty, someone who might use a new employee to start a rumor or stir shit up. Maybe it was also a test. Maybe he had seen something in me.

Bonnie and I walked to the top of Mont-Royal at Colline de la Croix, the path clogged with red and yellow leaves. Bonnie plopped down on the stone wall that marked the viewpoint. "Christ, is that it?"

"What did you expect?" I said.

"It seemed bigger when we started." The downtown buildings hadn't receded as we climbed. Bonnie ran her fingers through the dirt. "I've never been on a real mountain."

Montreal spread out in all directions from the base of the low hill, the backdrop of my entire adult life. My parka thinned as it lost stuffing each winter; the summer festival tents sprang up and were torn down. Every Sunday, I could hear the drum circles in this park for Tamtams, see the marijuana smoke like a fog through the trees, see the slack-rope walkers, the dancers, the fighters with medieval swords made of foam. The love song to the city that marked the loss of another week.

Beside us, a tourist couple took pictures of each other and the deep blush of the foliage. "I haven't seen you much lately," I said.

"You should be able to get lost on a mountain," Bonnie continued, as though she hadn't heard me. "They should have to hunt for your body if you're out after dark."

"Been busy?"

The wind picked up. The tourists went inside the chalet, an empty hall with a Coke machine. After a moment, Bonnie said, "You're always waiting for the mountains to come to you. It's exhausting."

She turned and saw my face. "I'm sorry. I didn't mean that." She patted the wall beside her. "Come here."

I sat down and she leaned her head on my shoulder. She said, "Do you remember when we would pretend to be Adele?"

"Yes. You got tired of it first."

"I didn't get tired of it. I just . . . Being me wasn't all that different. And it was more fun."

The wind whipped her hair into my cheek. "Lucky you," I said.

The daytime shift at Le Carré ended at three, when the night staff came in, and the switchover was lively. The restaurant was officially closed until dinner. The day staff sat at the bar in half-buttoned jackets and charged drinks to their paychecks, leering at the waitresses as they filed in. Servers of both genders wore white-collared shirts and bow ties. The uniform had a strangely eroticizing effect on the women; they looked sexier in the bow ties than in their street clothes. I had a flash of longing to try one on. The night cooks shouted complaints about the state of the kitchen and the prepped food, and the day staff shouted corrosive comebacks.

John followed me to the small coatroom. Changing around others made me uncomfortable, but there were so many people who needed to get in or out of uniform that there was no time to protest. The door didn't lock. I faced the corner as I unbuttoned my jacket. "Stay and hang out with us," he said. He pulled his chef's jacket over his head like a sweater and it snagged on his T-shirt.

I glanced over my shoulder. John's bare chest was revealed

for a moment. No bound breasts, no scars, the skin smooth and tan. The waiter had lied. I relaxed. "I'm pretty tired," I said. "I think I'll just go home."

He shrugged. "All right. Well, I'll see you at the crack of dawn tomorrow." He threw the door open before I had finished changing. Two waitresses stood there, holding their bow ties and shirts over their arms and looking at me pointedly. I decided to change at home. I ducked out with my head down.

As I passed, John was leaning over the bar from his stool, grabbing at one of the tumblers like he was going to make himself a drink. "Get out of there!" the bartender shouted, whacking his hand. Everyone laughed. I paused at the door, pushing against the wind that held it shut. I watched from a distance as John said something that made them all laugh again. Another cook gave him a high-five. Of course it wasn't true.

I paced my apartment. For the first time in a long time, it felt too small. I put on my sisters' decades-old makeup. It was hard to get the color to transfer from the dried-out lipstick. I wiped it on over and over again, chafing my lips, willing it to work.

I pulled the white—everything was so fucking *white*—winter blanket off the bed and spread it out on the floor. I set out a toy tea set, also from my mother's house, painted pink flowers and gold edging on plastic that looked like real china. I sat down with the dolls. Adele's and Bonnie's childhoods had been so far apart that the dolls represented different eras, forays in and out of realism. Helen had never played with dolls.

I lay down with my head on a cushion. It was my husband's lap. His rough hand stroked my hair. The dolls—small children running barefoot through the grass, a game of chase and tackle.

There was a knock at the door. My hair dissolved and ran through his fingers like sand. The children died where they stood, stiffening into painted smiles and stickers for eyes. I rubbed my mouth with the back of my hand and succeeded only in smearing the dry color onto my chin.

I threw open the door. Bonnie stood there wearing a camping backpack almost as tall as she was, her long hair in braids. I remembered when she'd first arrived in Montreal, fattened on Los Angeles, looking like a freshly shorn sheep.

"How did you get into the building?" I asked.

Bonnie held the straps of her backpack against her chest. "Is that Helen's?"

I looked down at the dress I was wearing, an austere, long-hemmed thing that buttoned from top to bottom. "Probably."

She looked past me to the dolls arranged on the blanket. "What are you doing?" She sounded genuinely perplexed. Her question exhausted me. I thought of the wig Adele had sent, of Helen's terse conversation while I stood naked in the shower.

"How is it," I said, "that you know me best and least of all?"

Bonnie shuffled uncomfortably. "Can I come in?"

I stepped aside. She sat down on the blanket next to the doll that said Mommy when squeezed. She flicked its pigtails with her finger. "I came to say goodbye. I'm going to Europe with some friends."

"How long will you be gone?"

"I don't know." She threw her hands up theatrically and smiled. "Forever! I'm retiring from stripping. Nobody wants to see my thirty-year-old tatas."

Sitting among the dolls with her braided hair, Bonnie looked twelve. "Are you going to visit Adele?" I asked.

"I don't know. We haven't really decided where we're going. We fly into Paris, and then we'll just train around until we get bored."

"I can give you her address."

Bonnie stood up. She tugged at the collar of my dress, flattening it out properly. "I'll see if I can work it into the trip." Her face came so close that I was sure she could smell the fruit-skin smell of the expired lipstick. "I didn't actually come to say goodbye. I came to ask you to come with us."

I shook my head. It was just like Bonnie to invite me on an indefinite overseas trip on her way to the airport, giant backpack and all. "I just got a new job."

"It's just a job. You have nothing here."

"There's Mother."

"Fuck Mother." Bonnie kicked at the picnic. The empty teacups tipped over. The head popped off one of the dolls and rolled in a weighted half circle, like a bocce ball. "I know for a fact that you have a shit-ton of money in the bank, sitting around doing nothing."

"Is that why you want me to come?"

"No! I think it could be fun." Bonnie bent down and picked up the doll's body and head. She examined the neck like she was trying to figure out how to reattach it. "We could . . ." She hesitated. I could see her weighing her words in her head. "We could tell people that you're my sister."

My mouth opened.

Bonnie stepped closer. "Paris," she repeated, like she was casting a spell. "And maybe Adele."

I saw it: *Sabrina*'s Paris in 1950s black-and-white, the city that made her a woman. The Eiffel Tower as seen through her window, the shutters thrown open to the night. Two figures went running through my imagined streets, rain-soaked cobblestones lined by gaslights, girls in matching polka-dot dresses and gold earrings. *This is my sister.*

I looked again at Bonnie, teetering under the weight of her backpack, ready to uproot her life in an instant. She was leaving right now. There was no time to think. No time for the doubt that held me in place. I knew this, these dolls and dresses, this miserable little life.

I was saying no. I could hear my voice saying no and I could see Bonnie nodding sadly; I could see her putting the broken doll gingerly onto my bed, apologizing for knocking its head off. Or maybe for her hubris, or for not asking earlier. For not saying it sooner. For not saying it all along: *Sister, my sister, I've always known.*

I slogged through my next shift in a haze, my head full of Europe. Now that the opportunity was lost, my fantasies were free to break with reality. No awkward lies and costumes. Bonnie and I sprawled in matching white bikinis on a Mediterranean beach, our thirty-year-old tatas on display.

The bug-eyed waiter came to the window and said a customer wanted to talk to John. A girl came to the kitchen door and John rushed over.

The girl couldn't disguise how good-looking she was, not with her severe haircut and round, unfashionable glasses, not with her oversize T-shirt and denim overalls. I was used to the waitresses who compensated for the high-collared uniforms with glittery eyelashes and torturous shoes, who were more young than attractive. This girl pushed her femininity away and it sprang back as though coiled.

"Hi, babe," John said. They leaned toward each other

without touching, like dogs straining against leashes. "What table are you at? What did you order?"

She pointed into the dining hall. "The fish stew. That's your job, right?"

"Yep. I'll make it special."

They gazed at each other with some profound, unknowable intent. It was uncomfortable to look at—worse, somehow, than if they'd just started making out on the floor.

That past summer, at the café, someone had left the skins from the roasted hams in the metal garbage bin out back. They sat baking in the sun. When I lifted the lid off at the end of the day, a cloud of black flies poured out and engulfed my head. Their wings brushed my cheeks and hissed in my ears. I thought of a picture I'd seen of a calf dying from black-fly bites, its sores red and swollen. No one heard me screaming in the alley. That moment, flat on my back in the filth around the bin, and this moment, watching John watch his girlfriend back out the kitchen door, felt the same. Loneliness exploding out of nowhere in a screeching swarm, dark and dense enough to blot out the sun.

The other cooks stopped what they were doing to make fun of John as he made a heart out of chopped scallions to top the cream garnish of his girlfriend's stew. The music playing in the kitchen was the pop hit of the season, sung by a group of boys who must have speaking voices like John: perky, irrepressible.

"What are you doing here so early?" John asked. It was a Friday morning. He stood yawning in his rumpled street clothes at the kitchen door, his blond hair sticking up at angles.

"I'm on the schedule for six."

"Yeah, but nobody shows up for their six until six thirty, at the earliest. Jeez. What have you been doing?" He surveyed the kitchen. "You already set up your station? Oh man. Don't let Chef find out about that. You're ruining it for everybody. Sit down and let me make you some coffee."

I sat at the bar. John danced around behind it, though there was no music playing, making a show of preparing the espresso. He flipped the small cup and caught it like a coin toss. "How about that? Pretty cool, huh?" He did the same thing with the tamper and tried to catch it behind his back. It clattered on the floor.

I laughed. He handed me my espresso. It burned my mouth. I coughed. "It's hot," he said helpfully. He sat down on the stool beside me with his cup, his elbows on the bar. I leaned away from him. He had a habit of getting too close.

"So," he said. "Where do you go after work every day? Why are you always in such a hurry?"

"I don't go anywhere," I said, surprised.

"You run out of here like your house is on fire. Why don't you stay and hang out?"

I felt like he was questioning some fundamental aspect of my person. Why are your eyes brown? Why do you like your steak rare? "I don't know."

"Stay today. I'll buy you a shot."

"Why?"

"Because I like you?"

"You don't know anything about me."

He laughed and put his hands up in defense. "Okay, fine. Don't stay, I don't care."

I nursed my espresso in my hands. John hopped off his stool and headed to the coatroom, still dancing to the music in his head. It took a moment before I felt bad. Yes, I could be friends with this simple-minded kid. I liked him. Everyone liked him. And he was right: with Bonnie gone, I had no-where to go.

I went to the coatroom to apologize. I knocked and pushed the door open without waiting. "Hey, John . . ."

He was stepping out of his jeans, his gray boxer briefs wadded up against his sweaty skin, wedged into the crease where his thighs met his hips. His chef pants were on the floor. He reached for them. I had startled him, and he tried to dive into both legs at the same time. He finally yanked them up and turned his back to me. For a moment, I doubted what I'd seen. I wouldn't have noticed if I hadn't been looking.

His voice stayed cheery. "What's up, Peter?"

Did I burst in on him on purpose? Did I want it to be true? This door didn't lock. People were constantly walking in on each other. With the wait staff, it had turned into a game. The waitresses went in two at a time and one of them held the door shut.

He turned around. Our eyes met. He was depending on me not noticing; it was such a subtle thing, an empty fold of fabric. I was frozen.

John was still smiling, though it had tightened. "Did you talk to Damian?"

"Who?" I took a step back.

"The waiter with the . . ." John held a hand over his eye in the shape of a ball. "With the eyes."

"Yes." I scanned John's body: the stout muscle, the teen-age facial hair, his natural voice. His flat, unmarked chest. "Is it true?" I asked. Before he could answer, I said, "It's not true. I've changed in here with you before."

"I keep my pants on." John shrugged. "Look, it's not a se-cret, exactly, but not everyone knows. I tell people only if it comes up and I feel like they can handle it." I could see the horror in my expression reflected in John's face. His smile dimmed.

"How?" I choked out.

"I don't really want to —"

I grabbed him by the shoulders. I couldn't stop myself. *"How?"*

John pushed me hard. I stumbled back and slammed into the wall, one of the coat hooks striking my spine, before I fell to the ground. I started crying. Loud, ugly weeping, heaving in staggers like a child astonished by his own tears.

"I'm sorry! It was a reflex. I thought you were going to hit me." John knelt down. "Are you okay?"

"How?" I whispered.

John considered my pathetic form, slumped on the ground. "I don't know what you want me to say."

I waved my arm around his body viciously. *"This.* How?"

He straightened up. "Look, I don't know you that well, and it's really none of your business. I'm a guy. That's all you need to know." He hovered over me, still more concerned than threatening. "Why are you crying?"

"It's not fair. Give it to me." *Give me your girlhood, John, I* thought nonsensically. *You don't want it? Give it to me. I want to be the woman you would've been: blond, simple, sunny.*

"What's not fair? What are you talking about?" John was too close again; we were almost nose to nose.

I lifted my head. John searched my face. His eyes widened. He sat down beside me and looked at his hands, his fingers thick and stout as the rest of him. A moment passed in silence. The hooks above our heads were crowded with left-behind clothes and junk. Toques and scarves, a T-shirt, a bow tie, a nude-colored bra.

Another of John's smiles, this one small and solitary, for himself. "Did you think . . . you were the only one?" he said.

"No, I thought . . ." Yes, and I still did. John wasn't like me. Whatever he was, whatever he called himself, he was something else entirely. He had to be.

"Are you a woman?"

He threw off this question readily, like it was nothing at all. My whole life summed up in a question I never got to ask. "I can't do this," I said.

"I'm sorry, you don't have to tell me what—"

"I can't work today." I stood up. "Tell them . . . something." John followed me out of the coatroom. He followed me all the way to the door. I didn't turn around, and he didn't speak.

I realized I had left my coat and bag with my transit pass inside of it. I walked for an hour to get home through the October slush, that first, strange snow that doesn't quite take.

John called me that night. I asked him how he got my number. "From your resumé. I also have your bag, your wallet, and your coat."

"Am I fired?"

"No. I told them you called in sick. No big deal."

"Then I'll get my stuff on Monday."

"You're going to go all weekend without your wallet?"

It was also my only warm coat. "Yes."

"Where do you live? I'll come drop it off."

"That's okay."

"We're having some people over for dinner tomorrow. You could come, and pick up your stuff then."

John had a girlfriend, without the quotation marks around

the term that came with a Margie or a Claire. I remembered their electric stares. "I'm busy."

He exhaled. The mouthpiece crackled. "I want to help you. Tell me how to help you."

I looked down into my lap. I picked at the skirt I was wearing: white denim, yellowed with age, ending several inches above my knees. Bonnie's. My mouth was gluey with lip gloss. His questions bothered me a lot. *What are your life goals? Why don't you hang out with us? Tell me how to help you.* As though all people understood themselves and had neat, one-word answers. "There's a lot about you that I don't understand." I tried to be honest. "I'm not sure I want to understand."

"We don't have to talk about anything you don't want to talk about. It's just dinner."

I rubbed my shin. The stubble prickled against my hand. *Time to shave,* I thought, not without pleasure. "Maybe."

"Maybe?"

"Maybe."

"Well, hot damn," John said. I could picture his smile.

John's girlfriend, Eileen, pointed to each dish spread out on the coffee table. "The chickpea salad has mayo in it. The green salad has soy sauce in it. The pasta has cheese and gluten in it. But the macaroons are gluten-free, and nothing has shellfish or meat."

I'd been introduced to the five faces who were now nodding solemnly, but none of their names had stuck. They appeared to be memorizing this information. We sat on cushions on the floor. All of the furniture in the living room consisted of piles of cushions, aside from the coffee table and a wide, backless bookcase.

"What else is in the chickpea salad?" I asked.

"Fruit and spices," Eileen said, passing around a stack of plates.

"So why did you mention the mayo?"

"I don't eat eggs," said a blond girl. Her eyeliner was drawn in sharp points nearly an inch away from each eye.

"And some of us can't eat dairy," added the boy in the skin-tight baby-blue pants.

"Mayo's not dairy," Eileen said.

"Oh."

The floor was now open. "I can't eat wheat," explained a thick-bodied girl with a deep voice.

The girl with aviator glasses said, "Me neither. And shellfish gives me hives."

"I'm allergic to nuts and soy," Blue-Pants chimed in. "And mushrooms."

John said, "I don't eat mushrooms either, but that's not an allergy. Something about the texture just makes me want to retch."

Deep-Voice said, "Oh, I'm like that about potatoes."

Eileen turned to me. "I'm sorry, Peter. I forgot to ask you if you had any food sensitivities."

"Um, no," I said. They seemed to be waiting for me to say something else, so I added, "It's sort of funny that you all do, isn't it? Have so many allergies, I mean. For one group of friends."

"They're not all allergies. Some are intolerances," Pointy-Makeup-No-Eggs said. She started gathering food onto her plate.

"I read somewhere it's a generational thing," said Blue-Pants-No-Soy. He was waiting for Pointy to relinquish the tongs, his plate hanging limply from his hand. "Something about us not getting tapeworms, or parasites, or something.

Like, we're the no-tapeworm generation, so we're the food-allergy generation too."

Deep-Voice-No-Wheat said, "Or maybe it's all in our heads. We're the hypochondriac generation."

Aviators-No-Shellfish replied, "My EpiPen would disagree with you."

"My stomach hurts so bad when I eat dairy. Like, I can't get out of bed," Pointy-Makeup-No-Eggs said.

"Maybe in previous generations, they wouldn't have figured it out, and you would've just died," I said. "Maybe there wasn't as much choice. Maybe you just had to eat what was there or starve."

Blue-Pants tapped the tongs together like a castanet to get my attention. "What are you saying? That we should just suck it up and deal with it? Lisa would asphyxiate, you know. Her throat closes up."

"No," I said. Even though we all sat around the table, it felt as though they were all facing me. "Sorry. I just meant that no one would have thought to blame the nuts."

"Shellfish," said No-Shellfish, apparently Lisa.

"Shellfish." It was rare for me to talk so much at once, especially to strangers. "You wouldn't realize it was the shellfish. You wouldn't try it out and think about how you felt afterward. If you lived somewhere where the dominant food was shellfish, you'd just have a reaction and die, and no one would know why."

"Why are you talking about Lisa dying?" asked Pointy.

"Sorry," I repeated. I turned my eyes down to my plate. It was the only one still empty.

Blue-Pants and I stayed after everyone else had left. Eileen washed the dishes and I dried, while Blue-Pants sat at the table behind us typing into his phone. John was outside fiddling with the compost in the small garden of their first-floor apartment.

"Way to help, asshole," Eileen said casually to Blue-Pants. "What are you doing?"

"Coming up with a short, pithy summary of the evening to share with the Internet," Blue-Pants said, in a self-mocking drawl.

"Yes, the Internet needs to know what you thought of my macaroons."

"They were acceptable," Blue-Pants said. His chin was lit from below by the screen. At dinner, everyone had been fascinated by the fact that I didn't own a computer. "I didn't know there were dinosaurs like you still left in the world," Blue had said.

Eileen handed me a wet glass. My small hand, with a dishcloth wrapped around it, fit inside. We worked to the soft clinking of dishes and Blue's tapping thumbs. "May I ask you something?" I said.

"Shoot," she said.

I paused, holding the glass aloft. John's friends had a brittleness he lacked, hardened and delicate at the same time, as though the wrong touch or the wrong word would blow them apart. I couldn't figure out how to talk to them.

Eileen said, "You're wondering about John, right?" I nodded. She opened a cupboard above our heads so I could put away the glasses. "He's always bringing home curious strays. Thinks it's his job to educate the whole fucking world."

"Never mind," I said, burying my face in the cupboard. "It's none of my business."

"I'll make this short," she said. "John's parents came around to the idea when he was in kindergarten, though he'd been demanding it since he could talk. He went on puberty blockers early enough that there were no breast buds to be removed, and then on testosterone. His family moved to Toronto for better care, and so nobody knew him from when he was a girl. He hasn't had bottom surgery and doesn't plan to, although he thinks all M-to-Fs should do it, because, as he says, 'Your surgery works.' Enough? Does that answer your question?"

She was holding out a bunch of utensils. I didn't take them. The world took on the unimportance that it has in dreams where you know you're dreaming and you can leap off buildings without fear.

Eileen shook the utensils so they dripped onto the counter. I reached for them, and as I felt the knife edges and fork tines through the cloth, what I was feeling gave itself a name. Rage. I was so angry I could've driven the tiny blades into her side. I hadn't understood some of the terms she used, but I understood the tone. Who were these kids? What right had they to be born into a world where they were taught to look endlessly into themselves, to ask how the texture of a mushroom made them feel? To ask themselves, and not be told, whether they were boys or girls? You eat what's there or you starve.

I started yanking open the drawers, pulling them all the way back until they snapped at their farthest opening, then slamming them shut again, looking for the one where the utensils went. *Moved to Toronto* made it sound like he came from somewhere like Fort Michel. "What about your parents?" My voice came out as a snarl, surprising both of us. "Are they happy with this?"

"My father is dead," Eileen said, "and my mother is a born-again Christian, so we don't talk about it much. She calls every other week to remind me that we're going to hell. We spend all our holidays with John's parents."

I found the drawer. The utensils inside rattled like chains as I pulled it free. "How did your father die?"

"Cancer," she said.

"What kind?"

She handed me a mug and our fingers touched. "Does it matter?"

"I suppose not." The mug rattled against the others.

"Pancreatic. It spread to his bones and then he was gone. Swift, painful, and very ugly."

"How old were you?"

"Fifteen. Is your father dead?"

I blinked at the directness of the question. I nodded.

"From what?" We were out of dishes. She scrubbed a pot while I dried my hands on my thighs.

"I don't know."

Blue glanced up, as though I had finally said something interesting. "How can you not know?"

I thought about that. "My parents are very private people," I said finally.

Eileen worked away at a stubborn spot, a lock of hair falling into her eyes. "That's fucked-up."

"I guess." The curve of Eileen's back flexed with effort. I wanted to tell her she was going to scratch the bottom of the pot.

"My mom found Jesus more or less the day after my dad died," she said. "I remember, at the funeral, everyone was comparing drugs and doctors. Traditional medicine, alternative therapies. Eating roots, giving up meat. Prayer. So-and-so tried that and she still died. So-and-so tried that and she lived five years longer than the doctors said she would." Eileen threw down the sponge and pushed her bangs away. "Every-one had so many examples, so many dead friends and rela-tives. And I thought, *My God*. At a certain point, everyone you know has cancer. I bet your dad had cancer."

There was a bang from outside, and a yell. John's head poked up from behind the compost bin, grinning. "It's okay! I got it!" He waved at us.

Eileen waved back. If I had to name this thing I was born with, I would've called it misery. Yet there was John, with os-tensibly the same thing, and of the three of us, he was the one with that smile, as though he had always been loved and always would be.

John came back inside, his clothes muddy, as if he were returning from an adventure. Eileen ruffled his hair with her wrinkled-sponge hand. They kissed. John turned to me, his hands still at her waist. "Do you guys want to open a bottle of wine?"

I felt sick of these kids. The space between us had only grown, a field strewn with words. They never had to invent anything. Not who they were, not even how their bodies fit together in the dark. They probably made the same kinds of declarations in bed as at the dinner table. This is me, this is what I'm willing to do. "I think I'll just go home," I said.

John stopped me with an odd, sweeping gesture, like he'd tried to punch my arm and stroke it tenderly at the same time. "Hey. Come to Tams with us tomorrow." I started to shake my head. "What else do you have to do?"

Laundry. Dressing up alone in my apartment.

By the time I rode the bus home from John and Eileen's, I'd been awake for twenty hours. I drifted in and out of sleep, my head lolling. I rested my elbow on the windowsill, feeling the comfort of my small, soft hand against my face.

"Hey."

I snapped awake. There was a man sitting next to me, his legs spread open so he covered two seats. He had an open bottle in a plastic bag and wavy, shoulder-length white hair. His chin was smooth but didn't look clean-shaven—rather, it looked like hair didn't grow there anymore, a fallow field. "Where you from?"

"Ontario," I said. "Near Toronto."

"No," he said. "Where are you really from?"

There were only a few other people on the bus. They were listening, along with the driver. "My parents are from China," I said. Disoriented and half awake, I added, "Where are you from?"

"I'm an Indian," he said, almost shouting. I hadn't heard the word used that way in a long time. "But I look white, don't I?"

He did. I nodded.

"Where in China are your parents from?"

"I don't know."

He snorted and drank from the bottle. Some of it ended up in his lap. "You gotta know where you're from. It's important."

"They never told me."

"They dead?"

I heard Eileen's question echoed. "My mother's still alive."

The man poked me in the chest. "Then you go home, and you call your mother, and you ask her." He pointed his thumb at himself. "Me, I'm part Ojibwa, part Mushkegowuk. From the Great Lakes." He poked me again. "Part Ojibwa, part Mushkegowuk," he repeated. "You remember that, now. You remember where I'm from."

He turned to the window. It was hard to make out where we were, but you could see it was starting to snow again. I wondered if it would stick this time. He pulled the stop cord, as though the snow had told him it was time to get off.

"Remember where I came from," he said, one last time, and stumbled toward the exit.

I'd fought against sleep on the bus, but when I welcomed it into my bed, it wouldn't come. I sat up in the dark. I felt for the phone by my bedside. It was after four in the morning. I called my mother.

"Peter?"

"I'm sorry for calling so early."

"I was already up. I'm making my oatmeal!"

I saw my mother, talking on her new cordless phone in one of her new tracksuits, standing over the stove, eager to greet the day. I had planned to ask her about Father's death; it suddenly seemed cruel. "Mother? Where are you from?"

"What?"

"Where in China are you from?"

"I was born in Guangzhou." Anticipating my next question, she added, "Your father was born in Beijing."

I was silent. What did I learn from that? Mother didn't push me to talk. She stayed on the line, humming distractedly. I could hear her scraping the bottom of a pot. "How are you doing?" I asked finally. "Do you want me to come visit?"

"Oh, sure. If you like."

I felt like I knew her less and less. She seemed impatient to get off the phone. "Mother?"

"Hmm?"

"Are you . . . dating anyone?"

She laughed sharply. "Dating? Are you kidding? Why would I do that? Men are tyrants."

"All of them?"

"All of them!" Her oatmeal spoon clanked against the side of the pot. "The ones my age, they were raised that way. They think that's how you show love." With strange glee, she added, "And their sons are going to be *very* disappointed."

I slept until the afternoon. When I woke, I could already hear the Tamtams in the distance, like the boots of an advancing army. John and his friends were easy to spot: an androgynous rainbow of hooded sweatshirts near the base of the central statue in Parc du Mont-Royal, passing a joint back and forth. They regarded me with the same distant interest as they had at dinner. Blue-Pants was there again, this time wearing yellow skinny jeans and a matching yellow sweatshirt. It no longer seemed possible to ask his name.

The day before it had been fifteen below, and today it was fifteen above with a reassuring sun — a false summer. A group of circus students were stringing up a long band of red silk in the tree above us, two of them in the highest branches and two of them at the bottom. The sky bled.

"What are you guys doing for Halloween?" Yellow asked.

"Warehouse party in Parc-Ex," Eileen said.

"Sounds cold," Yellow said. "Dressing up?"

"Of course. What about you, Peter?"

One of the circus students, a woman, wrapped herself up in the silk *tissu* and self-propelled upward. She turned herself upside down, spread her legs in a V. "Nothing," I said. "I'm too old."

John sat bolt upright. He reminded me of a dog who

hears the kibble bag being shaken in the next room. "Come with us!"

I could feel Yellow's incredulity without looking up. The V tumbled and inverted, the sky dripping silk. "That's okay."

"It'll be fun!"

I reminded myself that John was high. It was hard to tell, as he seemed no more slack and joyful than usual. "It's too late to get a costume."

"No way. We'll help you. We'll go to some thrift stores. What do you want to go as?"

"I don't—"

John cut me off. "It's Halloween. You can be whoever you want."

Eileen raised her eyebrows. She gestured at Yellow to pass her the joint and gave me a heady, almost cross-eyed stare as she took her first inhale. "So, Peter. Who do you want to be?"

A snake of red silk around the woman's ankle, up her leg, around her waist. Legs windmilling for two turns, a song of desire. I suddenly remembered the Luther, the theater from my childhood where Adele had taken us to see *Sabrina*. I wanted to be Adele, the way she looked silhouetted by the screen, more striking than the thirty-foot-tall Sabrina. Was Bonnie still in Paris? Had she moved on?

I heard myself say, "Audrey Hepburn."

The circus student touched ground. Eileen let out a long stream of smoke. "We can do that."

I walked home with John and Eileen through the Portuguese district. A warm, meaty smell came from the small restaurants and bakeries. "Want to have dinner at our place again?" John asked. "It would be good for me. You can criticize my cooking."

Before I could answer, something in the near distance caught John's eye and he ran ahead without us. He rounded the corner and disappeared. "Peter! Come here! I want to show you something!"

When we caught up to him, he was standing on an unremarkable street. The road curved downhill, bordered by a row of faded, matching condo buildings that had once been painted in different bright colors. John had his hand on the wall of the yellow one.

"This again?" Eileen said.

"Peter hasn't seen it," John said. "My mom is a real estate agent. She showed me this." He patted the wall. "Put your hand here."

I did.

"Push. Really hard."

The stucco wall responded like it was a sponge. The belly of an animal inhaling and then exhaling, shrinking back and then expanding.

"Isn't that cool?" John asked.

"That's terrible," I said. "It's going to collapse." I pictured the rubble rolling downhill with the floods of the spring thaw. I rubbed the wall gently, as though I could encourage it to stay in place.

John whacked the building with his palm and it shuddered in response. "It's also sinking, see? The whole complex is. But you look at it from far away and it's this solid thing, like it's been here forever and it's going to be here forever."

I felt like I was missing something. "Somebody lives here," I said. "It's their home."

Eileen laughed suddenly and tossed her arm around John's neck. "Leave Peter alone. You're so fucking high."

We walked back to their apartment. John beelined for the

bathroom. Alone with Eileen in the living room, I could hear John singing through the walls as he pissed. I started scanning the spines on their giant bookshelf.

"You want to borrow a book, Peter?" Eileen said.

"Like what?"

"Whatever you need." She glanced at me sideways. "You okay with being called Peter?"

"What else would you call me?"

"John hated his old name." Eileen said. "Sometimes his parents slip up and call him by it, or use female pronouns. Even after all these years."

"Did he pick his own name?"

"Of course."

I shook my head at that. Of course.

She let me stare into their bookshelf for a long time without comment. Textbooks and college-course packs on queer theory and gender theory, books of memoir and poetry with heady, academic subtitles, political tracts—they were defined by these things, it was their hobby, their subject of scholarly study, their political fight. They had no other books.

John reappeared at Eileen's side, and she fed her hands into his. They beamed at me like proud parents. They'd made me into a project. Out of nowhere, I missed Claire—our ecstatic confessions on the couch. Mired in self-hatred up to our knees, trudging toward the approval of her God and my father. It had been easier to detail explicit dreams to Claire than it would be to say *I should have been a woman* to these kids. As soon as I said it, as soon as I said what they wanted me to say, everything would change. And I still didn't believe them—you couldn't just rename yourself, you couldn't tear down the skyline and rebuild and think there wouldn't be consequences.

· · ·

The day of the party, Eileen led us through the Village des Valeurs. She ran her hand along the dress rack without looking, seeking out satin by feel. She picked a violet strapless gown and a fake pearl necklace, four rows deep. We went to a costume store that was nearly cleaned out, but John found a brown wig in a high bouffant, a twenty-five-cent tiara to slip into it, opera gloves, and a long-stemmed cigarette holder.

We got dressed at their apartment. They had to explain to me that Eileen was supposed to be Michael Jackson and John was supposed to be Justin Timberlake, as their costumes were a lot less elaborate than mine. Eileen just had a white suit jacket and John dressed the way he always did, in a hoodie and his red skate shoes.

Eileen did my makeup first. She wouldn't let me look in the mirror while she worked. "For effect," she said. I'd never seen her anything other than bare-faced. She curled my eyelashes, filled in my eyebrows with a pencil, and applied mascara, blue-gray eye shadow, and maroon lipstick. She zipped the dress as far as she could up my back, then closed the top with a series of safety pins. John arranged the wig and tiara on my head. I put on the gloves and necklace. I borrowed some clunky, too-big shoes of Eileen's. I didn't tell them I already had my own collection of heels.

I almost didn't want to look. Nothing would be as good as how it felt: the sweet constraint around my hips from the dress, tight as a sausage casing, squeezing joy into my skull, making it swell. The satin on my hands, my spidery eyelashes, the weight of the hair and the jewelry. I loved the sound of the gown's train swishing behind me. It felt like something restored: a tail cut off and regrown.

They each held one of my arms and guided me to the full-length mirror in their bedroom. There she stood, at last: the iconic Audrey, only with Adele's almond eyes, her sloping cheekbones. The face a little more drawn, a little harder, but undeniably her.

"Let's take this on the road," John said.

I panicked at the threshold, after Eileen had already opened the door. "I can't go outside."

"Why not?" John said. Eileen went to the kitchen.

I thought about walking on the street, riding the Métro. I shook my head.

"It's Halloween," John insisted. "Everybody's dressed up." I kept shaking my head. I was trembling, the outside world blowing in, so close I could trip and tumble into it.

Eileen reappeared with a water bottle of what looked like orange juice. She held my head and brought the bottle to my mouth as though coaxing a baby to drink. The alcohol stung my nostrils. "Drink," she said.

I pulled away. "I don't like—"

"This is exactly why God invented vodka," Eileen said.

I stared down into the bottle. "You look beautiful," John said.

Eileen had filled up three large bottles with her orange-juice mixture. I supposed she meant for us to sip on them all night. I took the one she was offering. I tilted the bottle up so the liquid ran straight down my throat. I swallowed. I inhaled. I swallowed. I had some memory of doing this before.

They watched me chug the whole bottle. Eileen said, "Ready to go now?"

We stepped out. They stayed on either side of me, arms looped through mine, so I couldn't turn back. The Métro was crammed with other people in costumes. I watched my reflection racing past in the windows, blackened by the underground tunnels. Audrey looked back in flashes, moving jerkily, like a filmstrip. I winked.

The party in Parc-Ex was partially in a warehouse loft and partially on the street. Two sets of speakers played two different pop songs in the same key and time signature, melding them together. "Inside," Eileen yelled. A firecracker skidded along the pavement and popped in agreement.

People were dressed outlandishly, but no one seemed to be wearing a costume. Kids went by in garbage bags cut to fringes, cling wrap that showed through, homemade medieval armor, latex suits, corsets, wigs. From a distance, I couldn't tell the humans from the art and the furniture. Studio lights and a backdrop were set up in one corner, and someone took pictures with a blinding flashbulb. The teenagers in front of the camera struck dramatic, sexual poses. More and more, I liked the feeling of Eileen's and John's elbows against my ribs, dragging me as they greeted people, drifted away again.

"This is Audrey," John said to some group of half-naked monsters, slits of flesh and bright colors under a strobe light. I saw Yellow among them. He'd dyed his hair pink, shaved off his eyebrows, and painted them back in to match the hair.

I bit my cigarette holder coquettishly. "Hell-*o*," I said. I added a melodic whistle to the name when I said it myself, the voice effortless. "My name is Audrey."

I knew how to stand: hand on one hip, cigarette holder in the other. A boy in regular clothes and face paint leaned in so I could hear him. "Your ass looks great in that dress."

Lights kept pulsing over us. I couldn't see him clearly, just the butterfly painted over his entire face. "Thank you," I said.

John grabbed my arm and started to drag me away, shouting directly into my ear, "Dance with me!" I looked back at the boy apologetically. He waved.

The music inside was different than outside — some grating, industrial chaos. We drifted to the edge of a slam-dancing crowd that jumped and fought, bodies crushing and bruising like fruit. John took a step away from me, stood stiffly upright, mock formal, and held out his hand. I took it, and he pulled me in, one hand on the small of my back, one hand still holding mine up in the air. My hand settled on his shoulder. He led a three-four step, ignoring the crashing music around us, and I stumbled to follow. The hand on my back guided me in, and my head rested on his chest, ignoring the shift of my wig. He held me as though my bones were made of glass, the way you would hold Audrey. The voice in my head whispered grimly, *It's Halloween, it's just a game, it isn't real,* but I was too busy being spun, the room whirling along the hem of my gown, and John was Humphrey Bogart on an empty tennis court, and I didn't care that William Holden would never come.

We walked south from Parc-Ex on avenue du Parc, a deceptively straight road, familiar downtown buildings visible when still hours away. The neighborhoods changed drastically as we went along: smashed-in laundromats, manicured lawns, bars and diners with names like Chez Gary, pretentious bistros, richer and poorer and richer again. Eileen and I walked at the front, arm in arm, and John followed with a small crowd. They were singing a song in French that I didn't recognize. John's accent was the worst but he sang the loudest.

Eileen and I had walked in silence most of the way. She reminded me of Helen, how she held her liquor with a straight back, how her thin frame seemed to be holding my weight.

"Faggots!"

I felt Eileen tug sharply in the direction of the voice. Two boys across the street, not in costume, about the same age as Eileen and John.

"What did you say?" Eileen yelled back.

"Let it go," John said.

"I said, what did you say?" Eileen yelled, louder now.

I had immediately turned to the group to see who among us had prompted the shout. I'd blamed Pink and his eyebrows; I'd even thought that the boys somehow knew about John. But I was the man in the dress.

Without coming any closer, the boy called back, "I said you're a bunch of faggots!"

"You got us there," John said.

Someone in John's group laughed. I kept watching Eileen, who pulled harder at the crook of my arm. "What are you going to do about it?" she shouted.

"Eileen," Pink warned.

My shoulder jerked in its socket as Eileen tugged in their direction. "You going to come here and make something of it? There's ten of us and two of you."

"Eileen!"

She finally released my arm. "Come over here! You want to see what a bunch of faggots can do?"

John and Pink grabbed Eileen. John murmured her name. "Calm down."

The boys were too far away for us to see their faces. They stayed where they were. "Fuck you," the first one said. His voice was weaker than before.

Eileen struggled free. "Fuck you!" she answered. The boys turned and left, walking away at a normal pace. Eileen kept screaming, "Cowards! Assholes!" The one who hadn't spoken glanced back at us, his face just a flash of white.

The next morning, I came in at six thirty like everyone else. I sang along with the radio as I prepped. Everyone looked pale and ill. One of the cooks snapped at me. "Would you shut up? I drank my weight in tequila last night."

I'd hardly slept. Night had rolled giddily into morning. The makeup hadn't washed away cleanly, and shadow and sparkle lingered around my eyes. Alcohol sweat dripped from my temples.

John walked in with a newspaper under his arm. His expression was grave. "You hear about Dana Jackson?" He put the paper down on my station.

"Eh! Not near the food!" shouted the sous-chef.

"It's important," John said.

The lead story was about how it had been an unusually difficult Halloween for police; more vandalism and violence than most years. John tapped his finger at the bottom right corner of the front page, at a photo caption.

*"Dana" Jackson, née Daniel, dies after Halloween beating, p. 7*

I heard John talking but couldn't register what he was saying. Something about the quotation marks. A school portrait of a teenage boy in glasses, a little effete, sweet-looking, something his parents could explain away. And a grainy, blown-up photo taken at a party, a red-eyed flash, opaque eye shadow and puffy lips, a striped minidress, overstuffed high heels. The photos were stretched so that they fit, side by side, into one frame. An art director or a layout director—someone had made the choice to do that. People all over the city, opening the paper over their morning coffee, using their cereal bowls to pin it down, looking at the sideshow of "Dana," née Daniel.

John flipped to page seven. He read aloud bits and pieces. Ten people outside a nightclub. Police believe two participated in the beating while another eight stood and watched. All could be charged as accomplices. Bartender saw them leave together, didn't have the chance to check until hours later. Already dead.

"There's a candlelight vigil tonight," John said. When he shut the paper, clutching it closed, the front page faced me again. I stared into the red at the back of Dana's eyes, blood caught in the flash.

"How could they have planned that already?" another cook asked.

"We're organizing it," John said.

I knelt down to the fridge under my station. "We still have a restaurant to open," I said. I slammed a container of iceberg heads down onto the counter. As I chopped them into strips, the knife kept skidding on the board, making a conspicuous noise.

"So," John said, "I'll meet you at your place at eight, and we can walk over together?"

"What? For what?"

"The vigil."

"I'm not going to that."

I tried to ignore his surprise, his dogged faith. "Of course you are."

"I don't know this person."

John continued to stand there, arms hanging down. The knife skidded so much I lost my grip and had to pick it up again. "It could've been you," he said finally.

"No," I said, chopping bluntly, breaking more than slicing the lettuce, "it couldn't. I've worked my whole life so that it couldn't be me." White flash of a face. Where did they go, those boys, after they left us behind?

"Last night," John began. He paused, still looking wounded. "You were so happy."

I gathered the lettuce into a bin and held it against my stomach like a barrier. "If it had been me, it would've been your fault."

John reeled as though I'd struck him. "You're a coward," he said. "You've worked your whole life because you're a coward."

"What do you know? What do you know about anything?" His family moved for him. The hormones. The surgery he was allowed to accept or reject. I waved my arm around the kitchen, at the stunned cooks watching us. "Nobody has to know about you! You can blend in whenever you want!"

"You honestly believe that? You think my life's been *easy*?"

"Yes, I think it's been fucking easy!" I screamed. "They don't know! I didn't know! I wish I still didn't know!"

I tried to shove past him. He touched my back. I remembered Humphrey Bogart's hand, I remembered dancing, I remembered the gown twirling, I remembered the boy who complimented my ass, I remembered being told I was beautiful. I remembered the woman staring back at me in the Métro windows, her wink. I tried to pull away. John embraced me with my arms pinned to my sides, the lettuce bin between us, its raw, wet smell pushed toward our faces.

In full view of the entire kitchen, he kissed me. A kiss that made me think of the woefully few people I had kissed in my life. A kiss that reminded me I had never been loved. A kiss that said I could not be John unless I risked being Dana.

My bedside clock rolled past eight. Somewhere, Dana on the cross. I remembered something Claire said, in a vulnerable moment, her blond hair against my mouth: "Even Jesus didn't want to be Jesus. He cried out at the last minute." I missed her, and Margie, and Chef, and Ollie, and Bonnie and Adele and Helen — the comfort of being only partly understood. Eileen and John saw straight through me, past me, like a hole had been bored through my chest.

I tried to imagine eight people watching. Their shadows in the box lights of a deserted parking lot. Their impassive faces. Stepping back as I bled on the ground and reached for them.

I found the newspaper in my bag. John had stuffed it inside before I left. In the second picture, Dana was laughing, looking right into the camera. Who took this picture? Ten of them and one of her. Ten of us and two of them.

Teenage Daniel had dark circles under his eyes. He seemed caught by the camera, paralyzed by worry. I folded the newspaper over, tucking his picture underneath. Dana continued to laugh.

I dug through the kitchen drawer until I found the scissors. I cut both parts of the story out of the paper and sealed them into an envelope. Addressed it, stamped it, tucked it into the inner pocket of my winter coat, my down parka riddled with punctures. It left a trail of feathers. The empty fabric sagged but still kept out the wind.

. . .

The postcard would come weeks later, signed by both Bonnie and Adele. A vintage oil painting with *GERMANY!* across the top—a church in the far background, futuristic neon in the foreground, boxy cars rushing in between. A phone number, an e-mail address, and these words: *Come to Berlin, sister.*

I watched them from far away, in a small crowd gathered across the street. A few police cars stood between us and the field of candles, under a barren, starless sky. Thin paper skirts between their fists and the dripping wax, their faces wrapped in hoods and scarves and lit from below. A prayer, a plea for witnesses, a song. Silence. Silence settled in like a chill.

I waited as they blew out the lights, as the onlookers around me left and the shadows on the field spread out. Two of them walked toward me, stopped short.

"You came," John said.

Something quiet and solemn between us now. I slept with them in their bed that night, a heap of blankets on a foam mattress on the floor, huddled like nesting animals. The ambient lights of their phones and computers and music players glowed green and blue.

I woke sometime after midnight. I untangled from their limbs and went out into the living room, turning on one of their weak, opaque lamps. I'd spent the evening listening to them talk. Listing Dana in a long line of martyrs. Pulling out books they meant for me to read. The larger fight, against doctors and bureaucracy, against hate.

On the back cover of one of their manifestos, a close-up of a naked woman, spread-eagle on her back, showing the results of her surgery. I had started to tune out their voices. She was perfect. She held her lips open with her fingers, staring straight into the camera, straight at me, with an expression of pure joy.

I'd taken the slim book out from under Eileen's fingers to look closer. "It's not just about that," Eileen had said. "You don't have to look like that to be a woman. That's not what being a woman means."

I passed through the living room, sliding on my shoes, leaving my coat. I shut the door quietly and stood on the steps of their walkup, away from the close, lulling heat of John's and Eileen's bodies, alert in the cold.

I took out my phone.

"Hello?"

"Helen?"

"Peter? What's wrong? Is Mother okay?"

"Everything's fine," I said.

The air was heavy, smelled of wet steel: the snow was coming, the one that would last for months, the one that buries, that always wins. After a moment, Helen said, "Does no one in this family sleep?"

"Bonnie went to Europe," I said.

"To visit Adele?"

"Not only that. But yes."

"That's nice."

I paused, uncertain what I wanted to say.

"You know," Helen said, "even though it was hell most of the time, I kind of liked having Bonnie live with me, back in Los Angeles. Christ, that was a long time ago, wasn't it? I had this stupid idea, when I bought the house, that . . ." She trailed off. "Never mind."

"No, what?"

"I thought . . . I figured someday I'd buy an even bigger house, and that house, the one in California, it would be our summer place. All four of us. Like, maybe we'd retire there, a bunch of randy old ladies on the beach. It was that kind of place." Her tone curdled. "It was all wrong for me. Too far from the city, too many little rooms. The yard had all these motherfucking *flowers* —"

"I had the same idea," I said.

A beat passed. "It doesn't matter now," she said. "I sold it."

The land between us, five states, the Eastern Seaboard, a border. Helen felt near, a voice in the dark.

In John and Eileen's bedroom window, I thought I saw a flicker of movement. I shivered. "I should go."

"Sure. Good night."

The light came on in their room. They were probably wondering where I was. They'd looked younger asleep, their faces smooth in the blue and green blaze of idling electronics. The right people to help me, to guide me through whatever came next. And yet. "It's not just about that," Eileen had said. Not just about me and my body. There were marches, vigils, hate crimes, unjust laws, a world that needed education. There were other people like me and Claire and Dana. There were the forces that had crushed us.

I walked down the stairs. It was still just about that, for me. Let them fight their war. I appreciated it. But I'd fought long enough. I wanted to go home. I would send them a letter, apologizing for this last act of cowardice. I would send them a picture.

Guangzhou and Beijing. Father in an airport, after his father bribed a doctor and a bureaucrat and a friend in Hong Kong who pretended to be a relative. The waiting plane gleams on the tarmac, propellers roaring, louder than God. Go, his father says. Go and be reborn.

Four grown women sit in a pub, raising their tourist steins to the camera. The waiter who holds the camera comments on how much they look alike. "We're sisters," Bonnie says. *"Wir sind Schwestern.* This is Adele, Helen, and Audrey."

# Acknowledgments

Thanks to:

Keith Maillard and andrea bennett, my ideal readers, who understand me and my work as every writer longs to be understood; Linda Svendsen, Andreas Schroeder, and Kaitlin Fontana, for their practical advice and sustaining faith, and for repeatedly putting their names on the line; Ben Rawluk, Erika Thorkelson, Tetsuro Shigematsu, Bill Radford, Melissa Sawatsky, Kevin Spenst, Karen Shklanka, Meredith Hambrock, Margret Bollerup, Lauren Forconi, Emily Urness, Indrapramit Das, Emily Davidson, Chris Urquhart, Sigal Samuel, Michelle Deines, Taylor Brown-Evans, Anna Maxymiw, Jay Torrence, Nancy Lee, Ray Hsu, Deborah Campbell, Steven Galloway, and all the staff and students of the UBC MFA program for their talent, support, friendship, humor, alcohol tolerance, long hours, and all-around brilliance. I love you all.

Lauren Wein, Lorissa Sengara, and my agent, Jackie Kaiser, who saw the book as I wanted it to be, helped me get it there, and fought for that vision at every step; Tracy Roe, Stephanie Fysh, and everyone at HMH, HCC, RHA, and WCA; the Social Sciences and Humanities Research Council of Canada, for their financial support.

My loving family, who set an incredibly high bar for excellence just by living, and understand when I need to approach the bar sideways; Tim Mak and Jacob Sheehy, whose thought-provoking conversation and lifelong, globe-hopping friendship inspired much of this book.

My husband, John-Paul Lobos, who is everything.